Praise for Laura Griffin's thrilling romances:

'Top-notch romantic suspense! Fast pace, tight plotting, terrific
mystery, sharp dialogue, fabulous characters'
Allison Brennan, *New York Times* bestselling author

'A stunning page-turner with the perfect balance of romance and suspense
and a relentless pace that will keep you glued to its pages long into
the night. You won't be able to put this book down!'
Melinda Leigh

'*Hidden* has Laura Griffin's trademark strengths: a fast-paced
twisting plot and characters you want to know in real life'
Kendra Elliot

'Laura Griffin never fails to put me on the edge of my seat' *USA Today*

'Griffin pulls out all the stops in a phenomenal twist ending
that will leave readers stunned' *Publishers Weekly*

'A gripping, white-knuckle read. You won't be able to put it down'
Bren·· ···· ···· ···· ···selling author

'A··· ···· ···· ···· ···in deftly balances
···· ···· ···· ···· ···hington Post*

'··· ···· ···· ···· ··· Laura Griffin'

'A hig··· ···· ···
of ···

By Laura Griffin

LAST SEEN
ALONE

LAURA
GRIFFIN

HEADLINE
ETERNAL

Published by arrangement with Berkley,
an imprint of Penguin Publishing Group,
a division of Penguin Random House LLC.
First published in the United States in 2021

First published in Great Britain in 2021
by HEADLINE ETERNAL
An imprint of HEADLINE PUBLISHING GROUP

1

Cataloguing in Publication Data is available from the British Library

ISBN 978 1 4722 7603 2

Offset in 11.5/13.225 pt Times LT Std by Jouve (UK), Milton Keynes

Printed and bound in Great Britain by Clays Ltd, Elcograf S.p.A.

Headline's policy is to use papers that are natural, renewable and recyclable
products and made from wood grown in well-managed forests and other
controlled sources. The logging and manufacturing processes are expected
to conform to the environmental regulations of the country of origin.

HEADLINE PUBLISHING GROUP
An Hachette UK Company
Carmelite House
50 Victoria Embankment
London EC4Y 0DZ

www.headlineeternal.com
www.headline.co.uk
www.hachette.co.uk

For Kerry

CHAPTER ONE

═══╡═══

H E WAS LATE, AND she shouldn't have been surprised.
Vanessa buzzed down the window a few inches and cut the engine. Crisp, piney air seeped into the car, along with the faint scent of someone's campfire. She checked her phone. Nothing. She settled back in her seat to wait.

Her headlights illuminated a clump of trees—spindly fresh ones, along with the pointed gray spires that had burned years ago. She looked at the stars beyond the tree-tops. Once upon a time, she'd stretched out on a patch of grass not far from here with Cooper, gazing up at the sky and trying to pick out constellations. Orion. Leo. The Big Dipper. The memory seemed strange. Fanciful. Everything like that was gone now, replaced by a dull ache that never went away. Her emotions felt like tar, thick and heavy in her veins, and even swinging her legs out of bed required effort.

Yet here she was.

She was sick of the dread in her stomach. She was sick of being a silent bystander in her own life.

Vanessa eyed the bottle of Jim Beam peeking out from

beneath the passenger seat. She reached for it and checked her phone again before twisting off the cap.

Late, late, late.

She took a swig. The bourbon burned the back of her throat, but then she felt a warm rush of courage. She could do this.

Headlights, high and bright, flashed into her rearview mirror. Her shoulders tensed as she listened to the throaty sound of the approaching truck. It pulled up behind her and the lights went dark.

Vanessa stashed the bottle on the floor and wiped her damp palms on her jeans. Her stomach flip-flopped as he slid from the pickup and walked over. She couldn't believe she was doing this.

He stopped by the car, and she pushed the door open. He watched her from beneath the brim of his ratty baseball cap, and she could smell the smoke on his clothes. Marlboro Reds.

"Long time," he said.

"Do you have it?"

He held up a bag.

It was a lunch sack, like her mom used to pack for her. PBJ and a pudding cup. Vanessa took the bag, and the paper felt soft and greasy. She looked inside.

"That's four hundred."

Her head snapped up. "You said three-fifty!"

He pulled the bag away. "I need four."

"I don't have it."

His gaze dropped to her breasts, and she knew that look. Her gut clenched. The thought of sex right now made her want to throw up.

Twisting in her seat, she grabbed her leather tote from the back. She pulled the stack of bills from her wallet and counted twenty twenties. She turned and held them out.

Tucking the sack under his arm, he took the cash and thumbed through it.

"You look different," he said, and she caught the disapproval.

Vanessa gritted her teeth and waited. His attention fell to the bottle on the floor, and his brow furrowed as he leaned on the door.

"You all right, Van?"

"Yeah."

Something flickered across his face. Pity? Tenderness? She had to be imagining it.

He passed her the bag. "That's not really for your sister, is it?"

Vanessa didn't respond. It was none of his damn business. He stepped away, and she yanked the door shut.

For a moment he didn't move. But then he turned and walked back to his truck, stuffing her money in his back pocket.

The lights flashed on. Wincing, she watched in her rearview mirror as he backed up and made a three-point turn. When he was gone, she rested her hand on her stomach and let out a breath.

Vanessa started her car. She retraced her route over the pitted road until she reached the two-lane highway. When her tires hit smooth pavement, she pressed the gas and a wave of dizziness washed over her—probably the whiskey. She sighed with relief as the Austin skyline came into view.

Done.

She looked at the houses scattered on either side of the highway, some with lights on, some without. Through a gap in the pines she caught a glimpse of the lake glimmering under the half moon.

Eyeing the brown bag beside her, she felt a pang of yearning. She checked the mirror, then pulled onto the shoulder and parked. She grabbed the bag and reached inside.

Seventeen ounces.

It felt heavier than she'd imaged. She held the pistol in her palm and ran her thumb over the textured grip. For the first time in months, the knot of fear in her stomach loosened. She'd never been brave, never in her life. But people could change.

Headlights winked into the mirror, and she glanced up. High and bright again, probably a pickup truck. Squinting, she watched them get closer and closer.

Vanessa's nerves skittered. Was it slowing down?

Had someone followed her here? But she'd been careful. Not just careful—vigilant. She'd taken every precaution.

The truck started to slow, and an icy claw of fear closed around her heart.

Vanessa scooted across the seat and reached for the passenger door, jerking back as her sweater snagged on something. She yanked it free, then grabbed the bag and pushed open the door.

The truck rolled to a halt. Vanessa scrambled from the car, tripping as she glanced back at the headlights. Adrenaline shot through her, and she sprinted for the trees. The ground sloped down, and she ran faster, faster, losing control as she hurtled toward the woods.

Her toe caught and she crashed to her knees and elbows but managed to hold the bag. She pushed herself up and raced toward the line of trees.

Then the headlights switched off, and everything went black. She ran blindly through the knee-high weeds, huffing and gasping and clutching the bag to her chest like a football. A car door slammed, sending a jolt of terror through her. She pictured him running after her, closing the distance, grabbing her by her hair.

Thorns stabbed at her as she reached the thicket. She swiped at the branches, desperate for cover as she imagined him behind her. She couldn't see anything, not even her hand in front of her face as she groped through the razor-sharp bushes.

The thorns disappeared as she stumbled into a clearing.

Panting, she stopped and glanced up at the moon. Her heart thundered as she looked around and tried to orient herself. An arc of pines surrounded her. She could hide. Take cover. Defend herself, if she had to. With trembling hands, she fumbled inside the bag and pulled out the gun. Dear God, was it loaded? She hadn't thought to ask.

He's coming.

On a burst of panic, she raced for the trees.

B RANDON ALMOST MADE it home.
　　Almost.

His stomach grumbled, and he eyed the pizza box riding shotgun in his truck. Mushroom and pepperoni, thin crust. It wasn't nearly as good cold, but he wasn't picky.

His cell phone buzzed in the holder, and he tapped it.

"Almost there," he told his partner.

"Where are you exactly?" Antonio asked.

"About two minutes out."

"Okay. Take it easy on the curve. You'll see a black-and-white on the eastbound shoulder near my car. That's the best place to park."

"Got it."

Brandon drove another mile down the highway and slowed. He spotted the whirring yellow lights of a tow truck blocking the eastbound lane as it dragged a pickup from the ditch. Brandon passed them, making note of the disabled vehicle—a black Chevy Silverado.

He tapped the brakes before the curve and saw the reason for Antonio's warning. A silver car occupied the shoulder, just barely off the roadway. Traffic flares flickered on the pavement. Directly across the street, Antonio and a uniform stood talking with a man. Tall, goatee, green camo jacket, and a baseball cap turned backward on his head.

Brandon pulled a U-turn and parked behind Antonio's

personal vehicle, a black Mazda. Grabbing his phone, he gave his pizza a last wistful look and slid from the warmth of his truck.

A cool October breeze blew off the lake as Antonio trudged over. He wore dark slacks and a white button-down, same as Brandon, but his sleeves were rolled up. Looked like he hadn't made it home yet either. Their workday had begun at five thirty a.m. with a gas station holdup on the south side of town, and it was almost eleven p.m.

"How's it look?" Brandon asked.

"Weird."

Antonio stopped in front of him and ran a hand through his black buzz cut. His partner was short but powerfully built, like an MMA fighter.

"When did you get here?"

Antonio sighed. "'Bout ten minutes ago."

Brandon turned to look at the man being interviewed by the patrol officer.

"Guy's name is Tom Murray," Antonio said. "He called it in. Says he was driving westbound when a deer ran in front of him. He slammed on the brakes and swerved. Nearly hit the silver car there, then overcorrected and skidded off the road."

Brandon turned back toward the tow truck. The orange flares illuminated twin skid marks leading to the ditch.

"Tire marks corroborate his story," Antonio said. He'd spent four years on highway patrol, so he should know.

"And the driver of the car?" Brandon asked.

"Nowhere. But all her stuff's in the vehicle. Wallet, keys, phone, everything."

"Her?"

"Yeah, Murray said he walked over to see if anyone was inside and found a purse. Vanessa Adams, twenty-six. He checked the wallet."

Brandon muttered a curse.

"I know, right? Now his prints are everywhere."

Shaking his head, Brandon turned back toward the car. "What do you make of the guy?"

"Seems credible. Passed a Breathalyzer." Antonio shrugged. "We ran the name from the wallet. No wants or warrants. Vehicle's registered to her, too." Antonio looked at him, his brow furrowed. "I gave the car a once-over."

"Did you—"

"Didn't touch anything. There's a smear on the door. Looks to me like blood."

Hence, the reason he and Antonio had been called out to an otherwise routine abandoned vehicle.

Brandon scanned the area. The highway was lined with trees. North of the road, the forest was thick and healthy. South, not so much. Years ago, the highway had acted as a firebreak, but several hundred acres to the south had burned, and now it was a mix of jagged gray points and fresh saplings. The terrain sloped down to an area dense with scrub trees. Beyond the brush was a man-made lake created in an abandoned quarry. East of the lake was a public park.

Brandon opened his truck and reached into the back. "You have time to look around yet?"

"Not yet." Antonio gave a sheepish smile. "I don't have a flashlight."

Rookie mistake. But Brandon didn't state the obvious, even though he was Antonio's training officer.

Brandon reached into his truck and grabbed his high-powered Maglite, then tucked it into the back of his pants and handed his spare to Antonio. Opening the tackle box that lived in the back of his cab, he dug out two pairs of latex gloves and handed one to his partner.

"You want to talk to the driver?" Antonio asked.

"I'll take a look at the car first." Brandon pulled on the gloves. "Tell him to hang out. Then go get started in the woods."

"Roger that."

Antonio headed off, and Brandon took a last look around before approaching the vehicle.

It was a silver Toyota, ten years old, give or take, with a purple *namaste* sticker on the back bumper. The tires were bald, but there was no sign of a flat. A thin layer of grime covered the paint, except for streaks along the back, where someone had opened and closed the trunk a bunch of times. Brandon switched his beam to high and checked the back seat. Empty. He stepped to the driver's side. The door was closed, but the passenger door was wide open. He didn't like that.

No interior light on, no *ding-ding-ding* warning sound. Brandon circled the vehicle, making note of the license plate and the dented side panel. The damage looked old. Taking care not to mar any footprints in the dirt, he approached the open door and leaned in.

The smell hit him immediately. Piña colada. He swept the flashlight over the seat and spotted the pineapple-shaped air freshener tucked inside the door pocket.

Brandon crouched beside the car. On the floor was a half-empty bottle of bourbon and a big leather bag. It seemed more like a tote bag than a purse. A red leather wallet sat on the passenger seat. He shined the light on the Texas driver's license peeking through the plastic window and studied the smiling picture.

Vanessa Adams had long auburn hair. She wore red lipstick, and her blue eyes were accented with gray eye shadow. *Smoky eyes.* That was how his ex-girlfriend Erika described it when she did her eyes that way before they went out to clubs. Yet another thing he definitely hadn't missed over the past six months.

Brandon swept the flashlight over the door again and found the smear. It wasn't big—just a swipe near the handle. But it looked to him like blood.

In the cup holder was an old iPhone with a glittery white

case that had a pink heart on the back. The heart case seemed young for a twenty-six-year-old.

Brandon stood and examined the car's exterior again. No sign that she'd hit an animal in the road or anything else. So, what was the deal here? Was it a simple case of car trouble, and she'd hiked out for help?

Brandon could see her leaving her stuff behind, maybe even the tote bag and wallet if she was inebriated enough not to be thinking clearly. But her phone?

He looked over his shoulder toward the dark woods where a white light bobbed behind the trees. He called Antonio, and the light went still.

"Anyone check nearby gas stations?" Brandon asked. "There's an Exxon half a mile east of here where Old Quarry Road meets the highway."

"I'll get patrol on it."

"Thanks."

Brandon turned back to look at the car. The iPhone bothered him. Even shitfaced, he couldn't see someone leaving it behind. For most twentysomethings, a phone was like an appendage. Plus, it was late. He couldn't picture a woman leaving here without her phone if she'd gone somewhere by choice.

He swept the light over the dashboard. The ashtray was open slightly and a white business card poked out. Brandon took a pen from his pocket and used the end to slide the tray open enough to read the card.

LEIGH LARSON. ATTORNEY-AT-LAW.

Beneath the name was a Tenth Street address and an Austin phone number. So, was Leigh a man? A woman? What kind of lawyer? The generic white card didn't offer a clue. Brandon took out his cell and snapped a picture, then slid the ashtray shut.

His phone buzzed as he stood up. "Yeah?"

"Hey, I'm in the woods about fifty yards south of you." Antonio sounded out of breath, and Brandon caught the excitement in his voice. He turned and spotted the distant white glow through the row of trees.

"What is it?" Brandon asked.

"Man, you need to come see this."

CHAPTER TWO

L EIGH WAS SEVEN MINUTES from being in contempt of
court.

She checked her watch again and cursed as the line outside the Travis County Courthouse inched forward. She
craned her neck, but even in her four-inch heels, she had
trouble seeing over all the heads.

This was her fault. Mondays were jury selection, and she
should have built in extra time to get through security. But
this hearing had cropped up at the last minute, and she
hadn't thought about the timing.

Leigh's stomach knotted as she eased forward in line.
The Honorable Randolph J. Thielman was a ballbuster. He
despised unmuted cell phones, baseball caps in his courtroom, and late attorneys. Punctuality was a particular fe-
tish, and he didn't hesitate to slap lawyers with stiff fines if
they showed up late more than once. Leigh had long ago
used up her free pass.

At last, she stepped through the propped glass door into
the shade of the courthouse. She heaved her leather satchel

onto the table, then grabbed a plastic tray for her phone. She checked the time before sending it through the X-ray.

Five minutes.

Leigh stepped through the metal detector and set off a nerve-grating beep. Damn it, she didn't need this now.

A barrel-chested sheriff's deputy waved her over. "This way, ma'am."

Cursing her choice of lingerie, Leigh stepped out of the traffic flow and scanned the guys manning the X-ray machine. Where was Deputy Gronkowski? That one knew she was a regular and always waved her through without a hassle. Leigh didn't actually know the man's name, but he was big and beefy and reminded her of a football player.

Leigh lifted her arms and felt a half dozen male gazes on her as the deputy ran a wand over her body, pausing beneath her breasts. She dropped her arms before he could nod and rushed to retrieve her belongings.

Four minutes.

She quickly silenced her phone and stuffed it into her bag. Glancing up, she spotted Gronk near the water fountains talking to a pair of plainclothes cops, a tall one and a short one. They were detectives—she could tell by the guns and gold shields.

And they were looking right at her.

Gronk nodded in her direction, and she felt a jolt of shock as she read the words on his lips: *There she is.*

Leigh turned and hurried for the elevator. The car was full. The door started to close, and she made a dash for it.

"Wait!" she yelped.

The door slid shut.

"Leigh Larson?"

She whirled around. The tall detective's gaze homed in on her as he strode toward her.

"Shit." She cast a glance at the red digits above the elevators. The second elevator was on floor three and moving up.

She stomped her foot.

"Are you Leigh Larson?"

She turned around, and the detective was right behind her now. His sharp gaze pinned her, and she took a step back. *I'm in trouble,* she thought. Which was ridiculous. She'd never even laid eyes on this man. One of her *clients* was in trouble—that was much less ridiculous. Leigh had gotten her start with the public defender's office, and some of the people she'd represented weren't exactly pillars of the community.

"Are you Leigh Larson?" he asked again.

"Yes. Who are you?"

"Detective Brandon Reynolds, Austin PD."

"If it's about De Silva—"

"Who's De Silva?"

She paused to look up at him. He had strong cheekbones, brown-black eyes, and thick dark lashes that any woman would kill for. And he definitely looked annoyed.

Leigh shot a glance at the elevators. "Listen, I'm late for court, so whatever it is you need—"

"I need information."

"You'll have to call my office."

Leigh moved toward the stairs, and he fell into step beside her, undeterred. She pushed through the door, and he followed her into the cinder-block stairwell.

"It's about Vanessa Adams," he said.

She glanced at him as she hurried up the stairs.

"Who?"

"Vanessa Adams."

She checked her watch. "I really can't talk right now. I'm due in court in two minutes."

"I just have a few questions."

"My office is on Tenth Street." She rounded the landing, but he kept pace with her. "You can make an appointment and—"

"Stop."

He halted on the landing, and an invisible force made Leigh stop, too.

"I need information now, not later."

She stared up at him and summoned her very last shred of patience.

"If you insist on doing this now, you have thirty seconds," she said.

The corner of his mouth curved up in a smile, and she felt an unwelcome rush of warmth.

She glanced at her watch. "Twenty-five."

He rested his hands on his hips. "Vanessa Adams, Austin resident, twenty-six years old. Can you tell me if she's a client of yours?"

"No."

He frowned. "No, she's not a client? Or no, you can't tell me?"

"I don't have a client by that name."

"No?"

"No."

She hurried up the last flight of stairs.

"You sure about that?"

She shot a look at him as she pulled open the door. *"Yes."*

Leigh glanced around, disoriented as she emerged from the stairwell and not the elevator bank, like she normally did. Her gaze landed on room 305, and she hurried for the door. Through the rectangular window, she spotted the bailiff standing beside the bench. But no Judge Thielman, thank goodness.

Leigh turned to face the detective, giving him her full attention for the first time. He was tall and powerfully built. Short dark hair, tanned skin. He was actually fairly nice-looking, in a cop sort of way. But his timing was crap.

"One more thing," he said.

"I have to *go*."

"What about Gertrude Soltis?"

"Gertie Soltis, the defense attorney?"

"Yes."

"What about her?"

"She ever send you referrals?"

"Sometimes. Listen, I need to get in there." She cast a glance over her shoulder, and her pulse jumped as the door to the judge's chambers opened.

"All rise," intoned the bailiff as everyone stood up.

Leigh grabbed the door handle. She closed her eyes for a moment to collect herself. Five years in, and she was still prone to panic attacks.

Focus. You can do this.

Leigh squared her shoulders and stepped into the courtroom.

B RANDON FOUND HIS partner exactly where he'd expected. Antonio stood beside the food truck in front of the courthouse, pumping ketchup onto a pair of hot dogs.

He glanced up from his lunch as Brandon approached.

"How'd it go? She know her?"

"I don't know," Brandon said.

"Well, did you ask her?"

"Yeah. She said Vanessa Adams isn't a client."

Antonio frowned. "So, what's the problem?"

"She lied."

"How do you know?"

"I could tell."

Brandon couldn't say how, exactly. But he had a nose for BS. And Leigh Larson, attorney-at-law, had been lying through her pretty white teeth.

"But why would she lie about knowing Vanessa?" Antonio asked.

"No idea," Brandon said.

With his hot dogs fully loaded, Antonio stepped away

from the food truck. Day or night, rain or shine, his partner never missed a meal. Even after grabbing less than three hours of sleep, he'd shown up for work this morning with a bag full of breakfast tacos. The kid worked out like a maniac and was constantly scarfing down food.

"These are good," Antonio said around a mouthful. "You want one?"

"No."

Brandon glanced back at the courthouse, where the security line still stretched all the way to the park.

"She's hot, though."

He turned around. "What's that?"

"The attorney." Antonio smiled. "Don't tell me you didn't notice."

Brandon didn't comment. He'd have to be dead not to notice. Leigh Larson was definitely hot. The skirt, the heels, the sleek dark hair pulled back in a prim bun.

But the main thing he'd noticed was her eyes. They were forest green, and they'd gone from surprised to wary the moment she noticed him watching her. She'd taken one look at him and tried to hightail it out of there.

Not exactly the response he usually got from women. Criminals, yeah, but not women in general. She'd said she was late for court, and that explained the rush, maybe, but it didn't explain the lie.

Leigh Larson had lied to him—he was sure of it. What he didn't get was why.

"Well, we may have a better lead anyway." Antonio crumpled his first wrapper into a ball and pitched it into a trash bin before chomping into the second hot dog. "The lab called while you were in there. They just got the Toyota in. Who'd you talk to over there?"

"Jane," Brandon said.

"Oh yeah? Well, she must like you because they bumped us to the front of the line. They've already started processing the vehicle, and get this. The smear on the door? They did a quickie test and confirmed the blood is human."

Brandon wasn't surprised. After four years in homicide, he was good at reading stains. The real question was, did the blood belong to Vanessa Adams, who was still apparently missing after abandoning her car on that highway more than fourteen hours ago?

And then there was the pool of blood Antonio had discovered in the woods. It was no small amount, and one look at it had prompted Brandon to get on the phone with his lieutenant to request a team of CSIs out there, stat, to process the scene.

Brandon took out his phone now and pulled up the photo he'd taken last night. The blood pool—still coagulating—had been discovered beside a burned tree stump. The sight had put a lead weight in Brandon's gut as he tried to imagine what happened. Someone had been injured or worse, and the logical candidate was Vanessa. Had she been shot? Stabbed? Bludgeoned?

Despite combing the area, they'd turned up no shell casings or drag marks—nothing beyond that one pool of blood by the stump in the woods.

At this point, they didn't know if that blood matched the smear in the car, or if it was Vanessa Adams's. To determine that, they needed DNA tests, which meant submitting samples to the notoriously backlogged DNA lab, and jumping to the front of *that* line would take a hell of a lot more than a friendly phone call to Jane, especially since their case wasn't even officially a homicide.

Yet.

Brandon had a feeling about it, though.

He looked over his shoulder at the courthouse. Counting three levels up and three windows over, he zeroed in on Judge Thielman's courtroom. He thought of Leigh Larson just before she'd gone in there. For a moment, she'd looked like a deer in the headlights. But then she'd opened the door and walked straight up the aisle, all confidence. It was the damnedest thing.

"You still stuck on that lawyer?"

Brandon turned around. "What? No."

"Hey, don't take it personally." Antonio smiled. "Lawyers lie, man. It's part of the job."

CHAPTER THREE

=======||=======

M ENDEZ & LARSON OCCUPIED the bottom floor of a re-
furbished 1930s house six blocks west of the capitol.
It was a prime location, and when Leigh first started working there, everything about the place had seemed romantic—
the wide front porch, the dormer windows, the flower
boxes. It was so impossibly *quaint* that Leigh hadn't fully
realized the maintenance headaches in store when she
committed to the lease.

She walked up the steps and glanced at the porch swing
where their resident tabby lazed in the sun. Watermelon
yawned and gave her a perturbed look, possibly holding her
responsible for the racket going on overhead. Leigh stepped
into the office and looked at the ceiling.

"What are they doing up there?" she asked Bella.

Their receptionist leaned back in her swivel chair and
moved the mouthpiece of her headset out of the way.
"Something in the bathroom," she said.

Leigh winced. "Don't tell me it's a leak."

"It is, but it's the sink, supposedly."

Bella's curly blond hair was piled on top of her head today and secured with a pencil. Her expression brightened as Leigh set a pair of coffee cups on the marble reception counter.

"Is one of those for me?" she asked.

"Yep. Skinny latte."

"Oh, *bless you*. I missed lunch." Bella adjusted her headset and held up a finger telling Leigh to wait. "Yes, I'm on hold for James Khagan?"

Leigh reached over the counter for the iPad where Bella kept a log of phone calls. She swiped at the screen and scrolled through what looked like a busy afternoon.

Bella adjusted the headset and sighed. "Still holding," she said, then took a sip of coffee.

"So, any chance a police detective came by here earlier?" Leigh asked.

"*Yes.* Oh my lord, talk about packin' heat! Did he find you?"

"Yeah."

Bella grinned. "You're welcome." She adjusted her headset again. "Yes, I'm still holding for James Khagan?" She rolled her eyes and then turned to Leigh. "What are you looking for?"

"I'm not sure. Have we had anything from a Vanessa Adams lately?"

"No. Why?"

Leigh tapped on the previous day and scrolled through the calls.

"You can do a search, you know. Just—hello? Mr. Khagan? Hi there, it's Bella over at Mendez and Larson. How was your fishing trip?"

Leigh grabbed her coffee and left Bella to her work. Besides being a kick-ass receptionist, she had a knack for collecting unpaid invoices. Leigh thought it was her voice. The sugary Southern accent caught people off guard, and before they knew it, they'd pulled out their credit card and agreed to pay over the phone.

Leigh's heels clacked on the restored oak floor as she made her way down the corridor. The law firm occupied just over half of a four-thousand-square-foot building. Upstairs was a two-man accounting shop, and a space at the very back of the building was leased by a private investigator who mostly kept to himself. It was an amicable arrangement, but at any given moment at least one of the office suites was undergoing some sort of maintenance.

Leigh stepped into her office, which had a lovely view of an ivy-covered wall. After finding the building, Leigh's partner had gotten first dibs on the front office, which suited Leigh fine. She didn't want a front-facing window where any creep on the street could peer in at her while she worked.

Leigh's office was small, but sumptuously furnished with a blue velvet sofa and a brown leather armchair arranged around a coffee table. Her desk was tucked into the corner, almost like an afterthought. On the end table was an amber-shaded lamp and a box of tissues. The room was designed to be soothing, like a therapist's office. Many of Leigh's clients showed up distraught and needed calming. Often, she was their last stop on a desperate journey.

Leigh set her satchel on the coffee table and sank onto the sofa to kick off her shoes. Groaning, she rubbed the balls of her feet. The pointy heels killed, but she'd long ago decided they were worth it. They gave her a couple inches of height and distracted male attorneys while she stuck it to them in court.

On a good day. Unlike today.

She leaned her head back against the cushion and slurped her Frappuccino, letting the creamy chocolate goodness take her mind off her afternoon.

Javier stuck his head in the doorway. "How'd it go with Thielman?" His gaze fell on her Frappuccino. "Oh, shit. That bad?"

She answered with a long slurp that gave her a brain freeze.

Javi stepped into the room and shut the door behind him. Leigh's partner wore a custom-tailored blue dress shirt and espresso-colored slacks. Even at three in the afternoon, the creases looked sharp enough to cut butter.

"What happened?" he asked.

"He granted the TRO."

His dark eyebrows arched. "Hey, that's good."

"He denied our request to make him take down the posts. Doesn't want to violate his First Amendment rights." Leigh rolled her eyes, making the head freeze worse.

"Well, it's Thielman. What'd you expect?"

"I expected to convince him! I made a damn good argument."

"I'm sure you did."

She sat forward and plunked her cup on the table as Javi looked her over. She felt especially crappy because Javi's sister had referred the client. The woman was going through a messy divorce and her ex-husband had been bad-mouthing her for months on Facebook. When he showed up at their kid's birthday party and called her a cunt in front of a room full of eight-year-olds, she decided she'd had enough.

Javi leaned against the doorframe, and she noticed he was wearing his favorite alligator belt, which meant he'd been in court earlier.

"How'd *your* day go?" Leigh asked.

"Still going. I've got a client at five."

"Here?"

"Her place."

She took a last sip of coffee, and Javi grimaced. "How do you drink that stuff? It makes my teeth ache."

A knock sounded on the door, and Javi scooted aside as Bella leaned in.

"Sorry to interrupt. You were asking about Vivien Adams?"

Leigh perked up. "Vanessa. Why?"

Bella stepped over and handed her a stack of mail. "That

was in your box. The manila envelope on the bottom is from a V. Adams."

"Thanks."

"There are some bills in there, too. All that's been in there a few days."

Bella stepped out as Leigh shuffled through the stack, which did indeed contain some neglected bills.

"Who's Vivien Adams?" Javi asked.

"*Vanessa* Adams. A couple of cops tracked me down at the courthouse to ask about her."

His eyes sparked with interest. "What'd she do?"

"I don't know."

"What kind of cops?"

"I don't know that either."

She flipped the envelope over. It was addressed to Leigh in a woman's loopy handwriting. The return address was only a name.

"Well, were they sheriff's office? Austin PD?"

"APD. Detectives." She glanced up. "You know Brandon Reynolds?"

"Never heard of him."

Leigh opened the envelope and took out a familiar two-page document. It was signed by Vanessa Ann Adams. Paper-clipped to the last page was a check for five hundred dollars.

"Well, look at that."

Javi stepped closer, and she caught a whiff of his Gucci cologne.

"What is it?" he asked.

"She freaking hired us."

Leigh stood up and handed the client agreement to Javi. It was the standard boilerplate contract used by the firm. Leigh stepped over to her desk and powered up her laptop.

"She came to see me two months ago," Leigh said. "Some problem with her landlord, if I remember right."

24   LAURA GRIFFIN

She opened her email and searched. Nothing from Vanessa. She clicked into a browser and googled **Brandon Reynolds** and **Austin police**.

"You'd better get a driver's license number on this check," Javi said. "If the cops are after her, it might bounce."

A list of news stories appeared. Leigh clicked the top one: **Suspect Arrested in Greenbelt Attacks**. Leigh's stomach tightened as she skimmed the story. It was from a year ago. The accompanying photo showed Brandon Reynolds addressing reporters on the steps of the police station. Several uniformed officers stood alongside him, but Brandon seemed to be the one fielding questions.

Javi whistled. "Is that him?"

"Forget it. He's straight."

Javi lifted an eyebrow.

Leigh scrolled through the story, skimming for info.

"Oh no," she murmured.

"What is it?"

"He's a homicide cop."

B RANDON SCANNED THE faces at the bar and spotted a few he recognized. He walked to the back and slid into a booth as a text landed on his phone.

She show up? Antonio wanted to know.

Instead of answering, Brandon called him. "What happened with the sister?" he asked.

"She still hasn't heard from her," Antonio reported. "What about you? Is she there yet?"

"No."

From the music in the background, Brandon figured Antonio was in his car on his way home, finally, after another marathon day.

"So, what's with the Ice House?" Antonio asked. "I thought you hated that place."

"She wanted to meet here."

"Why?"

Leigh Larson strode into the bar and looked around. Same blouse, skirt, and shoes as before, same hairstyle. She hadn't been home either, apparently.

She spotted him, and something flitted across her face. Relief?

"Hey, lemme call you back," he told his partner.

Leigh walked over, and Brandon scooted from the booth to greet her.

"Thanks for meeting me," she said.

"No problem."

She glanced around curiously before sliding into the wooden seat. She set her purse on the bench with her phone sticking out, as though she might be expecting a call.

She turned those green eyes on him. "I appreciate your time. I'm sure you'd rather be headed home right now."

Brandon didn't comment, and she didn't seem to notice. She looked around again, as though this place were something more interesting than a dive bar down the street from the police station.

A server stopped beside their table. "Anything to drink?" She directed the question at Brandon, but then settled her gaze on Leigh.

"Um . . . You have Shiner Bock?" Leigh asked.

"Tap or bottle?"

"Bottle, please."

"And you?"

"Water," Brandon said.

The waitress left and Leigh sighed.

"Just water?"

"I'm on call tonight," he said.

"Oh."

Her smile faded, and she rested her hands in front of her on the scarred wooden table. Her hands were pale and slender. No wedding ring, but she wore an intricate silver band on her left thumb.

"I've never been here," she said.

"Why'd you suggest it?"

"Proximity." She looked around again. "It seems like a cop hangout."

"How can you tell?"

She smiled slightly. "You guys have a certain look."

Brandon watched her, waiting for her to talk. He'd been surprised to get her call at the police station, and she'd been brisk on the phone.

"So, earlier you asked me about Vanessa," she stated.

"And you said you didn't know her."

"No. I said she wasn't my *client*."

He arched his eyebrows, even though none of this came as a surprise. If she didn't know Vanessa, she wouldn't be here.

"Semantics," he said.

Which was one reason he wasn't crazy about lawyers.

"No, not semantics," she said. "It's an important distinction. I met Vanessa exactly once, and she wasn't my client. But then this afternoon—"

"Wait. You *saw* her?" He leaned forward.

"No." She huffed out a breath. "Let's back up."

The server returned with a tray filled with drinks. Balancing carefully, she placed the beer in front of Leigh and set a super-full glass of ice water in front of Brandon.

Leigh eyed his drink as she picked up her Shiner. She took a sip and set the bottle down.

"Vanessa came to see me," she said.

"When?"

"About two months ago. She was having a legal issue with her landlord."

"All right."

"Then today—when I got back from *court*," she said pointedly, "I had a package from her at my office."

"A package?"

"It was a signed client agreement and a retainer check.

So, as of this afternoon, Vanessa is officially my client. And, no, I did not lie to you earlier when you asked."

Brandon watched her, waiting. There was more to this story, or she wouldn't have wanted to meet him.

"The thing is," she said, "I reached out to her this afternoon."

"Call or text?"

"Both. And email. She hasn't responded." Leigh frowned slightly. "And since a pair of police detectives tracked me down at the courthouse to ask about her, I have to admit I'm worried." She paused and looked at him. "What's going on?"

Brandon didn't respond.

"You're a homicide detective, right? You and your partner?"

"Crimes against persons."

She lifted her eyebrows. Now, who was guilty of semantics?

Brandon took a sip of water, stalling for time. He didn't want to tell her much. He didn't want to tell her anything, really, but he needed information, and he sensed he'd get more if he gave something in return. She hadn't said the words *attorney-client privilege*, but he could tell they were on the tip of her tongue.

"Last night, we got a callout to an abandoned vehicle on Old Quarry Road at the east edge of town."

Her eyes filled with concern. "Is it Vanessa's?"

"It's a Toyota Corolla registered to her name, yes. And her identification was inside."

"She left her wallet?"

"Her wallet, her keys, her phone."

Leigh's expression turned grim. "That doesn't sound good."

"No."

"Anything else?"

"Not that I can share."

She turned away, settling her gaze on the crowded bar. But her thoughts seemed to be miles away.

"The phone thing is weird," she murmured.

"Agreed."

"When she came to visit me, she had it in her lap the whole time."

Brandon watched her, absorbing details he hadn't noticed at the courthouse. Her dark hair had glints of red in it, and loose strands fell around her neck. He liked the bun, and he couldn't look at it without wanting to pull it loose. She wore a chunky man's sports watch that seemed at odds with her feminine clothes, and for some reason the combination was unbelievably sexy.

Brandon sipped his ice water.

"Was Vanessa having a problem with anyone?" he asked.

"A legal problem?"

"Any kind of problem. The thing with her landlord, for instance."

"I can't discuss her legal issues."

And there it was, the dodge he'd expected. If it had been a homicide investigation, he could have compelled her to give him at least some information. As it was now, though, he needed to rely on persuasion.

"How'd she seem when she came to see you?" he asked, going for the indirect approach.

Leigh's expression turned wary. "How do you mean?"

"Did she seem stressed out? Upset? Scared?"

"She was stressed out. But that's not remarkable. I mean, people don't generally come see me to tell me how *great* their life is going."

"What kind of law do you practice?"

"All kinds."

He tamped down his impatience. "Does Mendez and Larson have a specialty?"

"Officially, no. But we do a fair amount of work going after psycho exes, stalkers, and online perverts."

He eased forward. "Psycho exes?"

"You know, pissed-off boyfriends and husbands. Guys who harass and trash and post revenge porn, that sort of thing."

For the first time since he'd shined his flashlight on that abandoned Toyota, Brandon felt like he was getting somewhere.

"Is that what was going on with Vanessa?" he asked. "And before you say anything about privilege, you should know that time is working against us here."

"I don't know. I wish I did." Leigh looked sincere, but he figured that was an expression she had in her arsenal after years as an attorney. "We had a short preliminary conversation—mostly about our fee structure, to be honest with you. She seemed to be concerned about money. And then she left. When I didn't hear back, I assumed she decided not to hire us."

"Until today."

She nodded.

Brandon leaned back in the booth. He hadn't had time for more than a quick Internet search, but he hadn't come up with this psycho-stalker angle when he'd run Leigh's name. She must not be established in the specialty yet. Which meant Vanessa might not have gone looking for help with some guy giving her trouble. Maybe she simply needed some legal advice.

"You guys keep pretty busy with cases like that?" Brandon asked.

"Online harassment, you mean?"

"Yeah."

She nodded. "There's no shortage of bad actors out there. Same reason you stay busy, right? Some people are sick. And a depressing number of them use technology to terrorize women and upend their lives."

"Just women?"

"Mostly. At least the ones who come see us." Her expression darkened. "Social media is rife with misogyny, you know. Harassment, rape threats, extortion. Some people do it for profit or for fun or because they're sadistic. Some people are just flat-out crazy, and someone in their life becomes a target for that."

Target. Exactly what Brandon was worried about with this missing-person case.

"Who referred Vanessa to your firm?" he asked.

"No idea."

He shot her a look.

"What? She didn't say."

"Don't you make it your business to find out where your clients are coming from?"

"Yes. But in this case, I don't know. She didn't mention a referral or anything, and it's not like I grill people the second they walk in the door."

He sighed, and she leaned forward.

"Listen, Detective. I'd like to help you."

"Call me Brandon."

She nodded. "I'd like to help you, Brandon. Really. You have no idea how often I have a client who's pushed to the brink because the police won't take her seriously. Some of these guys are experts at skirting the law. It's maddening. But in this case, I really don't know about a problem Vanessa might or might not have been having with anyone."

"What about the landlord? Who is it?"

"I don't know offhand."

"I need a name."

She watched him, and he could see the debate going on in her head. Attorney-client privilege versus helping police with what was potentially a murder investigation.

A chime emanated from her purse, and she checked her phone. He watched her reaction, hoping maybe it was Vanessa returning her phone calls, and they could all go home, mystery solved. But Leigh's face gave nothing away.

She tucked her phone away and looked at him.

"It's late," she said, "and I still have work left to do tonight."

He didn't doubt she had work tonight, but her tone told him that was an excuse to leave.

"I'd like to get that name," he said.

She pulled a twenty from her purse and tucked it under the beer. "I'll think about it." She slid from the booth.

"Don't think too long." He gave her a stern look. "A case like this, the clock's ticking."

A HIGH-PITCHED BEEP GREETED Leigh as she stepped through her front door. She tapped in the alarm code, then kicked off her heels in the foyer, eyeing her running shoes with a twinge of guilt. She'd meant to go this morning before work, but she'd gotten sidetracked with an email. Then tonight she'd gotten sidetracked at the Ice House.

Leigh crossed the living room, dropping her bag on the sofa, and stepped into her kitchen. Opening her fridge, she sighed. Her refrigerator was just as neglected as her running shoes. She grabbed a yogurt and took it into the sunroom that doubled as a home office.

The sunroom had been the primary selling point of her one-bedroom condo. It looked out over a private patio. Leigh had spent her first three weekends after move-in pulling up half the bricks and putting in flower beds so she'd have a slice of nature to look at whenever she worked from home, which was often.

She had overestimated her gardening skills at first, planting azaleas and hydrangeas, even though her mom had warned her they might be difficult to grow. Of course, her mother was right. Not only did she know plants, but she knew Leigh, and by midsummer the plants had withered under Leigh's sporadic care. At her mom's suggestion, she had switched to some knockout roses. The heartier flowers didn't mind when she put in marathon days at the office prepping for trial, only coming home at night to crash and change clothes.

Grabbing her laptop, Leigh turned on the water fountain and stepped onto the patio. Her home faced a busy street, and she kept the front windows covered for privacy, but the patio was her oasis, and the lotus-shaped fountain drowned out the traffic noise. She sank into her favorite chair and turned on her computer. After logging in, she opened the file she'd created after her meeting with Vanessa.

Leigh made notes after every meeting, even those in which the person didn't commit to hire her, because as Javi always said, *A "no" today could be a "yes" tomorrow.* Clients could be indecisive as hell. In that respect, Vanessa was typical.

It was everything else that seemed bizarre.

Leigh skimmed her notes, which were written in the choppy shorthand she'd developed her first semester of law school. She'd reviewed everything this afternoon, but she wanted to see if anything new jumped out after her conversation with Brandon.

Vanessa had come to see her on a rainy Friday in August. She'd been wearing surgical scrubs and said she was on her lunch break, and Leigh remembered Vanessa's sneakers squeaking on the floor as she'd led her back to her office. Leigh had ushered her to the sofa, where she'd sat down and unfolded the four-page lease agreement she had signed for an apartment in North Austin. Vanessa had been visibly shaken as she recounted getting a letter from her landlord threatening to sue her for illegally subletting her apartment.

"He says I'm in breach of contract, but I'm *allowed* to sublet," she'd insisted. "It's right here in black and white."

Vanessa hadn't brought the letter, unfortunately. She'd said it was from the law offices of Heinrick & Toole, which Leigh knew to be a boutique firm on the south side. She'd also said the letter wasn't signed by a specific attorney, which

Leigh considered a red flag. Yet another red flag was the correspondence coming digitally versus an actual letter.

Leigh's advice had been simple: Wait. The email message could be an empty threat. If the suit was legit, Vanessa would receive something further, and at that point Leigh could get involved. Vanessa had asked questions about fees and then ended the meeting, saying that she had to get back to work, but she'd be in touch.

That was the last Leigh had heard from her, or about her, until today.

Leigh pictured Vanessa with her rain-dampened hair, smoothing the lease agreement out on the coffee table.

Did she seem stressed out? Upset? Scared?

Brandon's questions came back, and Leigh realized now that Vanessa had been all of those things. And she realized there might have been much more going on with her than a litigious landlord.

Leigh thought about how she'd looked that day, with her bloodshot eyes and wan complexion and her nails bitten down to the quick. The woman had been distraught, and Leigh wished now that she had spent more of her time with Vanessa asking questions rather than answering them.

Why had she sublet her apartment in the first place? Leigh had done a little digging this afternoon, and the home address Vanessa had listed on the client agreement was less than a mile away from the apartment she was subletting. And based on the websites, both apartments were one-bedroom units of similar cost.

So, what had prompted her to move? Had she simply wanted a change of address? And if so, why? Moving was a hassle. Period. It wasn't something people did for no reason, and Leigh had her suspicions.

She caught a blur of movement as a skinny black cat leaped onto the wall separating Leigh's courtyard from the one next door. Leigh's neighbor was a software exec who worked even longer hours than Leigh did.

Sherlock pranced along the wall and settled himself directly above the fountain, watching Leigh with a scheming look in his eyes. He was typically aloof, but he'd been known to sniff out sandwich crusts or abandoned yogurt cups.

Leigh finished her yogurt and set it on the ground. She resettled her computer on her lap and launched a social media search. She combed three platforms but came up with nothing for a Vanessa Adams living in Austin. Finally on Twitter, she found a Vanessa Adams who listed her location as Texas. The profile picture was a white daisy, and the account was private. It seemed like a longshot, but Leigh sent a follow request anyway.

Her phone chimed on the table beside her. The number was blocked, but Leigh knew who it was.

"Hey," she said.

"I ran your friend," C.J. told her.

C.J. Foley was Leigh's go-to guy for background checks, mostly because he was good, but also because he was free. The private investigator occupied the office at the back of their building, and Javi had helped him out of some legal scrapes over the years, pro bono. It was a symbiotic relationship.

"That was fast," Leigh said.

"Slow day. And it was easy. She's clean."

"No record at all?"

"Nope. No wants or warrants. Not even a traffic ticket."

"You're sure?"

"Yep."

C.J. didn't sound offended by her skepticism. He didn't offend easily.

Leigh was surprised by the result, though. When Brandon had asked if Leigh got referrals from Gertie Soltis, a public defender, she'd figured Vanessa had had some sort of brush with the law in her past and Brandon had learned about it.

"I did find one thing," he said.

Leigh's pulse picked up. "What?"

"She reported a burglary back in June. Her name's on the report."

"She had an intruder?"

"Car burglary. It was parked on the street. Anderson Lane."

"Do you know what was stolen?"

"Nope. I know the cop listed here, though. I could see if he remembers it."

"That would be *great*, C.J. Thanks. I owe you."

He clicked off.

C.J. wasn't big on pleasantries. Or lawyers, for that matter. But he and Javi seemed to have a good arrangement, and he never pushed back whenever Leigh called him up.

Sherlock rubbed his head against her ankle, and Leigh reached down to scratch his ears. He was in a rare friendly mood after finishing off her yogurt.

Leigh stared at her computer screen, thinking about Vanessa. Something about her had struck a chord during that meeting. Leigh had seen something desperate in her eyes, and she'd been pulled in from those very first moments. Subconsciously, maybe Leigh had sensed that Vanessa had more going on in her life than a nuisance lawsuit, more than she'd let on in that meeting. Leigh wished she'd followed her instincts and asked more questions when Vanessa was right there in front of her and it would have been easy to get answers. Leigh had a knack for getting people to open up.

Now the answers would be much, much harder to come by.

Sighing, Leigh pulled the pins from her bun and tugged her hair loose. What a day. She thought of Brandon back at the bar and the somber look in his eyes as he'd told her about the investigation. He had twelve years on the force, and he was treating this case like a homicide, because that was what experience told him this was.

What happened to you, Vanessa?

It was a question for the detectives, and Leigh should leave them to it. She didn't have the time or the bandwidth or even the skills, really, to get involved in this case. Logically and objectively, she knew she should back off.

But it was too late. She was already hooked.

CHAPTER FOUR

THE GARAGE SMELLED LIKE a Jiffy Lube, but the concrete floor was so clean you could eat off it.

"Shoes at the door," Jane said as Brandon stepped into the room.

He stopped beside a metal storage rack and pulled off his shoes, dropping them on a mat by the door.

Antonio looked at him. "Seriously?"

"Seriously," Jane said from across the room. "We can't have you tracking mud in here. Or any other grossness you picked up at a crime scene."

Jane wore white coveralls and plastic visor with a shield that covered her face, and her dark hair was in a braid. She walked over and grabbed a bottle of water off the counter. Looking them over, she flipped up the shield so she could take a swig.

Brandon glanced around the cavernous room. Vanessa's little silver Toyota sat in the center bay with all its doors open. It looked like an insect about to take flight.

"Anything interesting?" Antonio asked Jane.

The CSI set her bottle on the counter. "Oh yeah. Come take a look."

They followed her across the garage. All the other bays were empty, except for the one on the far end, where a technician in coveralls was photographing a white van that looked like it had been T-boned.

Brandon stopped beside the Toyota and peered inside. He hadn't had the time or the lighting to thoroughly examine it the other night. Looking at it now, he noticed the black dirt on the back floor mats.

"Let's start with the blood," Jane said. Despite the overhead lights, she took a mini flashlight from her pocket and aimed it at the front passenger door. "I can tell you it's human blood and it's fairly fresh."

"Fairly?" Brandon looked at her.

"Last forty-eight hours, I'd say."

So, consistent with the timing of Vanessa's disappearance.

"Do you know if this blood is from the same source as what we found in the woods?" Antonio asked. Having made the discovery, he'd been focused on the blood pool as their primary lead.

"I can't tell you," Jane said. "That's a question for the DNA lab. I sent them a swab, and I'm sure they'll run it eventually."

"Who'd you send it to?" Brandon asked.

"Brie Matheson. She's good. You know her?"

"No. But I know everyone's backlogged. You mind putting in a call for us to speed things along?"

Jane looked skeptical. "I can try, but last I heard, this case wasn't a homicide. Has it been upgraded?"

"No," Antonio said.

"Not yet." Brandon shot him a look. "A lot of signs are pointing that way. The missing woman's sister lives in town, and she hasn't been able to get a hold of her. She's gone by her place and left messages."

Jane looked down at the blood smear. "That doesn't sound good. I'm happy to put in a call to Brie, but it may not help, depending on how slammed they are."

"We'd appreciate it."

"Let me show you the rest of what I found." She dropped into a crouch beside the car and aimed her light at the bottom of the passenger seat. "Have a look."

Antonio crouched beside her. "What are we looking at?"

"Cotton fibers on the metal track there, where the seat slides back. See?" She glanced at Brandon. "And using luminol, I found a small droplet of blood on the floor mat here. So, I have a theory. You told me the driver's-side door was closed when you found the car, right?"

"Correct." Brandon leaned closer, careful not to touch the door.

"I'm thinking she pulled over in a hurry and slid across the seat here to get out this side. She may have snagged her clothing here, then jerked it loose and pushed the door open, and that's when she smeared the blood."

"You're saying she cut herself as she was fleeing the vehicle," Antonio said.

"It's just a theory, but the fabric fibers support that scenario."

Antonio stood up and looked at Brandon. "So, she ran into the woods and then got injured, or worse, when someone caught up to her."

There were a lot of assumptions in that statement. But the physical evidence fit. Still, it wasn't going to be enough evidence to convince their lieutenant to upgrade the case to a homicide investigation—which would give them not only more resources but also more pull with the DNA lab.

Brandon looked at Jane. "This is helpful. Anything else?"

She stood up and tucked her flashlight into her pocket. "There's the damage on the vehicle—the scratched paint and chipped taillight. But it looks old to me. And Keith checked the car out." She nodded at the CSI working on the minivan. "He said there's nothing mechanically wrong with it, except for a dead battery, which could have happened after she abandoned the car and left the door open. The lights could have drained the battery."

"Or, she could have pulled over and parked for some reason, and then couldn't get the car to start again." Antonio looked at Brandon.

But Brandon didn't buy that scenario. His gut told him Vanessa had pulled over because she was afraid of something and then either fled her vehicle or was forced out.

"There's something else," Jane said. "I'm hoping it will help." She walked around the front of the car, and they followed.

"I lifted fingerprints throughout the car. Got a good set from the steering wheel, plus several clear prints from the dashboard and the lock switch on the driver's door. Those prints likely belong to your missing woman, assuming she was the person behind the wheel."

Brandon didn't like assumptions, but that one seemed logical unless, of course, Vanessa had been carjacked, and someone else had been behind the wheel. Either way, when combined with the pool of blood in the woods, the scenario pointed to a possible homicide.

"I found two more prints on the vehicle on the outside of the driver's-side window. These two prints *don't* resemble the others I got inside the car."

Jane shined her flashlight on the glass at an oblique angle. Brandon saw smudges of fluorescent green powder where the prints had been dusted, and his heart rate sped up. It was their first trace of a possible suspect in Vanessa's disappearance.

He looked at Antonio. "Think it was the guy who swerved off the road? Tom Murray?"

"He didn't touch the driver's side, according to his sworn statement. Murray said he went around to the open side and only touched the wallet to check the ID. We got his prints for exclusionary purposes, in case there's any doubt."

Brandon looked at Jane. "And you're sure these prints on the glass don't match the others inside the vehicle?"

"No, but I'm telling you what I *think*. Also, the prints are larger, and my guess is they belong to a man. It was a good lift," she said, and he caught the pride in her voice. Jane was a master at lifting fingerprints. He'd once seen her get a usable print off an old brick. "I digitized everything and sent it to our expert for further analysis. I think you're going to find that those fingerprints on the glass belong to someone besides the driver."

"The question is, who?" Antonio said.

"That's *your* job," Jane told him. "I'm just showing you what I found."

V ANESSA'S SISTER DIDN'T answer her door, but the TV was on and Antonio saw a Roomba buzzing around the living room floor. He rang the bell again and glanced down the tree-lined street just as a school bus rumbled past the stop sign.

A woman and kids turned the corner. Even from two houses away, Antonio recognized Kate Morris from her driver's license picture. Two little girls with backpacks walked alongside her while another girl in pigtails rode in the wagon Kate pulled behind her.

Kate spotted Antonio and halted. Her gaze darted to the unmarked police car parked in front of her house.

Shit.

He walked down the sidewalk to meet her. She had the same coloring as her sister—auburn hair and blue eyes— but her skin looked ghostly pale as she stopped in front of her house.

"Kate Morris?"

She nodded.

"I'm Antonio Peña." Something told him not to mention *police* in front of her children. "We talked on the phone earlier."

He glanced at the two girls with backpacks, who were eyeing him curiously. They looked to be seven or eight and were so close in height, they could be twins.

"Girls, take Sylvie inside," Kate said, handing off the wagon.

Still watching him, one of the older girls towed the wagon up the walk. The kids went inside, and Kate turned to look at him.

"No news or anything," Antonio said.

Her shoulders sagged.

"Sorry to just drop by. You said you'd be home today, so—"

"No, it's fine. Come in. I appreciate you not saying you're with the police."

"Sure."

"I haven't told the girls about all this."

She started up the sidewalk, and he followed. She wore an oversized T-shirt and black leggings, and her hair was pulled up in a long ponytail. She grabbed a pink sippy cup from the wagon before ushering him inside.

"Excuse the mess," she said.

"It's fine."

She smiled, and he was struck by how young she looked to have so many kids. Despite her resemblance to Vanessa, she looked oddly younger—maybe because she wasn't wearing any makeup.

She led him past a dining room that seemed to serve as a home office. A computer was set up on the table beside stacks of manila files. He followed her into a living room that smelled like a bakery. Antonio's stomach started to growl. Toys littered the floor, and *Mickey Mouse Clubhouse* was playing on the TV.

The girls had dropped their backpacks by the breakfast table and were in the kitchen raiding a pan of cookies.

"Rachel, Becca, y'all take your snack outside."

They loaded up two cookies each and headed for the back door.

The little one grabbed her mother's leg and plugged her thumb into her mouth, gazing up at Antonio with big brown eyes. She wore a glittery lavender dress with a princess on the front.

He smiled down at her. "Are you Elsa?"

She ducked behind her mom.

"She's Anna today. This is her Halloween costume." Kate grabbed a cookie off the pan on the counter and handed it to her. "Go on outside and swing, sweetie. Get Becca to push you."

The girl took the cookie and went outside, and Kate watched through the window as she ran to the wooden playscape.

"So." She gave him a tense smile. "You're familiar with *Frozen*. Do you have kids?"

"Just nieces and nephews." He looked out at the back-yard. "Three girls must keep you busy."

"Four. I've got a fifteen-year-old, too. She's at drill team practice." She picked up a pan from the counter and held it up. "Would you like one? Oatmeal chocolate chip."

"I'm good, thanks."

"Have a seat. Please."

He pulled out a chair and tugged the notebook from his back pocket. He'd worn his blazer over here to conceal his gun, which was more formal than he liked. But he'd found that house calls went better when people weren't distracted by his weapon.

She sank into the chair at the head of the table and pressed her hand to her chest.

"When I first saw you, I thought . . ." She shook her head.

"I'm sorry." He knew what she'd thought, and he felt like crap. "I should have called first."

"No, it's fine."

He opened the notebook and took out a pen. "I won't take much of your time. I just have a few follow-up questions."

And he'd wanted to meet her. Phone interviews were okay, but he got way more information face to face.

He cleared his throat. "First, thanks for filing the missing-person report. It should help expedite things."

She nodded.

"We're still waiting on Vanessa's cell phone records. We're trying to understand her activities leading up to Sunday night, and who she was with."

"Can't you get a warrant for that? I would think since you found blood in the car, it would be urgent."

"We're working on it," he said. "I expect we'll have something soon. In the meantime, I wanted to see if you'd heard back from your family. You were going to contact your brothers to see if anyone had talked to her recently or knew what she's been up to?"

"I checked, and no one's heard from her. But that's really not unusual. Two of my brothers are in the military and one is on an oil rig in the Gulf. She doesn't really keep up with them much since our mom died. Mostly, it's me."

She watched as Antonio jotted that down.

"Ms. Morris—"

"It's Kate."

"Kate." He cleared his throat. "We went back to the location where Vanessa's vehicle was found and talked to several residents nearby, as well as employees at the closest gas station."

"The Exxon."

He looked at her, surprised. "You've been out there?"

"Yesterday, while the girls were in school. I wanted to see the scene for myself."

"Does Vanessa have any friends who live in that area, that you know of?"

She shook her head.

"Do you have any idea why she might have driven out there on Sunday?"

"I've been thinking about it ever since your call. I can't think of any reason. All of Van's friends live in town. The ones I know, at least."

He jotted that down in his notepad, mainly to stall for time because he was getting to the tougher questions.

"Does your sister have any issues with substance abuse?" he asked.

"What, you mean drugs?"

"Drugs, alcohol, anything like that?"

"No."

"What about her friends?"

Her brow furrowed. "I don't think so. Why?"

"There's been some methamphetamine activity out in that area. It's an angle we're looking into. Again, we're trying to figure out why she might have been out there at night on the outskirts of town."

"Well, it wasn't for meth. Not Vanessa. I mean, I don't know about her *friends*. But Vanessa isn't into that. She's really health conscious."

Antonio wrote down her answer, even though in his experience, people's families didn't always know what sort of drugs they were into.

"What about the campground near the lake there?" he asked. "Do you know if she ever went there?"

"No idea." She bit her lip. "Vanessa isn't much of a camper, though. She hates bugs."

She glanced down and looked like she might cry. Antonio flipped through his notes from their previous interview, trying to give her a moment.

"So, Kate—" He cleared his throat. "You said earlier that you're an accountant?"

She dabbed her eyes. "A bookkeeper." She took a deep breath. "Not a CPA. I haven't passed the test."

"Did Vanessa ever talk to you about her financial situation? Or maybe mention any money problems?"

"No."

"She ever ask to borrow money?"

"No. Well, once a few years ago. Her car broke down, and she needed to get it fixed. But it's been a while since she asked for money. She has a good job now at the dermatology clinic."

"How about problems with a boyfriend?"

"Like I said on the phone, she isn't dating anyone that I'm aware of."

"What about ex-boyfriends?"

"What about them?"

"Any problem with anyone from her past? In the last year, maybe?"

"I don't think so. She broke up with someone in the spring, but it sounded like no big deal."

He perked up. "When was this?"

"Maybe . . . after Valentine's Day? I think they're still friends. They sometimes go to movies together."

"You know his name?"

"I've never met him. Cooper somebody. They only dated a few months."

"You know where they met?"

She shook her head. "Online possibly? I know she uses some dating apps, but she doesn't talk to me about them. She knows I don't approve."

"Why not?"

Her brow furrowed. "I told her it was dangerous. I mean, who knows who you're meeting?" She stood abruptly and went over to the sink. She grabbed a sponge and started scrubbing down a cookie sheet. "You think that's what happened, don't you? She met up with some man that hurt her?"

Antonio watched as she furiously scrubbed the pan.

"She's always been too trusting. Always." She glanced up from the sink, and she looked like she might cry again. "Three older brothers looking out for her, she grew up with blinders on. She doesn't see the bad in people, especially men." She tossed down the sponge and looked out the window at her daughters.

Antonio just watched her. Sympathy churned in his stomach. She understood why he was here right now. She understood he was treating this as a homicide investigation, even though it wasn't official yet.

She grabbed a dish towel and dabbed her eyes. "I'm trying to keep it together for the girls, but this is hard. I'm scared."

"I understand."

His words seemed inadequate, but she didn't seem to be listening anyway. She took a plate down from a cabinet and filled it with cookies, then returned to the table.

"Here." She put the plate in front of him and forced a smile. "I can tell you're hungry."

"Thanks."

She sat down and took a deep breath, trying to regain her composure. "Sorry I'm emotional."

"You don't have to be sorry."

"I just wish . . ."

"What?"

"Nothing."

Antonio picked up a cookie and took a bite. The brown sugar melted on his tongue, and he forced himself not to wolf down the whole plate.

She looked at him. "Can I ask you something?"

He nodded.

"What do you *think* happened?"

"We're trying to piece that together. She might have encountered someone on the road, maybe a stranger. Or maybe she was meeting someone out there."

She watched him steadily, and he knew she wanted more.

"We're looking at all the possibilities." He paused. "You think she might have taken off with someone?"

"She wouldn't do that."

He just looked at her.

"I know my sister. She wouldn't run off with someone, not without telling me. Not without taking her phone and her wallet. It doesn't make sense."

He agreed, it didn't. Especially considering the pool of blood not far from the car. But he hadn't told Kate about that. It was one of the key details they were keeping under wraps.

She looked out the window again. "The thing is . . . there's been something going on with her."

He waited. This was why he'd come here—to get more than just yes or no answers.

"I wish I could pinpoint it. She's been, I don't know, withdrawn lately. Stressed. We haven't been talking very much, but I was too busy to really notice until this happened."

"Did she say what was wrong?"

"I asked once, and she dodged me, so I let it go. I know—selfish, right?" She looked at him, her eyes filled with guilt. "I'm her *sister*. I should have pinned her down."

BRANDON PUSHED THROUGH the door of the police station and was surprised to see Leigh. She was a block away, but there was no mistaking the high heels and the confident stride—not to mention the phone pressed to her ear. He stopped to watch her. Where was she going? He had a hunch he knew, and his hunch was confirmed when she noticed him standing there and ended her call.

She stopped in front of him and smiled. "Hey, just the man I was looking for."

He felt a warm rush of attraction, same as the last time he'd seen her.

"Why were you looking for me?" he asked.

"Do you have a moment?"

"Not really."

"It's about the case."

He'd figured as much, so he reached for the door he'd just walked through. He followed her into the lobby of the police station and gestured toward an empty bench near the reception counter.

"I only have a couple minutes," he said as she sat down. "I've got an autopsy at five."

Her eyes widened. "Oh God. Is it—"

"Different case."

She closed her eyes, clearly relieved. He took a seat beside her, leaving plenty of space between them but not enough to keep him from noticing her subtle perfume. She smelled good—much better than the bullpen where he'd spent the last two hours typing up reports. And a hell of a lot better than the place he was going next.

She crossed her legs, and he realized she was wearing another version of the outfit she'd had on yesterday—a snug-fitting skirt and silk blouse. Only the colors were reversed, and today her skirt was white and her top was black. The switch intrigued him, for some reason.

"I won't take much of your time." She glanced at her chunky sports watch. "I just had a follow-up question."

"Follow-up?"

"About Vanessa."

A "follow-up" implied that she'd been interviewing him, when it was the other way around.

"When we first talked at the courthouse, you asked me about Gertrude Soltis, the public defender."

"Yeah?"

She tipped her head to the side. "Why did you ask that?"

"What do you mean?"

"I mean, what's the link between Vanessa and Gertie, if there is one?"

He watched her, mulling how to respond. Again, he didn't want to tell her anything, but if she had anything useful, he needed her cooperation.

"Vanessa doesn't have a criminal record. I checked," she said. "So how did Gertie come up?"

"Why does it matter?"

"Well, I'm her lawyer. I'm trying to understand her legal issues. I'm building a comprehensive file—"

"Why?"

She looked startled. "So I can help. Why else?"

"Help Vanessa? Or the police?"

"Well, both, really. I'm trying to understand her legal situation at the time of her disappearance. It could be relevant what happened to her." She paused. "Don't you agree?"

Brandon gritted his teeth. When he'd first gone looking for Leigh Larson, he'd thought there was a chance she held the key to whatever had happened to Vanessa. She still might. But he'd underestimated how much getting a lawyer involved would complicate things. He should have known. And he should have resisted the temptation to loop her in. But she was smart and smooth and, yes, *beautiful*, and each time she reached out to him he convinced himself it only made sense to hear what she had to say.

"Well?" She leaned closer. "Do you?"

His attention snapped back to her question: Did he agree Vanessa's legal situation could be relevant?

"Absolutely. But that doesn't mean I want you involved."

She rolled her eyes. "Oh, come on. You're being territorial. I'm on your side here. I want to help you find Vanessa."

He just looked at her.

"Okay, here's another question," she said. "Has there been any activity on Vanessa's credit card? Purchases, ATM withdrawals? I assume you're monitoring her cards."

They were, and there hadn't been any activity, but Brandon didn't tell her that.

"Sorry," he said, although he wasn't, "but I can't discuss

details about the investigation." He stood up. "I have to head out."

She stood, too, looking annoyed now. "You still haven't answered my question about the link between Vanessa and a criminal defense attorney."

"Unfortunately, I have to get going," he said. If she was set on investigating, she could figure it out for herself. He didn't want to encourage her.

"Call me if you come across something that can help us," he said.

She scoffed and crossed her arms. "You refuse to answer a few simple questions and you want me to call *you*?"

He smiled. "That's right, counselor. That's how this works."

CHAPTER FIVE

===========

Vanessa adams rented a one-bedroom walkup apartment on the north side of town, in a neighborhood where rents that had once been affordable were steadily ticking up. By the time they arrived around midmorning, the parking lot was nearly empty and most of the residents appeared to be at work.

"Like I told you, I don't think anything's missing," Vanessa's sister said to Brandon as she unlocked the door. "I was here just yesterday."

Kate stepped into the apartment, and Brandon followed, casting a look over his shoulder. Antonio had stopped to interview a man in a paramedic's uniform who appeared to be leaving for work.

"It's kind of messy," Kate said from the tiny kitchen, which consisted of a small patch of linoleum flooring. She stepped toward the sink.

"Wait," Brandon said. He could see from her face that she wanted to do something about the pile of dirty dishes. "It's best not to move anything." He pulled a pair of gloves from his pocket and handed them to her. "If you want to open closets or anything, use these."

She bit her lip and looked at the gloves, as though accepting them might be some kind of admission. She took them, and he pulled out a pair for himself.

"Mind if I . . . ?" He nodded toward the hallway.

"Whatever you need to do."

Brandon left her in the kitchen, giving her some privacy. She was on the verge of tears. The reality of the situation seemed to be taking hold.

With every hour that ticked by, the benign explanations—Vanessa had had car trouble and hitched a ride to a friend's, she'd called an Uber, she'd gone away with a boyfriend—were becoming more and more implausible. What was becoming clear to her sister, and had been clear to Brandon the moment he saw that passenger door hanging open, was that something unexpected, and unexpectedly bad, had happened to Vanessa on that highway.

But right now they were stalled. They still had no body, so for now they were dealing with a missing-person case instead of a homicide, which meant everything was slower, including getting the warrant needed for Vanessa's cell phone records. Without that phone dump, they were flying blind, trying to piece together what she'd been doing in the hours and minutes leading up to her disappearance.

Brandon stepped into the bathroom, which had a prefab tub with a moldy white shower curtain. A pink razor and a jumble of plastic bottles were lined up along the side. On the Formica vanity, a zippered makeup bag and a scattering of pencils and brushes sat alongside the sink. A glass cup held a purple toothbrush and a tube of whitening toothpaste.

Brandon opened the medicine cabinet with a gloved hand and inspected the contents: mouthwash, acne cream, an array of vitamins. He closed the cabinet and caught Kate's reflection in the mirror.

"Do you know if your sister takes any prescriptions?" he asked.

"Nothing regularly." Her brow furrowed. "She gets allergies sometimes, and she has something for that." She scooted around him and opened a linen cabinet. Amid the stacks of mismatched towels, she found a plastic bin filled with over-the-counter medicines. Tucked among the bottles was a sheet of pills in foil blister packets.

"These are her allergy meds," she said. "That's the only thing I know about."

The apartment door opened. Brandon and Kate stepped into the hallway. Antonio gave Brandon a look that let him know he wanted to talk privately.

Brandon walked over.

"I talked to the tenant in 223," Antonio said in a low voice. "He hasn't seen her since Sunday morning, when he passed her in the parking lot. He was coming off his shift, and Vanessa was walking upstairs with some groceries."

"What time?"

"Around eight thirty. He's an EMT and he'd been working the graveyard shift. I got his contact info, if we need to follow up."

Kate watched them from the hallway, listening intently.

"I, um, I'll wait outside while y'all finish up." She walked past them to exit the apartment, quietly closing the door behind her.

Antonio turned to Brandon. "It's sinking in with her," he said.

"I know."

"Hey, did I tell you I saw the lawyer again yesterday?" Antonio asked.

"Who?"

"Leigh Larson. She was pulling up to Kate's house in her little blue Mustang just as I was leaving."

"What was she doing there?"

"I figure same thing I was. She wanted to talk to Kate."

"Well, what'd she say to you?"

"Nothing. Just smiled and waved."

Brandon felt a prick of annoyance, and he wasn't sure why. If Leigh wanted to talk to her client's sister, so what? It shouldn't bother him.

Except that it did. Leigh was obviously still poking around and asking questions. He didn't want her involved in his case, and he definitely didn't want her talking to potential witnesses before he did.

"You get a look at the kitchen yet?" Antonio asked.

"I was about to do the bedroom."

"I'll check out the kitchen."

Brandon walked to the back of the apartment. The bedroom was dim, with light coming in through slats of the closed miniblinds. Brandon scanned the space, taking in the unmade bed, the scattered shoes, the chair in the corner heaped with clothes. The room smelled faintly of vanilla, and he spied a fat white candle on the nightstand.

He stepped over and opened the drawer. Most people's nightstands were filled with personal clutter. Vanessa's was almost empty except for a plastic baggie with a few antacids and an individual blister tab that looked like her allergy medicine.

He turned to the closet, which stood open. Compared to the rest of the apartment, it was surprisingly tidy, with shoes lined up neatly on the floor and hanging clothes sorted by type—shirts, dresses, jeans. Tucked behind the hanging clothes was a black roll-on suitcase.

After checking a few more drawers, Brandon returned to the kitchen to find Antonio standing in front of the refrigerator.

"Looks like she just stocked up," his partner said. "Fruit, almond milk, Diet Snapple."

"Any beer or wine?"

"Uh . . . six-pack of Michelob Ultra. Two gone."

"Detective?" Kate leaned her head in the door. "Vanessa's neighbor just came home, if you want to talk to her."

"I got it," Antonio said. He walked out, leaving Brandon alone in the kitchen.

He stepped over to the sink, which was filled with dirty plates and mugs. Opening the cabinet beneath, he found a half-filled trash can. On top was an empty takeout box and a cardboard coffee cup with Vanessa's name scribbled across the side.

So, they now had a grocery run and a coffee stop, plus maybe some takeout food. What else had Vanessa been doing the weekend she disappeared?

On the counter was a phone charger and a yellow pad of sticky notes with a phone number scrawled across it, local area code. Brandon took out his phone and snapped a photo of the number. Beside the notepad was a bowl filled with coins, nail clippers, a red matchbook with the name of a sports bar on South Congress. Decker's Pub. Brandon had never been there, but he knew the location because it was near his favorite jazz club. On the inside flap of the matchbook was a scrawled address: 325 *Clark #104*. Brandon snapped a picture of that, too.

Antonio returned, and the look on his face made Brandon's pulse pick up.

"Just talked to the neighbor. She said she passed Vanessa on the stairs Sunday night around ten. Hasn't seen her since."

Not long before her abandoned car was discovered.

"Was Vanessa coming or going?" Brandon asked.

"Going." Antonio glanced back at the door. "This woman said they didn't say hi. Vanessa was talking on her phone, and she looked upset."

"Upset?"

"Yeah, she was crying apparently."

Brandon checked his watch. "Let's go."

"Where?"

"Time to light fires under some people. We need that phone dump."

L EIGH PULLED INTO the parking lot of Pura Vida just before her noon appointment. Since her meeting with Brandon yesterday, she'd begun to wonder if she was wasting her time with this quest. But she'd been distracted for days, and she knew she wouldn't be able to truly focus on anything else until she got some answers about Vanessa.

Leigh surveyed the sleek glass building that she hadn't visited in months. Pura Vida billed itself as a dermatology clinic, but it looked more like a day spa. Besides offering facials and chemical peels, the clinic did a booming business in everything from Botox and collagen injections to liposuction and facelifts. The office occupied the bottom two floors of a U-shaped building that looked out on a courtyard with a fountain.

It was lunchtime, and Leigh watched the front door as women in high-end workout gear streamed in and out, along with Pura Vida staffers in bright pink scrubs. At twelve sharp, Leigh spied her former client amid the stream of people. Tiffany had chopped her hair since their last meeting, but at five-foot-eleven, she was easy to spot.

Leigh waved to catch her eye as she walked over. Tiffany wore white Adidas sneakers with pink laces that matched her scrubs.

"Thanks for meeting me," Leigh said.

"Sure." She smiled. "You saved me from ramen noodles."

At the end of the building was a small café with yellow umbrella tables where Leigh and Tiffany had met before to discuss her case. The tables looked full, but they could eat in the courtyard.

"Love the hair," Leigh said as they walked over.

"Thanks. I just did it." Tiffany touched it self-consciously. "I needed a change, ya know?"

"Absolutely. It looks great on you."

They entered the restaurant and stepped up to the counter to order. They got food to go, Leigh's treat, and found a shaded bench near the fountain.

"So, what's up?" Tiffany asked, poking a straw into her iced tea. "I know you're too busy to call me just to chat."

Leigh peeled the lid off her fruit cup. "First, I wanted to thank you for the referral."

She arched her perfectly shaped eyebrows. "Referral?"

"Vanessa Adams." Leigh watched her reaction closely because she was here on a hunch. "That was you, right? She came to see me a while back about a legal issue, and she mentioned that she worked here at the clinic."

"Oh." Tiffany's expression clouded. "You heard what happened, right? That she's missing?"

"I did."

"A detective was here yesterday asking questions about her."

Leigh wasn't surprised. Brandon struck her as thorough. "Detective Reynolds?" she asked.

"And someone else, too," Tiffany said. "Detective Peña, I think it was. You talked to them?"

"Yeah. Did they interview you?"

"Just briefly. They talked to her supervisor, mostly, and then several of the other admins in her section. I don't know if we were able to help much." She put her tea down and looked at Leigh. "So, Vanessa hired you?"

"That's right."

"Why?"

Leigh chose her words carefully. She had to walk a fine line between asking questions and answering them. "I can't get into specifics."

"No, I get that. But was it something like *my* case?" She shuddered. "I sure as hell hope not. I wouldn't wish that on anyone."

"To be honest, I'm not sure exactly what she was dealing

with," Leigh said. "We only had a brief meeting in the summer. Her legal issue sounded pretty straightforward, but now I'm wondering if there's more to the story."

She watched Tiffany's reaction carefully. She picked the onions from her turkey wrap but didn't respond.

"Do you know if she was having any problems with harassment? Or anything online?" Leigh asked.

"She never said anything like that," Tiffany replied. "But she did ask me a lot of questions about all that shit with Julian. I told her about my settlement and everything, so maybe that's why she called you. I really don't know."

So, it sounded like Vanessa *had* gotten Leigh's name from Tiffany. That was one mystery solved, but not the most important one.

"But she never talked about problems with an ex or anyone?" Leigh asked.

Tiffany shook her head.

Leigh tried to mask her disappointment. Talking to Tiffany had been a long shot, but she'd hoped that if she and Vanessa were friends, Vanessa would have confided in her if she was having problems with a guy.

But many of Leigh's clients were very tight-lipped, due to a potent combination of fear and embarrassment. Some never talked to anyone about the pain they were dealing with until they came to Leigh's office and sat down on her couch. That was usually when the floodgates opened, and their misery spilled forth in a powerful torrent.

Tiffany had been one such client, not even telling her current boyfriend what was happening until she had formally filed a lawsuit.

Leigh looked her client over now and felt a renewed wave of sympathy. Tiffany's life had been forever changed by a vindictive ex who'd uploaded a sex video to half a dozen porn sites. The video was viewed thousands of times before someone recognized Tiffany and sent a screenshot to her brother, of all people. By the time Tiffany figured out what had happened and came to Leigh, the video had been passed around so much, it was practically impossible to get it removed, even with a court order.

Now, two years later, Tiffany was still checking online to see if her images had resurfaced. Each time she found one, she sent a takedown notice. Had the problem subsided? Yes. Had it gone away? No. That could take years. And—like so many of Leigh's clients—she would always carry the knowledge that her naked images could be out there somewhere for any dirtbag to see.

Tiffany was only twenty-four, but she'd been sentenced to years of punishment by a rage-filled man who couldn't deal with rejection.

"How are you doing with everything?" Leigh asked.

She sighed. "It comes and goes." She shrugged. "Me and Ross broke up. You remember the guy I was seeing when everything happened?"

She nodded.

"He just couldn't handle it. I guess I've become pretty paranoid about people. I don't know." Another shrug. "I've been seeing that therapist. The woman you recommended."

"Oh yeah?"

"We meet once a week. So, you know, the money helps in that way. But it's not like a cure-all. You told me that from the beginning, and you were right."

Leigh nodded. Money couldn't buy happiness, but it could by a crap-ton of therapy, which was what some of her clients needed after everything they'd gone through.

"I hope Vanessa's okay," Tiffany said now. "It was really a shock when those detectives showed up."

Leigh didn't comment. Clearly, Brandon and his partner had neglected to share certain information, such as the fact that they were treating the case like a homicide.

"You know, there is this one thing that's been bugging me," Tiffany said.

Leigh's pulse picked up at the tone of her voice. "What?"

"She was seeing someone over the summer. And she was weird about it."

"Weird?"

"Secretive." Tiffany looked away. "Sometimes we'd grab lunch together and swap stories. I told her all about Ross and our breakup, for instance. And she told me about breaking up with her boyfriend last spring."

"Do you remember his name?"

"Cooper Collins. He's a grad student at UT. But this thing was different. Early in the summer, she went on a date she was all excited about, but then she wouldn't talk about him. She said she didn't want to jinx it, but I thought maybe it was something else, like the guy was married or something."

"Did she tell you his name?"

"No."

"Was she still seeing him?" Leigh popped a grape into her mouth, trying to act casual.

"I don't know. I stopped asking because the topic was off-limits. But then it felt weird going to lunch, and so we stopped going. I really hadn't talked to her in months, and now all this happened."

"Did you tell the detectives about this?"

"Yeah. But they didn't react, really. It's not like I had a name or anything."

Any detective worth his salt could figure it out. Hell, Leigh could probably figure it out with some basic nosing around. It was a good lead.

As if on cue, a dark sedan pulled into the parking lot and slid into a space in front of the clinic. Leigh felt a flutter of nerves as she watched a pair of detectives get out, one tall and one short.

"Welp. Looks like they're back," Leigh said.

"Who?"

"Reynolds and Peña." Leigh replaced the lid on her fruit cup. She hadn't finished lunch, but she wasn't eager to cross paths with them. Detectives, as a rule, were protective about their cases, and that went double for Brandon.

Tiffany checked her phone. "I'd better get back," she said, gathering up her food.

"Same. Thanks for meeting. It was good to catch up."

They stood.

"Take care of yourself, Tiffany."

She gave a tired smile. "I try."

CHAPTER SIX

After a frustrating day, Brandon swung by Leigh's law firm. He found a space on Tenth Street and surveyed the old house from his truck. The front windows were dark, both upstairs and down, but light spilled from a window along the side of the building. Given the blue Mustang parked in the alley, Brandon suspected the office with the light on might be Leigh's.

He slid from his pickup and glanced around. This part of downtown emptied in the evenings as nine-to-fivers either commuted home or migrated to Sixth Street for happy hour. A homeless guy pushed a shopping cart through an intersection, watching Brandon with a wary look.

Brandon walked up the sidewalk to the old house and mounted the creaky wooden stairs. A brick sign in the yard advertised Leigh's firm, as well as an accounting business that apparently shared the building. The porch was dark. Shadows shifted as a fat gray cat dashed behind a planter.

Suddenly, the light switched on and the door opened.

"Hey," Leigh said, clearly surprised to see him. "What are you doing here?"

"Looking for you."

She stepped out, pulling the door shut behind her. She looked sexy again today in a tight black skirt and silky pink blouse. Instead of heels she wore sequined purple flip-flops.

"Headed home?" Brandon asked as she twisted around to lock the door.

"Nope. Dinner break." She turned to face him.

"Dinner?"

"Yeah, you know. Food. Water. Sustenance. In this case, tofu pad thai." She smiled. "Care to join me?"

"You want me to have tofu with you?"

"Have whatever you like. I'm going to Mei's." She nodded at the Thai restaurant on the corner. "They've got an eclectic menu."

"I'm good on food, but I'll walk with you."

He stepped aside, and she gave him an amused look before going ahead of him down the stairs.

"To what do I owe the honor of this visit?"

Her flip-flops made little thwacking noises on the sidewalk as they walked toward the intersection. The homeless man had disappeared, but now there was a man on a bike cutting through the alley near Leigh's car.

"You always park in the alley at night?" Brandon asked.

"Only when I show up in the afternoon and all the meters are full. You didn't answer my question."

They stopped at the intersection. A delivery truck roared by, giving Brandon another few seconds to come up with an answer. He'd driven by Leigh's office on the off chance that she was working late. He hadn't really planned what he wanted to say to her.

"You've been poking around my case," he said.

She lifted an eyebrow. "Poking?"

"Digging. Meddling. Whatever you want to call it."

The light changed, and they crossed the street. The restaurant glowed like a lantern on the corner, and the other nearby businesses looked to be closed for the night.

LAST SEEN ALONE

67

"Well, I definitely wouldn't call it *meddling*." She neared the door, and he reached around her to open it.

Warm air wafted out as they stepped inside. The restaurant smelled like fried spring rolls, and Brandon's mouth began to water. A row of red vinyl booths lined the wall, all empty. Looked like they did a lot of carryout, though, and the Formica counter beside the cash register was filled with paper bags, each with a receipt stapled to the top.

"Am I early?" Leigh asked the woman behind the register.

Thin and fiftyish, the woman looked Brandon over before picking up a paper bag. "No, you're ready."

Leigh turned to Brandon. "What about you? If you order the special, it shouldn't take long."

"I'm good."

"You sure?"

"Yeah."

Leigh stuffed some bills into the tip jar beside the register and took the bag. "Thanks, Su."

"Come back soon."

"I will."

The spring roll aroma followed them out, and Brandon's stomach rumbled. They hurried across the street as the crosswalk light counted down to zero.

"Investigating," Leigh said, resuming their conversation. "Not meddling."

"What for?"

"Because. Vanessa's my client. I need to understand what's going on with her."

Like Vanessa's sister, Leigh was using the present tense. Brandon noticed things like that. When someone talked about a missing person in the past tense, he noticed that, too.

They reached the law firm again, and Brandon followed her up the steps. Without a word, she handed him the warm sack of food and unlocked the door.

As opposed to Brandon's last visit, the place was deserted. No harried-looking paralegals or smiling receptionist. Leigh flipped the latch on the door and jerked her head toward the hallway.

"I'm back here," she said, leading him down the corridor.

"Do you work late a lot?"

"Couple nights a week, usually. I've got a trial coming up."

He followed her into a small office that resembled a living room. It had a dark blue sofa and an oversized armchair arranged around a coffee table blanketed with paperwork. An expensive-looking rug added a homey touch to the room.

"Make yourself comfortable," she said before disappearing back into the hallway.

Brandon set the bag of food on the end table and looked around. A banker's lamp glowed on a small desk in the corner. No family photos on the desk—just a starfish-shaped paperweight and a stack of files. The framed diplomas on the wall snagged Brandon's attention. BA from University of Texas. JD from UT Law.

She stepped back into the room with a stack of napkins and a pair of water bottles.

"What's 'Order of the Coif'?" he asked.

"Honor society for law school."

"Nice. Why isn't that in your firm bio?"

She sank into the leather armchair and slipped off her flip-flops. "You've been checking up on me?"

He stepped over and hesitated a moment before taking a seat on the blue velvet sofa. It was even more comfortable than it looked, and Brandon felt strange being here. It felt like her private living room instead of an office.

She opened the bag and unpacked three small cartons.

"That water's for you," she said. "Sure you're not hungry? There's plenty of food."

"I'm fine, thanks." He grabbed the water and twisted the top off, watching her.

She was good at evading questions, but he had no intention of letting her off the hook.

"So, did you get anywhere?" He swigged his drink.

"What do you mean?" She unwrapped a plastic fork and stabbed at a carton of noodles.

"Did you figure out what was going on with Vanessa before she disappeared?"

"I made some progress." She dabbed her lip with a napkin and put her fork down. "You know, you could have just asked me nicely to help you instead of getting all pissy."

"Pissy?"

"Yes, and territorial." She opened another carton and took out a fried spring roll. "I mean, has it occurred to you that I might be in a better position to get info from people than a couple of cops flashing badges?"

He watched her, annoyed again, and again, he didn't know why. It *had* occurred to him that she might have better luck talking to people. That was why he was here. But he hadn't expected her to hang it over him. Or to be so cagey with information.

"You sound like you think this is a game," he said.

Her eyes bugged. "Are you kidding?"

"No."

"I do *not* think this is a game. I'm the last one who would ever think that."

He could tell he'd ticked her off. Good.

She dropped her half-eaten spring roll onto the napkin and dusted off her hands. "I'm *worried*, okay? That's why I'm doing this. That's why I've spent the better part of this week ignoring my caseload and driving around town interviewing Vanessa's friends and her sister and her co-workers. I've probably talked to more people than you, and I probably got more out of them, too. And I'm happy to share info, even though you're being defensive about it."

First, he was pissy. Now, defensive.

"What?" she demanded. "What's that look?"

He'd definitely pushed her buttons, and now he wondered whether it was the right tactic.

He took a deep breath. "I'm not trying to be defensive. I'm just not used to civilians horning in on my work."

"I used to work for the public defender's office," she told him. "I know how to investigate a case, and interview witnesses, and vet a story. I know how to sniff out bullshit and how to tell when people are lying."

He nodded. "Good for you."

"Is that sarcastic?"

"No. I mean it. I bet you're a skilled interviewer."

She watched him for a long moment. Heat flickered in those pretty green eyes, and he ignored the jolt of attraction.

She picked up a carton and held it out. "Have a spring roll."

"I'm fine."

She sighed. "Please. I can hear your stomach rumbling from here."

She held out the carton like a peace offering, and he took a roll. She put a napkin in front of him and then a little plastic container of mustard.

"Careful, it's hot," she said.

He pulled off the lid. "So, what did Vanessa's friends tell you?"

"Well, there were some common threads."

He dipped the spring roll in mustard and chomped into it. Fire wafted up his nose, and his eyes filled with tears.

"Damn," he choked.

"I warned you."

She smiled as he swigged water.

"Almost everyone said Vanessa had seemed distracted lately." She returned her attention to the noodles. "She was upset about something, but no one knew what, exactly. Her sister told me she'd seemed really stressed out."

"How long had she been that way?"

"A month or two, depending on who you talk to."

"So . . . since August."

"Right."

"That's around when she came to see you."

"Right. So, I'm thinking she was having some problems beyond what she told me in our initial meeting."

"Like what?"

"I don't know, but I've got some ideas."

He finished off the spring roll and watched her, waiting.

"I don't think she only came to see me because of that thing with her landlord. I mean, I think that was part of it, but not the only reason. I think she hadn't gotten around to telling me the rest yet. She was probably going to, which was why she signed our client agreement and sent me the retainer."

"How much was that?"

"Five hundred. Which is lower than our usual, but I quoted her our discount rate because she seemed worried about money."

She took another sip of water, and Brandon tried not to get distracted by her mouth.

"Like I told you the other day, I get all kinds of clients." She set the bottle down. "But the two most common problems I handle are revenge porn and stalkers. I've found several clues that suggest to me that Vanessa might have a revenge porn problem. The first one is that she found me through an informal referral from another client with a similar type of case."

"Informal? What does that mean?"

"This client of mine is friends with Vanessa. They work together at Pura Vida. Anyway, I talked to her, and she never actually gave Vanessa my contact info, but they discussed *her* case and she told Vanessa I represented her."

"And her case was revenge porn?"

"That's right." She slurped a noodle off her fork.

"Were you successful?"

"Yep. We got a big fat settlement—which doesn't solve my client's problem, but it helps."

"Okay. You said 'several clues.' What was the other thing?"

Leigh sighed. "The other thing is based on personal observation. Vanessa had cut marks on her left forearm."

"Cut marks?"

"A lot of people dealing with nonconsensual sexual images become depressed, sometimes suicidal. I would definitely describe Vanessa as under duress the last time I saw her, and she showed signs of self-harm."

"Why didn't you tell me this earlier?" he asked.

"I'm telling you now."

"It goes to her state of mind."

"I know."

Brandon watched her carefully. "Do you have any reason to think Vanessa might have taken her own life?"

Her eyes grew somber and she picked at her noodles. She looked up.

"I really don't know," she said.

Brandon hadn't told Leigh about the blood pool in the woods. Investigators were keeping that detail under wraps for now. But he and Antonio had considered the possibility that Vanessa could have gone into the woods and killed herself, maybe ending up at the bottom of that lake. He wished he'd known about the self-harming stuff before now.

Leigh watched him, her expression solemn. From the beginning, he'd known she was holding out on him. No doubt, she still was. But she was also providing lots of good information that he hadn't had, so it was probably better to keep her talking rather than nitpick her timing.

"So, that's one possibility," Leigh said. "Another type of case I handle a lot is stalkers. In most stalking cases I see— and you probably know this—the stalkers aren't strangers to their victims. Typically, they're intimate partners."

"The psycho exes you mentioned," he said.

She tipped her head to the side. "Exes, almost always. As

for the psycho part, that varies by case. I'm not a psychiatrist, I'm a lawyer. I don't know what all these guys' mental health issues are, and I'm not here to diagnose them. But what I see most often is a guy who's been rejected. He feels betrayed and humiliated—especially if she's met somebody else. So he starts stalking his ex in order to reassert control. Sometimes these guys post revenge porn, too. It's all a form of punishment, and it usually works, unfortunately."

"Have you ever seen a guy escalate from stalking to violence against one of your clients?"

"Oh yeah. Happens a lot. A big chunk of what I do is help my clients get restraining orders. But as far as Vanessa's concerned? We never got to anything like that." Leigh shook her head. "All she ever told me about was this lease problem. But that in itself is another red flag to me."

"Why?"

"Well, she was having this whole issue with her landlord because he said she was illegally *subletting* her apartment. So I'm wondering, why did she move? Did she feel unsafe in her home for some reason? Was someone coming around, bothering her? And when you combine that with Kate saying how Vanessa got a new phone—"

"Vanessa's sister?"

"Yes. Kate. She told me Vanessa got a new phone during the summer. She claimed she lost her other phone, but maybe she just wanted a new phone number. I see that all the time when clients are being stalked and harassed by an ex. A simple block-and-delete strategy doesn't work with these guys. You have to sever ties completely—which may have been what Vanessa was trying to do."

"So, this nightmare ex-boyfriend theory—"

"It's a *theory*," she told him. "I don't have proof or anything. Just, you know, some circumstances that raise red flags to me, based on talking to her friends and her sister."

"I need to interview the boyfriend. You have a name?"

"I'm a step ahead of you."

He felt a dart of annoyance. "You talked to him?"

"Went to see him this afternoon. His name's Cooper Collins, and she dated him last winter. He's a grad student at UT. Works at the bookstore near campus."

"How did you find him?"

"How I find anyone. The Internet. You can locate pretty much anybody if you know how to look."

"Jesus, Leigh."

"What?"

He leaned close, needing to get through to her. "You went to see a potential suspect in a woman's disappearance. What the hell were you thinking?"

"We met in a public place. And for what it's worth, I don't think he's a suspect. He doesn't strike me as the type."

Brandon shook his head.

"There's definitely a profile, and Cooper Collins doesn't fit," she went on. "Trust me. I deal with these assholes every day. They're sadistic and controlling and extremely manipulative. Cooper doesn't fit."

"Do me a favor. Don't talk to any more potential suspects, okay? You're putting yourself and the investigation at risk. The last thing we need is you tipping someone off before we get a chance to talk to them."

"Fine. You can handle the other one."

"What other one?"

"One of her friends told me about another guy she dated last spring. His name is Jason . . . something. Hang on, I wrote it down." She went to her desk and flipped open a notepad. "Mandrapilias. I haven't talked to him."

"Don't. Let me handle it."

She wrote something on a yellow sticky note and brought it to him. "You're welcome."

"Thanks," he said.

She sank into the armchair again, this time tucking her feet under her.

Brandon just looked at her, both impressed and annoyed as hell. He couldn't believe all the details she'd unearthed in a few short days. He also couldn't believe she'd had the nerve to go talk to all these people.

Brandon's phone buzzed with a text message. He pulled it out to check.

"Work calling?" she asked.

"Yeah. I need to go."

But he didn't move. He just sat there, staring at her, mesmerized by her sharp green eyes. Even with all the leads she'd given him, he still didn't know whether he should have come here tonight. She pushed his buttons, and he could tell she knew it. She seemed to enjoy it, in fact. Usually, he was better at shielding his reaction.

Leigh's gaze softened as she watched him in the dim light of the desk lamp. He needed to leave. They'd crossed some sort of line into personal tonight. He felt it, and he had a feeling she did, too.

"You okay?" she asked.

"Yeah." He stood up and tucked his phone away. "I should get back."

She stood, too, putting her at eye level with his neck. She wasn't as tall as usual in her bare feet.

She stared up at him with those catlike eyes.

"So, listen—"

"Don't." She held up a hand. "I already know what you're going to say."

"What?"

"You appreciate my help, but you can take it from here."

"You need to stop talking to people."

"That's not going to happen." She smiled. "But I can assure you I'll be careful."

"I mean it, Leigh."

"I do, too. And if I learn anything useful, I'll be sure to let you know."

CHAPTER SEVEN

=====

ANTONIO FOUND HIS PARTNER in a conference room in front of a laptop and a stack of paperwork. Brandon looked pissed off, and the loosened tie around his neck gave Antonio a hint as to why.

"How was the deposition?" he asked.

Brandon didn't look up. "Tedious."

Depositions were right up there with root canals. Antonio didn't know a single detective who liked to get all dressed up to get grilled by a bunch of lawyers.

He dropped a file folder on the table beside Brandon.

"What's this?" his partner asked.

"The phone dump for Vanessa Adams. It came in this morning."

His face brightened and he reached for the folder. "Anything in it?"

"Lots."

He let Brandon skim the records as he sat down and popped open a can of Red Bull. He'd skipped lunch and needed a sugar boost. Brandon flipped to the last page, just as Antonio had known he would.

"Nine fifty-five Sunday night." He glanced up. "That's the call she was taking when the neighbor passed her on the stairs and said she was crying."

"Reina Chambers," Antonio said. "I tracked her down already."

"And?"

"And she didn't know Vanessa was missing. Whole thing took her totally off-guard. She sounded really rattled over the phone."

"Who is she?"

"A friend of Vanessa's. They know each other from a therapy group, apparently. She said Vanessa called her Sunday night and told her she'd had a rough weekend."

Brandon's eyebrows arched. "Why?"

"She didn't elaborate, according to the friend. Just told her she'd been struggling with cutting and needed to talk."

"Cutting herself?"

"Yeah, they're in a support group for it. I didn't even know that was a thing, right? She said they talked about that, mostly. Vanessa said she'd see her at the next group meeting, but she skipped it."

"When was this?"

"Tuesday at noon. They meet at St. Michael's church over there on the south side."

"Vanessa say anything to her about trouble with a boy-friend or an ex? Anything like that?"

"Nope."

"Shit."

"I know. I was hoping for a break, given the timing."

Brandon leaned back in his chair and sighed.

"So, this cutting thing has me thinking about the quarry again," Antonio said. "That lake out there's really deep."

Brandon nodded. They'd already talked about the pos-sibility that Vanessa had slashed her wrists or maybe downed a bottle of pills and gone for a swim. It was possible, especially in light of this new info from her girlfriend. But something about that scenario didn't feel right.

"I keep coming back to that blood in the woods," Antonio said.

"Same. This doesn't feel like a suicide to me."

"Me either."

Brandon flipped back through the pages, which Antonio had spent the morning marking up. "What else is in here?"

"A couple calls to her sister. A couple to the clinic where she works. One to Leigh Larson."

Brandon's head snapped up. "When?"

"A week ago, I think. I made a note in the margin."

He frowned down at the papers. "M & L."

"Yeah, looks like she called Mendez and Larson at five thirty p.m., so could have been after hours." He paused. "I can contact Leigh about it, see if there's a record of the phone call."

"I'll do it."

His reaction confirmed Antonio's suspicion. Brandon had a thing for the lawyer. Antonio didn't really blame him, but it might make the case a little dicey if it turned out she was withholding information.

Brandon glanced at him. "What?"

"Nothing."

"What's this 725 number? It's in here twice."

Antonio nodded. "That's the one I'm looking at, too. I haven't been able to track it down yet. Think maybe it's a no-contract phone. I tried calling it from a blocked number, but no one picks up."

"Interesting."

"Yep."

There were plenty of legit reasons to have a no-contract phone, and plenty of sketchy reasons, too.

"Maybe it belongs to one of her exes," Antonio said. "If either of them has a burner phone, I'd like to know why."

Brandon checked his watch and pushed his chair back.

"Where you going?"

"Time to hit the road," Brandon said. "These suspects aren't going to come to us."

L EIGH STUCK HER head into Javi's office as he ended a phone call.

"Hey, Part Time. You're here."

She stepped into the office. "Um, excuse me? I was here till eleven last night."

"Doing what?" He leaned back in his chair and propped his Bruno Maglis on the desk.

"Prepping for the Tannehill trial."

Javi frowned. "When is it?"

"Opening arguments next Wednesday."

"How's the other thing? Your missing client?"

Leigh shut the door behind her. The firm had six other employees, and every one of them had big ears.

"Still missing," Leigh said.

"That's not good."

"I know."

"You deposit that check yet?"

"Javi."

"What? I'm just asking. You're putting a lot of time into this."

"*No*, I didn't. I didn't have the heart to."

Javi sighed. They had a strange partnership, but it worked for them. Javi paid attention to the money, pushing everyone in the firm to hold costs down and bill as many hours as possible, so they could keep the lights on and make payroll. Leigh was more the rainmaker, bringing in new clients and keeping the cases flowing. She put a lot of work into her role, attending seminars and networking and staying in touch with friends from law school. She also handled recruiting and was responsible for all three associates who'd joined the firm.

"There's more to this case than I thought," she told Javi. "I'm getting sucked in."

He lifted an eyebrow. "I can't imagine why."

It was a reference to Brandon, but she ignored it.

"Gertie Soltis finally called me back," she said. "She remembered Vanessa's case. She was arrested for shoplifting when she was nineteen, but the charges were dismissed."

"Gertie remembers that? Sounds routine."

"She remembers it because Vanessa's mom had just died, so her sister shepherded her through the process, apparently, and later helped her get her record expunged so she wouldn't have it hanging over her head. Gertie said Vanessa was kind of a basket case, and she felt sorry for her."

"Is she still a basket case?" Javi asked.

"I don't know. But I think she may have had a stalker."

"Why?"

"Red flags everywhere. She changed her number, changed her address. She'd been under stress right before she disappeared."

He steepled his hands under his chin. "Ex-boyfriend?"

"I'm looking into it."

"Sounds dangerous. Why don't you leave that to your detective?"

She shot him a look. "He's not *my* anything. And I feel like he needs my help. I'm familiar with these types of cases."

"You mean these types of psychos."

"Well, I am. You are, too. Most people don't deal with the sort of toxic assholes we handle on a daily basis. I feel like I can offer some insights."

"Well, don't *offer* him too much. Remember, he's a cop."

She crossed her arms. "So?"

"So, when have you ever met a cop that wasn't bossy and controlling? Those guys are alpha with a capital *A*. I thought you were done with that. What happened to Yoga Man?"

She rolled her eyes. "Jonathan was never serious. That was, like, a couple of dates and we had no chemistry."

"You bought a freaking Lululemon wardrobe for the guy."

"I did not. I bought it for *me*, and I'm still going to classes. Whenever I get time."

Which hadn't happened in weeks, but whatever. Javi was needling her. He didn't like that she'd been distracted from her other clients—ones who paid. She didn't take it personally, though. He cracked the whip on everyone.

"You need to watch out for yourself," he said. "Leave the policework to the police."

"You sound like Brandon."

"Oh yeah? Told you he was bossy."

A knock sounded at the door, and Bella leaned her head in. "Oh, hey, you're here," she said to Leigh. "I thought you were out today."

"I was at the courthouse. What's up?"

She stepped into the office and handed a FedEx envelope to Javi. "This just arrived." She turned to Leigh. "And that detective called earlier. Brandon Reynolds? He needs you to call him. As soon as possible, he said."

Javi shot her a look. "See?"

"See what?"

"Controlling, just like I said."

CHAPTER EIGHT

======I======

THE GUY WAS NERVOUS. No question.

But there was nothing relaxing about having a cop show up at your workplace.

"So, when was the last time you saw her?" Brandon asked.

Cooper Collins darted a glance at the barista behind the counter. He and Brandon were seated at a too-small table in the coffee shop attached to the bookstore where Cooper worked. The twenty-six-year-old had an ice water in front of him with a long straw. He hadn't taken a sip of it yet, just kept playing with the straw wrapper.

"I told you," Cooper said. "It was back in April sometime. We met for a beer."

"And since then? Has she called you?"

"Just that time in May, like I mentioned."

Another glance at the beautiful barista. He seemed interested in her reaction, even though the woman was about six feet tall and looked way out of his league.

Cooper Collins was a grad student in the UT physics department. He was five four, skinny, and wore rimless round glasses. He had sandy blond hair and freckles that covered his forearms. No scratch marks, though, or signs he'd been in a struggle recently.

"What else can you tell me about the phone call?" Brandon asked. He kept asking the same questions in different ways, zeroing in on any inconsistencies.

He sighed. "She wanted to grab a movie, like I said. But I couldn't go. I had to work."

"What was it?"

"Huh?"

"The movie."

Another glance at the woman behind the counter.

"Uh . . . *Breakfast Club*."

Brandon lifted an eyebrow.

"They were running a John Hughes marathon at the theater that weekend."

Brandon leaned back in his chair comfortably, as though he planned to stay awhile. "So, you couldn't make the movie with her. Did you make a plan for later?"

"What? No. I told you, that was the last time I talked to her."

Cooper twisted the straw wrapper around his finger.

"And when you guys got together, did she usually call you, or did you call her?"

"She called me."

"Where did you meet?"

Cooper looked confused. "Meet?"

"Where did you first meet her?"

"Oh." He sighed. "This place on South Congress. Decker's. We were there with some friends and they introduced us."

"And what happened?"

A shrug. "Nothing. She came by my place later. No big deal."

"So, 325 Clark Street, number 104."

He went pale. "How did—"

"I looked you up, Cooper."

His Adam's apple moved up and down. The kid had no

criminal record, so he wasn't used to dealing with cops. He looked like he wanted to bolt out of there.

"Have you ever been to *her* apartment?" Brandon asked.

The tip of his finger was purple now as he strangled it with the straw wrapper.

"A couple times, yeah."

"When was the last time?"

"I don't know. April, probably? I picked her up for a movie."

"Anything else you guys did together?"

"I don't know. Movies, mostly. Sometimes we'd meet for beers."

"You ever go out of town together?"

"We went camping once."

"Oh yeah? Where?"

"A state park off Highway 71."

"Rustling Pines?"

"Yeah, that one. We did an overnight there back in February, I think."

Brandon glanced at the straw wrapper. He unwound it and dropped it on the table.

Cooper cleared his throat. "Look, my break is over now, so . . . I should get back."

Brandon didn't move, and the kid just stared at him.

"Is there anything else or . . . ?"

"That about does it." Brandon checked his watch, and Cooper scooted his chair back, eager to escape.

"Oh, one more thing," Brandon said. "Vanessa's sister says she got a new phone recently. You happen to have that number?"

"Uh . . . no."

"You sure?"

"Yeah."

"All right. That's it for now." He handed the kid a business card. "If anything comes up, or you think of anything that might help us, please give me a call."

He stood and nodded as he tucked the card into his pocket.

Brandon exited the bookstore and put on his sunglasses. He spotted the unmarked police unit in front of a meter down the street.

"How was he?" Antonio asked as Brandon slid into the passenger seat.

"Jumpy."

"Yeah?"

"Yeah."

"Jumpy, like he just offed his girlfriend?"

"No. Just jumpy. He copped to being in her apartment."

"Damn."

If he'd denied ever being there and then they lifted his fingerprints, that would have been useful.

Some of the things Cooper had told him tracked with evidence. For example, the Decker's matchbook in Vanessa's apartment with Cooper's address scrawled on the inside. Other things he'd said seemed evasive.

Brandon was used to being lied to. It happened every day. Witnesses, suspects, even colleagues. People lied all the time, and usually it was to avoid awkwardness or to make themselves look better.

Suspects were no different. The key was figuring out which lies, if any, were relevant to his case.

"He also said they went camping together once," Brandon said, "over at Rustling Pines State Park."

"No shit? The one by the lake?"

"Yep."

Coincidence or not? Brandon didn't know. It might be significant. At the very least, it told them one of Vanessa's ex-boyfriends had spent time with her not far from the place where she disappeared.

Antonio put the car in gear. "That's weird."

"Yep."

"I think this guy just moved to the top of my list."

* * *

Leigh's car bumped over the pitted road. Rounding the bend, she followed the cloud of red dust kicked up by the white pickup truck ahead of her.

Another curve, another dip in the road. Then a gap in the trees opened up, revealing the bright blue lake glistening in the sunlight. A row of APD and sheriff's vehicles was parked along the grassy shoulder. The white pickup pulled off the road and parked beside them. Leigh kept going, getting as close to the lake as possible in what was probably a futile effort to save her shoes.

She parked beside a red Suburban with the Austin Fire Department logo emblazoned on the side. Beside the Suburban was a plain black sedan that looked remarkably similar to the one she'd seen at Pura Vida just the other day.

Leigh got out and looked around at the scene. She passed a couple of onlookers—nearby residents, she guessed—some openly gaping and others pretending to be out walking dogs as they watched the action unfolding. Leigh ignored their curious looks, just as she ignored the looks from cops and firefighters as she picked her way down the gravel road toward the lake.

Loblolly pines surrounded her, and she took a deep breath, inhaling the crisp scent that reminded her of trekking out to a big striped tent with her father to pick out their Christmas tree. Leigh felt a jolt of sadness at the memory. Those were the years when they'd been a normal family and her biggest gripe was not having a younger brother or sister to play with. Those were the years before arguments and divorce lawyers and heated phone calls about canceled weekend visits. At twelve, Leigh's carefree childhood came to a halt and she entered the brave new world of "just the two of us now" with her mother.

At thirty, Leigh didn't see her dad much anymore, but

she knew his wife had a nine-foot blue spruce that she folded up and stored in the attic every year.

Leigh trekked past the towering row of pines and reached the grassy slope, where she scanned the group of cops near the dock. The heels of her Jimmy Choos started to sink, so she stepped back onto the gravel to wait.

A diver on the end of the pier shrugged off his tank and set it on the dock. He unzipped his wet suit and peeled off the top half, revealing a muscular chest and six-pack abs. He was definitely nice-looking, but it was Brandon who commanded Leigh's attention. He stood at the end of the dock, hands on hips, gun and badge clipped to his lean waist. He talked to the diver, nodding and pointing out at the lake. Brandon's eyes were covered by mirrored aviators, so she couldn't see his expression when he turned toward her. But the instant he spotted her, she knew.

He traded a few more comments with the diver and another cop and then moved toward her. A warm tingle settled in her stomach as he homed in on her like a guided missile.

He stopped in front of her, and she saw her reflection in his shades. "What are you doing here?" he asked.

"I got a message you needed to talk to me."

"How'd you know we were out here?"

"Word travels." She nodded over her shoulder. Parked at the far end of the emergency vehicles was a gray minivan with Kate Morris behind the wheel.

"Shit," Brandon muttered.

"She told me she drives out here every day."

"Why?"

"I don't know. Anxiety, I guess?"

"No, why did she tell you that?"

Leigh shrugged. "We've become friends, sort of. She's under a lot of stress. Needs someone to talk to."

Brandon's jaw tightened, and she could guess what he thought of her befriending relatives of a potential victim.

"So, have you guys found anything?" she asked.

Brandon peeled off his shades and wiped his forehead with his sleeve. It was a mild sixty degrees, but he and his team had been out here awhile, according to Kate. His brown eyes were intense as he gazed down at her, and she could practically see the debate going on in his head.

"Not a thing," he said, surprising her. She'd expected another one of his non-answers. "No body, no clothing, no weapon."

She looked at the dock. "They searched the whole lake?"

"This side, anyway."

"Why only this side?"

His mouth clamped shut, confirming what she'd suspected from the beginning. There was evidence Brandon hadn't shared with her, evidence of foul play. Had they found tire tracks out here the night Vanessa disappeared? Maybe footprints or drag marks?

"What about shell casings?" she asked.

"Nope."

"You look frustrated."

He turned toward the lake, where a second diver was hoisting himself onto the end of the pier. "Hard to investigate a homicide without a body. Damn near impossible, in fact. Slows everything down. Warrants, questioning, everything."

"Well. Maybe it's good, right? Maybe it's not a homicide."

His jaw tightened again as he looked down at her, and she could tell he didn't believe that.

"We got Vanessa's phone records," he said, changing the subject. "That's the reason I needed to get a hold of you. There's a call to your law firm from Vanessa last week."

"Really?"

"Wednesday at five thirty p.m."

"Huh."

"You didn't know?"

"No, I didn't. I told you from the beginning, I hadn't

heard from her in weeks until that package showed up at my office."

He gazed down at her, and she started to get annoyed. "You don't believe me?"

"Any chance your receptionist lost a message?"

"Bella doesn't lose things. And anyway, she keeps track of all our calls electronically. She has a phone log." Leigh looked out at the lake. "Which reminds me . . ."

Brandon eased closer. "What?"

"Nothing." She had an idea, but she didn't want to share it with him yet.

His partner tromped over, looking tired and even more frustrated than Brandon. He had his sleeves rolled up, and his nice black dress shoes were caked with mud.

"Leigh Larson." She stuck out her hand. "I saw you at the courthouse, but we haven't been introduced yet." She shot a look at Brandon. "I'm Vanessa's lawyer."

He gave her hand a firm shake. "Antonio Peña. It's nice to meet you."

"Vanessa's sister is here," Brandon told him.

"I know." He turned toward the minivan. "Let me talk to her, and then we can head out."

He walked up the hill, and Brandon looked at Leigh.

"Bella wouldn't have lost the message," Leigh reiterated. "But on the subject of messages, I was going to suggest you check the messages on Vanessa's cell phone."

"We'd love to, once we get a warrant."

"Also, her computer. If she was having the kind of trouble I think she was, then you'll probably find evidence of it. You should check her search history."

"According to the sister, she doesn't have a home computer. She used her phone and her computer at work for everything."

"Well, check the computer at work, then."

His phone buzzed, and he pulled it out. Leigh could tell from his expression he had to go.

"I need to take this."

She nodded. "And I need to get back to the office. Keep me posted, okay?"

He gave a brisk nod and stepped away to take the call.

A NTONIO'S CHEST TIGHTENED with dread as he approached the minivan at the end of the row. Kate buzzed down the window.

"Hi," he said.

"Hi."

She didn't look good. Her eyes were pink and puffy, and it was obvious she'd been crying. Sylvie was strapped into her car seat in back, watching cartoons on an iPad.

Antonio leaned his arm against the roof of the van.

"You all right?" he asked, and immediately regretted it.

Kate started to say something, then bit her lip.

"The divers haven't found anything," he said.

She glanced over her shoulder. Sylvie had her thumb in her mouth and seemed absorbed with her show.

"I know I shouldn't come here," Kate said in a low voice. "But I can't stay away."

"You been coming here a lot?"

She nodded.

That was messed up. But who was he to judge? Antonio had four younger sisters, and if anything like this ever happened he'd be out of his mind with worry.

Kate looked through the windshield at the distant lake where search-and-rescue divers were packing it in for the day. Her hair was up in a ponytail again. She had no makeup on, and the end of her nose was red from crying, but she looked pretty anyway.

"I have to get back." She looked at him. "Will you do me a favor?"

"What's that?"

"If you all find anything, will you call me?"

"Yeah."

Another dumbass thing to say. Antonio couldn't promise that. But the look in her eyes got to him.

She started up the engine. "Day or night, just . . . let me know." She smiled slightly. "I'm not sleeping anyway."

He nodded and stepped back from the van as she pulled away. She did a slow three-point turn, careful not to side-swipe any of the law enforcement pickups parked everywhere.

Gravel crunched, and he turned around as Brandon approached. His partner's gaze narrowed as he looked him over.

"You all right?" he asked.

The same question he'd asked Kate.

"Yeah. I heard your phone. Who was it?" He could tell by Brandon's look there was some kind of news.

"Jane at the crime lab. The results are back from those prints on the car window."

Antonio felt a surge of relief. It was the first good news he'd heard all day.

"And?"

"And they're in the system. We got a hit."

BRANDON STEPPED INTO the bar and peeled off his sunglasses, and his eyes adjusted to the dimness as he scanned the room. High-top tables, all empty. A couple of wooden booths. On a raised stage in back, several guys were setting up a drum kit. The Backbeat Club offered live music five nights a week and no-cover Thursdays.

"There." Antonio nodded at the bar, where a man was unloading a tray of glasses. Six-foot-two, heavyset, shaggy brown hair. He looked just like his mug shot. He'd been arrested two years ago on drug charges.

"We don't open till six," the man said, not looking up from the tray.

Antonio stepped forward. "Jason Mandrapilias?"

He glanced up.

Antonio flashed his creds. "Austin PD."

Jason muttered a curse and cast a glance over his shoulder. He wore a black golf shirt and apron, and his forearms were covered in tattoos. He stuffed a rag into the back of his jeans and crossed his arms as Brandon and Antonio approached the bar.

"We need a word," Brandon said.

Jason darted another glance behind him again as someone walked out of the back room with a keg balanced on his shoulder.

"Yo, Alex, I'm taking a smoke break," Jason said. His gaze locked on Brandon as he came out from behind the bar and headed for the door.

Brandon and Antonio followed him into the late-day sunlight. The sidewalk in front of the bar was busy, and Jason sidestepped a guy on a motorized scooter as he led them around the side of the building. The alley smelled of piss and garbage. Jason pulled a cigarette and a Zippo lighter from his apron and lit up.

"I'm Detective Reynolds." Brandon nodded at Antonio. "And this is Detective Peña."

Jason squinted at them through a stream of smoke.

"Pruitt says hi," Antonio said, referring to Jason's probation officer.

"Yeah? Good for him." He looked at Brandon. "What's this about?"

"We're investigating an abandoned vehicle," Brandon said.

"What's that got to do with me?"

"It's registered to Vanessa Adams."

He squinted tighter. "Don't know her."

"You sure?" Antonio pulled a folded paper from his pocket and handed it over. The printout showed a copy of Vanessa's driver's license photo.

Jason sucked in a drag. Blew it out. "Yeah, okay. Vanessa. I didn't remember her last name." He handed back the page.

"So, you know her?" Brandon asked.

"I met her at work."

"When?"

"I don't know. A while ago. I was working at Decker's Pub as a barback. She and her friends used to hang out there."

"They still hang out there?" Brandon asked.

"I don't know. I switched jobs."

"Which friends?" Antonio asked.

"I don't know. I didn't talk to her friends. I talked to her." He sounded impatient, and he looked down the alley as though he wanted to be somewhere else.

Antonio crossed his arms. "So, how did you first meet?"

He took another drag, blew out the smoke. "The usual. She flirted, gave me her number. Later, we hooked up."

"You two hook up a lot?"

"You know, on and off. It was casual."

"And did you go to her place or yours?" Brandon asked.

He hesitated a beat. "Hers."

"She ever been to your place?"

"No."

Brandon eased closer, encroaching on his space. "When was the last time you saw Vanessa?"

He stepped back and flicked his ash. "I don't know. A few months, maybe?"

"When?"

He rubbed his chin, as if trying to remember. "May, I think? Somewhere in there." He flicked the ash again. "I was working at Decker's, so it was before summer, when I started here. Why? What's the deal?"

They waited, studying his reaction, watching for any tick of deception.

"Vanessa's missing," Antonio said finally. He looked at Brandon. "How long has it been now?"

"Four days." Brandon kept his gaze trained on Jason.

His shoulders were tense and practically hunched up around his ears, but his face looked unchanged.

"Are you sure you haven't seen her?" Brandon asked. "She didn't stop by the bar, maybe? You didn't go by her place?"

"No, man. I told you. I haven't seen her in a while."

The words hung there in the fetid air of the alley as rush-hour traffic whisked past.

"So, why'd you switch?" Antonio asked.

"Switch?"

"Why'd you change jobs?"

He tossed his cigarette butt down. "The pay's better here. We have live music."

"That right? And has Vanessa been by here to catch a show?"

"No. I told you." He sounded exasperated now. He tucked his hands into the pocket of his apron and looked at Brandon. "Is there anything else? I need to get back to work, so—"

"One more thing. When was the last time Vanessa called you?"

He tipped his head back, exasperated. "Before summer. May, probably."

A guy turned down the alley. He was dressed like Jason in a black polo and jeans and had AirPods stuffed in his ears. He eyed their huddle curiously and traded nods with Jason as he passed by.

Jason looked at Brandon. "I need to get back to work."

He eased back. "Sure, hey, no problem. Thanks for making the time."

Antonio handed him a business card. "Let us know if you hear from Vanessa."

Jason took the card without looking at it and walked off. They watched him round the corner. Without a word, they retraced their steps to their parking spot on Sixth Street. Brandon was driving today, and he popped the locks.

"You know he was lying, right?" Antonio looked at him over the roof of the car.

"Yep."

Brandon slid behind the wheel. Antonio got in and slammed the door.

"Why didn't you call him out on it?"

"Because." He started the car. "We got him on record with his bullshit story. That could be useful." He checked over his shoulder and pulled into traffic. "Especially when we figure out *why* he was lying."

Antonio shook his head, clearly not convinced. But Brandon was the lead detective, so it was his call.

"Guy's full of shit," Antonio said. "There's no way his prints are on her car window if he hasn't seen her since May."

"I know. And he's the second person to lie to me today."

Antonio looked at him. "Are you talking about Leigh?"

"I'm talking about Cooper Collins, the other boyfriend."

"What about Leigh?"

He glanced over. "What about her?"

"She still holding out on us?"

Maybe.

"She never gave us the name of that landlord, did she?"

"No," Brandon said. "But I don't think he matters."

"If he doesn't matter, why won't she tell you?"

Brandon shot him a look.

"What? I'm just saying."

He didn't answer. And Antonio had a point. He should probably bring it up again and lean on Leigh to give him the name, but he'd been focused on other aspects of the case.

And whenever he saw her, he tended to get sidetracked. Which was a whole other thing he didn't want to analyze right now.

Brandon stopped at an intersection as a stream of tourists and scooters moved through. "So, what'd you think of Jason?"

"Slimy."

"Yeah."

Antonio shook his head. "And I fucking hate being lied to."

Brandon looked at him. "Get used to it."

Leigh found a prime space near the streetlamp right in front of her office.

"Thanks for calling me back," she told Tiffany as she gathered her files from the passenger seat. "It's about Vanessa."

"I figured."

Leigh pushed open her door and got out. The street was deserted except for a trio of skateboarders probably headed to the parking garage on the corner, which had the allure of steep ramps.

"I wanted to see if you ever told Vanessa about your log." Leigh juggled her files and used her hip to shut the door.

"My log?"

"Your stalker log." She locked her car with a chirp. "The one I recommended you start keeping after our first meeting?"

"Oh, that. Yeah."

Tiffany sounded out of breath, and Leigh pictured her on a treadmill at home, or maybe at her gym. She knew Tiffany had stopped jogging outside at night because of safety concerns. Along with a sex video, her ex had posted her address on social media, leading to a torrent of harassment. Even after moving apartments, Tiffany still didn't feel safe going out alone at night.

"I may have mentioned it," Tiffany said. "Why?"

"If you told her about it, I was just wondering if she might have been keeping track of anything, like you were."

"You mean, like a stalker?"

"Yeah."

"She never said anything to me, but we hadn't really talked in a while. You know, come to think of it, I think I *did* tell her about my log. I talked to some of my friends about it when we were putting together the lawsuit. It really helped me feel, you know, more in control of the situation while everything else was so crazy. So I probably mentioned something to Vanessa."

Leigh walked up the porch steps and spied Watermelon asleep on the swing. She shifted her files to her hip and fumbled for her key.

"So . . . do they know anything more?" Tiffany asked. "I mean, about where she is?"

"I'm not sure. I know they're still investigating."

Silence.

Leigh was being purposely vague, and she sensed Tiffany knew it. But she didn't want to share anything more. She could already imagine Brandon's look of disapproval if he found out she was still talking to Vanessa's friends.

"I hope they find something," Tiffany said quietly. "I'm really worried about her."

"Yeah."

"Her family must be frantic."

"I'm sure they are." Leigh stepped into the dim lobby, where the only light came from the glow of Bella's screen saver at the reception desk. "Well, thanks for the call back."

"Sure. Let me know if there's anything else."

They clicked off, and Leigh glanced around. The office felt chilly, which usually meant the cleaning crew had messed with the thermostat.

She walked down the corridor and stepped into her office, switching on the light with her elbow. It was as messy as she'd left it, right down to the pastry bag on her desk from this morning. She dumped her stack of files on the coffee table, along with her purse and phone.

"Crap," she muttered, surveying the pile of work she had to do.

She was days behind on her trial prep. This was what she got for playing detective when she should have been combing through depositions. She was in for a long night, which called for caffeine.

As Leigh headed for the kitchen, her phone chimed. She doubled back to grab it, and her stomach did a little dance as she saw the familiar number on the screen.

"Hey," she said.

"It's Brandon Reynolds."

"I know."

"Are you at home?" he asked, and the deep sound of his voice sent a ripple of warmth through her.

"Nope. Working late." She went into the kitchen and switched on the light. "Why? What's up?"

"I need the name of the landlord who sent the letter to Vanessa."

"It wasn't a landlord." She spun the coffee carousel and grabbed a double-shot espresso.

"I thought you said—"

"The letter was from a law firm purporting to *represent* the landlord. And it was bogus, by the way. I followed up with the firm, and they knew nothing about it."

"They never heard of the case?"

"Right. It was a phony letter." Leigh popped in the coffee pod and then waited as the machine whirred and gurgled. "Hello?"

"So, you're saying she *wasn't* having a problem with her landlord?"

"I'm looking into that. All I know is the law firm was never hired by him, so either he phonied up a letter to put pressure on Vanessa or somebody else did."

"Who?"

"Good question. Maybe the landlord, maybe someone else." She opened the fridge in search of flavored creamer. No such luck.

"You think someone drummed up the threat of a lawsuit to hassle her?"

"Quite possibly. I see it all the time. Harassment, harassment, harassment—that's the goal. Turn a woman's life upside down in any and every way possible."

She grabbed the mug of black coffee and took a sip, scalding her lip.

"Damn it."

"What?"

"Sorry. Not you." She switched off the machine. "Like I said, I haven't finished looking into it yet. I was going to track down the landlord tomorrow and—"

"Don't. Give me his name, and I'll do it."

"But—"

"No *but*s, Leigh. What you just told me makes this relevant to the investigation."

She pursed her lips, annoyed by his tone, but also annoyed because she knew he was right.

"I'll text you his contact info."

Brandon didn't respond.

"Hello? Don't I get a 'thank you'?"

"Thank you," he said obediently, as though he knew he'd ticked her off.

"You're welcome. But now you owe me a favor."

Before he could object, she clicked off and stared down at her phone. She didn't even have a favor in mind, really— she just wanted to maintain the healthy push-and-pull of their newfound relationship. She'd learned that was a key to working with bossy men—never let them think they had the upper hand.

She stepped into the corridor and halted. It was dark.

Leigh's blood turned cold.

Her office was pitch-black, no light spilling into the hall-way. Her stomach clenched as she stood frozen in the corridor.

A shadow shifted. She gasped and stepped backward.

A hand clamped over her face.

CHAPTER NINE

LEIGH JAMMED HER ELBOW back, but it was like hitting a wall. Fingers dug into her skin, cupping tightly over her nose and mouth. Bucking and twisting, she tried to suck in air.

Another hand reached around and grabbed her wrist. Pain shot up her arm as her phone clattered to the floor.

Panicked, Leigh tried to stomp his foot, but he lifted her off her feet and slammed her into the wall. The grip on her wrist tightened and he twisted her arm behind her back.

Leigh's vision blurred. Shock and pain reverberated through her. She couldn't get air. She stomped once again, this time connecting with something, and a howl pierced her ear.

Leigh jammed her elbow back, dislodging his weight. She lurched sideways, accidentally kicking her phone, and it shot down the hall like a hockey puck. She lunged away, but then he was on her again with a grunt, and she crashed to her knees.

Pain zinged through her, and he slammed her to the floor, knocking the wind from her. She gasped for air as he reached for her wrists and tried to pin her arms behind her. *No, no, no!* She couldn't let him pin her. She squirmed and bucked, trying to pull her arms free. He shifted his weight to the side, and she twisted, trying to get a knee between his legs. A blast of hot breath hit her face, and she was staring into two bulging gray eyes glaring out from a black ski mask.

The ski mask sent a lightning bolt of panic through her. She jerked her knee up hard. He made a surprised *ooof!* sound, spraying her face with spittle. He rolled onto his side, and she seized the opportunity to scramble out from under him, kicking and shrieking as she stumbled to her feet and sprinted for the nearest door, the only door. She raced through and slammed it behind her, then threw the thumb latch.

Leigh's heart thundered as she stood in the darkness, gasping for air. She was in the windowless back office that they used as a storage room.

And he was out there. *Right out there!*

She flipped on the light and tried to catch her breath as she stared at the doorknob, her heart pounding a million beats a minute. Muffled cursing came from the hallway, and she could picture him climbing to his feet. The man was big. Strong. Much stronger than she was, and now he was probably pissed, too, because she'd kneed him in the groin.

Frantic, she looked around. There was no furniture in the little room—only stacks of file boxes lined up along the baseboards. She looked at the latch again. It was a flimsy interior door lock identical to the one in her own office. You could pick it with a paper clip! And it was the only thing standing between her and her attacker.

Leigh grabbed the nearest box. It was heavy, filled to the brim with case files, and she heaved it to the floor in front of the door. She grabbed another box and another and another, building a tower. Then she made a second stack with the three remaining boxes.

She glanced around the room, panting and sweating. No more boxes, only a clunky black paper shredder and a brown shopping bag. She knew from experience that the paper shredder was heavier than it looked. She limped over to it, and only then did she notice she was missing a shoe. Her other heel was in the hallway. She kicked off the remaining shoe, bouncing it off the far wall. Then she lifted the paper shredder and hefted it to the top of the second stack of boxes.

Panting, she studied the barricade. It was laughable. Tears sprang into her eyes, and she felt a fresh wave of panic. He was right out there, and he was huge. A man his size could probably bust through the door and the barrier in no time.

She pressed her cheek against the door and listened. He was out there. She could hear the scuff of his shoes on the floor, along with drawers opening and closing. Was he in her office? The one beside hers? What the hell was he doing? At least he wasn't talking to anyone.

Dear God, let him be alone.

She cast a look around the room, desperate for a way out. No windows. There was a vent, but it was much too small to offer any hope. Her gaze landed on the brown shopping bag and she hurried across the room to look inside.

Rummaging through, she found a stapler, legal pads, and several jumbo-size boxes of paper clips. But no box cutter or letter opener or anything else that might be used as a weapon.

A vision of Brandon's Glock popped into her head. God, why had she hung up on him so fast? A hot lump of frustration clogged her throat. Three more seconds, and he would have overheard the attack and no doubt sent help. But no, she'd wanted to have the last word.

At the bottom of the shopping bag was a cardboard shoebox. She opened it and found another jumble of office supplies—pens, pencils, dry-erase markers. Combing through everything, she discovered a wooden gavel with Javi's name engraved on it, along with the name of a judge he'd clerked for one summer. Not much of a weapon, but it was better than nothing.

Footsteps in the hallway. Frantic, she spun toward the door.

The footsteps stopped.

Leigh held her breath, gripping the gavel like a hammer as her heart pounded. Her chest felt tight. She stared at the twin towers of file boxes, expecting them to move.

Her numb brain registered the words scribbled on the side of the top box. *Tel Equip.*

Clutching the gavel, Leigh crept toward the door, not making a sound in her bare feet. Was he outside listening? Picking the lock?

Aiming a gun at it, maybe?

She didn't know whether he was armed, but the ski mask told her he'd come prepared. Prepared for *what*, she had no idea. Silently, she lifted the lid on the top box and peered inside at a pile of loose file folders and a tangle of black cables. She spied a curly black cord, and her heart skittered. She plunged her hand into the box and pulled out an old black desk phone. Whirling around, she searched the room for a phone jack, but didn't see one. *Four* electrical outlets, but no phone jack?

A small white board leaned up against the far wall. She rushed across the room and moved the board aside.

Jackpot!

Leigh dropped to her knees, wincing with pain as she set the gavel down and plugged the phone into the wall. She snatched the receiver to her ear and madly tapped the hang-up button. The hum of a dial tone sent an agonizing burst of hope through her. She jabbed at the numbers.

Please, please, please . . .

"Nine-one-one. Please state your emergency."

"Someone just attacked me!" Her voice was high and

shrill, and she hardly recognized it. "I'm at my office, and he's right outside the door." Her voice shook as she recited the address. "Come now! *Hurry*. He's right outside."

"Could you repeat that? He's *inside* the building? Or outside?"

"Inside my building. I'm locked in an office, and he's just outside the door. *Hurry!*"

"Stay on the line, please."

An eternity ticked by as she listened to the clack of a keyboard.

"Ma'am? Can you describe the person who attacked you?"

Leigh's chest constricted as she pictured his face just inches away.

"He's big and he's wearing a black ski mask. I think he has a gun."

"We have a unit en route to your location. Stay on the line, please."

"I am."

Leigh listened. More footsteps—farther away now. Then a dull *thud*.

Silence.

Holding her breath, she waited. Was he here? Had that been the door closing? She felt dizzy from pain and shock, and she didn't know if her brain was playing tricks on her.

"Ma'am? Are you there?"

Leigh didn't answer. Didn't say a word. Didn't even move, just stared at the door and strained to hear anything.

Minutes crawled by. Finally, she set the receiver quietly on the floor, picked up the gavel, and crept across the room. She leaned her head against the door, pressing her cheek against the cool wood as she strained to detect the slightest noise. But all she heard was the steady thrum of her own pulse.

He was gone.

She felt it.

At least, she thought she did.

He could be outside, standing in the hallway and waiting for her to venture out.

The silence stretched out, empty and endless. Sweat streamed down her spine in a cool trickle. Leigh took a deep breath, then released it. Clutching the gavel in her hand, she waited soundlessly.

She'd wait ten more seconds. Ten. Nine. Eight. Seven . . .

Summoning her courage, she reached for the door.

CHAPTER TEN

===—===

LEIGH WATCHED THE UNIFORMED officers traipsing back
and forth through the lobby. She'd counted five so far,
and three different vehicles. Seemed like overkill for this
particular incident, but it wasn't her call. And she got the
definite impression that the homicide detective in the hallway had some pull.

Leigh listened to Brandon talking to several cops in the
corridor. He'd shown up and taken charge, giving orders to
the pair of patrol officers that had arrived on the scene. One
of them walked past her now, casting a curious look in her
direction.

She sat in Bella's swivel chair, a cup of green tea clutched
in her hands. She'd hadn't had a sip in half an hour, and the
tea was cold, but she continued to hold it—she had no idea
why. It was from Mei's across the street, where Leigh had
waited for the police to arrive. She'd sprinted over there,
barefoot and panicked, after emerging from the storage room
to find her attacker long gone.

Leigh's throat tightened. She took a sip of tea as Brandon's footsteps approached. He'd shown up in jeans and

scarred leather work boots, and she'd learned to pick out the sound of his footsteps from those of the other cops tromping back and forth.

"Hey."

She glanced up. Brandon loomed over her, his expression stern. His tension level was off the charts, but Leigh didn't mind. Surrounded by strange men, she felt better having him around.

"Hi," she said.

"I'd like you to go to St. David's and get that wrist checked out."

"I'm fine."

She wasn't, but a crowded ER was the last place she wanted to be right now.

Brandon's jaw tightened. They'd had this conversation earlier after she'd relayed what had happened and he'd observed the red welts on her arm.

"I'll put ice on it when I get home," she said.

"Leigh—"

"Drop it, okay? I said I'm not going."

A uniform walked over, halting awkwardly as he caught the snippet of conversation. He glanced from Brandon to Leigh.

"Ma'am? Sorry to interrupt." The officer looked young, and clearly he was nervous. "I had another question about your assailant."

Leigh cleared her throat. "Sure."

"You recall his shoes?"

"Shoes?"

"Was he wearing athletic shoes? Boots? Business-type shoes, maybe?"

"I don't know." She tried to picture his feet, but the image she kept getting was those bulging gray eyes glaring out from the ski mask.

"What'd they find?" Brandon asked gruffly.

"We've got some shoe impressions in the flower bed next door. Could be nothing, but—"

"Have the CSI take photographs."

"He did."

"Sorry," Leigh told the officer. "I don't remember his shoes. I don't remember his clothes at all except the black mask, like I told you. And his eyes. Wait! One more thing. I remember onions."

The officer's eyebrows tipped up. "Onions?"

She looked at Brandon. "He had me pinned under him." Leigh's stomach clenched at the memory. "His breath smelled like onions."

The officer scribbled in his notebook. "Okay. Anything else?"

"That's it." She looked at Brandon. "Random detail, I know."

"No, it's good. Any detail helps."

The officer flipped his notebook shut and looked at Brandon, as if awaiting instructions.

"Tape off the flower bed," Brandon told him. "I'll be over in a minute."

The officer nodded and walked off, and Brandon turned to Leigh.

"I don't know why I remember onions, but I have no idea about his clothes or his hair or anything remotely useful."

"You gave us his size."

"Yeah, *big*. That's not much to go on."

"It's a start. And you remembered the gloves."

As the first responder interviewed her, she'd recalled the smell of latex as the hand clamped over her mouth. He'd been wearing gloves—yet another sign that the break-in was carefully planned.

Javi appeared in the open doorway. He wore a black silk shirt and slacks, and his hair had the moussed-up look that told her he'd been out at a bar when she called him.

"Shit, Leigh." He came straight over and knelt in front of her, resting his hand on her sore knee. "Are you okay? What the hell happened?"

Leigh had told him the basics over the phone, but she had a few updates.

"They think he came in through Samantha's office," she said. "Her window was open."

"But everything's locked. And we've got sensors on all the windowpanes."

"The alarm wasn't engaged," Brandon said.

Javi stood up, and she could tell he recognized Brandon from the news article she'd shown him.

"Detective Reynolds, APD."

Javi nodded. "Javier Mendez." He rested his hands on his hips and glanced at Leigh. "I activated the alarm around six when I left, so—"

"I *de*activated it," she said. "I ran home to get some files from my house, and I forgot to set it again. So when I came back, it was off."

Javi frowned. "What time was this?"

"I left around seven thirty. Then when I came back, I noticed it felt cold in here. I thought the cleaning people had fiddled with the thermostat again, but turns out the window in Samantha's office was wide open. Sometimes she smokes in her office and opens the window, so maybe someone figured it might be unlocked."

Javi's look turned grim. "I want to check around, see if anything's missing."

"I couldn't find anything," Leigh said.

"Talk to Detective Tate," Brandon told him. "He's back there now with our CSI."

Javi shot a look at Leigh to make sure she was okay. She gave a slight nod and he walked to the back of the building.

"That's your law partner?" Brandon asked.

"Yes."

"How long have you two had office space here?"

She blew out a sigh, grateful for the change of subject. "Two years in November."

"He mentioned the alarm system. You ever had a break-in before?"

"No. But we keep sensitive files around, so as soon as we moved in here, we upgraded the system."

"Any cameras?"

"No. At least . . . I don't think so. Ask Javi. He specced everything out at the time. I wasn't really involved."

Javi reappeared, looking grimmer than before. There was something deeply disconcerting about seeing their quaint little office filled with police officers. This whole thing felt like such a violation.

"Nothing missing, that I can tell," Javi said. "But I can't be sure until we check with everyone. I don't see any electronics missing. We've got tablets and laptops lying around everywhere." He looked at Leigh. "What about your office?"

"Nothing missing."

"You're sure?"

"Yeah. Even my purse and wallet are sitting right there."

Tension hung in the air as the implication became obvious. Why would someone break in and not steal anything? And why stick around *after* the confrontation with Leigh? While she'd been barricaded in the storage room, he'd moved around her office, opening and closing drawers. But she hadn't been able to determine a single thing missing.

So . . . was Leigh herself the target? But why? And how would anyone know she would show up here after hours?

None of it made sense, and just trying to apply logic to it was giving her a headache.

Brandon turned to Javi. "You said you left at six. You notice anyone loitering around at that time?"

"Besides the usual? No. But this is downtown. People loiter."

"Anyone casing the place? Or maybe sitting in a parked car?"

"No." Javi looked at Leigh. "You?"

"Not that I noticed. But I was on the phone when I pulled up, so I was a little distracted."

"What about security cameras?" Brandon asked. "Does your system include any?"

"Not ours. There are two in back, though, facing the alley."

Leigh looked up, startled. "There are? How come I never noticed them?"

"They're concealed." He looked at Brandon. "The tenant back there is a PI. Total gadget geek. If anyone approached from the back, he definitely would have caught him on tape."

CHAPTER ELEVEN

$$===|===$$

LEIGH STEPPED INTO HER house and heaved a sigh of relief before tapping in the alarm code. The digital clock on the keypad told her it was 11:45, but it seemed much later, probably because her limbs felt heavy with exhaustion.

She'd spent almost three hours with the police, answering questions and watching people stream in and out of the building. Then she'd walked through the office with Javi, relaying what had happened while trying not to look too long at the spot in the hallway where the attacker had pinned her to the floor. She'd felt claustrophobic just standing there, and at one point she'd been sure she was going to throw up in front of all the cops, but the moment passed. Tuning into her stress, Javi had offered to close things out with the police and lock up so Leigh could go home and put an end to her hellacious day.

The drive had been a blur. She couldn't even remember crossing the bridge and turning onto her street.

But she was home, thank goodness. After slipping off her shoes, she walked into the kitchen and set her computer bag on the drop-leaf dining table. Her place was a mess, but there was something comforting about the clutter, something infinitely reassuring about being back in her own house, away from all the cops, with their heavy footsteps and clipped voices and incessant radio chatter.

All night, she'd been the lone woman surrounded by men. It was a situation she'd found herself in before—usually in meetings, or in hearings, or when she'd been a public defender and had to visit a client in jail. Usually, being the only woman didn't get to her, and she held her own just fine. Or if not, she faked it. Tonight was different, though. Tonight she'd felt intensely vulnerable, and every stranger through the door made her think of her attacker.

Leigh's phone chimed. She fished it from her bag, and dread filled her stomach as she recognized Brandon's number.

Oh God. What now?

"Hello?"

"Hi. How you doing?"

The low-key tone of his voice made her relax a fraction.

"Okay. Just, you know, a little rattled."

He went quiet, and she wished she hadn't told him that.

"Would you like me to come over?" he asked.

"Oh. That's nice but . . . you don't have to."

The question caught her off guard. Was he offering to come over as a cop? As a friend?

Or as something else?

"What's your address?" he asked.

She laughed, caught off guard once again. "Can't you look it up?"

"I could, yeah."

She sat there for a moment, and it occurred to her what he was doing. Yes, he could use his position to find out where she lived. But he wanted to be invited. He was trying to respect her privacy, and that one simple thing touched her more than he could know.

Or maybe he did know. Maybe he'd sensed that privacy

was important to her and that she had walls up, carefully constructed walls that she'd spent years erecting between her private life and everything else. He was a detective, after all. And he was observant. Maybe he'd picked up on the fact that tonight's events had rocked her sense of security and left her nerves shredded. The only time she'd truly felt safe during the last three hours was when she'd been in Bella's swivel chair with Brandon standing over her, gazing down at her with that fiercely protective look in his eyes.

"One-sixty-five Ashby Lane." The words spilled from her mouth before she could second guess her decision.

"Off of South Lamar," he said.

"Yes."

"Be there in a few."

He clicked off, and Leigh stared down at her phone. Then she looked around her house.

"Crap," she muttered.

She'd invited him over and she didn't know why, exactly, he wanted to come.

The slovenly state of her living room spurred her into action. She collected mugs and cereal bowls and dumped them into the sink. Her coffee table was strewn with case files, much like the table in her office. She gathered everything into a semi-neat pile and glanced around. On the sofa was a heap of unfolded laundry, including three weeks' worth of underwear. She scooped everything into a laundry basket and carried it into her bedroom, where she set it on the bed. Passing her dresser, she caught her reflection in the mirror and stopped cold.

Yikes. Her mascara was smudged. The side of her lower lip was swollen from when she'd been slammed to the floor. Her silk blouse was rumpled, and tiny droplets of blood marred the collar.

Tears welled in her eyes. Her favorite blouse.

And damn it, she was crying over a stupid shirt! Disgusted with herself, she unbuttoned the blouse and tossed it on the bed, then walked into the bathroom and splashed water on her cheeks.

"Calm down," she told herself.

Nothing had happened, really. Nothing serious. Something *could* have, but she'd managed to get away.

Suddenly, she remembered the weight crashing down on her, the air whooshing from her lungs. Her heart started racing again.

Calm down.

She grabbed a towel and patted her face dry, then went into the bedroom and snagged her blouse off the bed. She took it into the utility room, where she dropped it into the basket for dry cleaning. On her way back through the living room she stopped to pick up the collection of flip-flops scattered around the floor.

The doorbell rang.

"Crap!"

How had he made it so fast? She scurried into the bedroom, dumped everything in the closet, and grabbed a UT Law sweatshirt. Pulling it over her head, she tugged loose her bun and hurriedly combed her fingers through her hair as she went to the door. A sweatshirt and miniskirt was a strange combination, but who cared?

She checked the peephole before opening the door.

"Hi," she said, trying for upbeat.

Brandon looked her over, taking in every last detail, it seemed, down to her bare feet and her hot-pink toenails.

"Hi."

She stepped back to let him in, then closed the door and flipped the lock.

He gazed down at her, and there it was again—that feeling of relief. Just seeing him in her foyer settled her nerves.

"You got here fast," she said.

"I was on my way home." He nodded at her hand. "How's the wrist?"

"Not too bad."

He frowned. "Did you ice it?"

"I was about to." She turned to walk into the kitchen. "Would you like a beer?" she asked over her shoulder.

"I'm good."

"You sure? I'm having one." She suddenly had a bone-deep need for something to take the edge off.

Leigh grabbed a Shiner from the fridge and set it on the counter, then opened the freezer and scooped a handful of ice. She pulled open a drawer.

"Damn it," she said.

"What?"

"No baggies."

Brandon stepped around her and opened the freezer again. He took out a bag of frozen strawberries that she used for smoothies.

"Oh. Good idea." She dumped the ice in the sink.

"Peas work better," he said, handing her the bag.

"Why?"

"They're smaller. The bag conforms to the injury better." He leaned against the counter and watched as she pressed the frozen strawberries to her wrist.

"Been in a few fights, I take it?"

"A few."

He held her gaze, and tension simmered between them. Brandon Reynolds was in her kitchen. At midnight. Not something she would have predicted when she got up this morning.

He eased closer—just a shift of his weight, really—and gazed down at her with those brown-black eyes. The bag against her wrist was cold, but she felt warm all over, and she was all too aware of her bedroom only a few feet away.

Leigh's heartbeat sped up. She battled the urge to take his hand and pull him into her room. The impulse burned inside her. Her willpower was nonexistent tonight, but she knew better than to use sex as an anesthetic. It never worked.

"Do you set your system?" he asked.

"What?"

"Your alarm system." He nodded toward the foyer. "It's top of the line. Do you use it?"

"Yes. Well, at night I do." She stepped around him and dropped the ice pack on the counter as she pulled out a bottle opener and popped the top off her beer. "I usually set it before I go to bed."

"Is it new? Old?"

"About two years old." She smiled. "You want to check out the rest of my security?"

"Yes."

She'd been joking, but he seemed dead serious, and she watched with amusement as he walked to the back door. It led to a one-car garage where she stored a kayak and a paddleboard, along with the camping gear she hadn't used since college. Brandon examined her locks and then stepped into the sunroom to check out her sliding glass door.

She could tell he didn't like the slider.

"You should get a brace for this."

"I know." She stepped around him and unlocked the door, then pulled it open and led him onto the patio.

The October air was crisp, and the bricks felt cool against her bare feet. She switched on the lotus-shaped water fountain in the corner to provide a bit of light. The fountain's soothing gurgle helped cover the traffic noise in front of her house.

She turned to look at him in the dimness. She'd never thought of her patio as small, but it seemed to shrink with Brandon on it. He looked so good standing there, all tall and broad-shouldered in his faded black T-shirt and jeans and his leather jacket.

He didn't say anything, just watched her in a way that made butterflies flutter through her stomach. What did he think of her home? It shouldn't matter, but for some reason it did. She wanted him to like it. She wanted him to think she was independent and accomplished and had her life together—even though most of the time she felt like she was faking all those things.

"So, what about you?" she asked. "Where do you live?"

"An apartment off Congress, near the bridge."

"Wow. Nice area."

He shrugged. "The place is small, but it's close to work, at least. Can't beat the location." He nodded toward the flower bed. "I like your Knock Out roses."

She turned to look at him, surprised. "Do you garden?"

"No." He smiled. "My mom grows those, but hers are yellow. She always keeps vases of them around the house. Growing up, she used to have me put coffee grounds in the beds."

Leigh turned to face him in the dimness, charmed by his talk of his mother.

"Is your family here in town or—"

"San Antonio," he said. "What about you?"

"My mother's in Houston. My parents split when I was twelve, so it was just the two of us for a long time."

Leigh needed to call her mom and tell her about tonight. She was dreading it, though, because her mother was always warning her about working late by herself.

She had a sudden flash of memory—being slammed to the floor, and all the air leaving her lungs in a big *whoosh*. The lack of oxygen and that massive weight on her body had terrified her.

Leigh shook off the memory and took a chair. She expected Brandon to take the one beside her, but instead he lowered himself onto the end of the chaise lounge. For the first time since she'd met him, they were at eye level.

She sipped her beer and offered it to him, but he shook his head. She set the bottle on the table.

"Leigh."

She looked at him.

"Are you really okay?"

The quiet question made her throat tighten.

She shrugged. "I'm not seriously injured or anything. Just freaked out."

He held her gaze, and there was something steadying about those deep dark eyes. He didn't give her BS or platitudes, and she felt grateful. She wondered how many assault victims he'd talked to over the years. And then her mind started going down the path it had been going down earlier, wondering if he was here as a friend or a cop or some less-defined role. Leigh was used to compartmentalizing her life. But so far their relationship—if you could call it that—defied classification. They'd met through work. But they kept crossing paths on their personal time. And they both knew it wasn't an accident.

"We talked to Charles," he said.

"Charles?"

"Charles Foley. The private investigator who offices in your building."

"Oh." She smiled. "He goes by C.J. Did you meet him?"

"Talked to him on the phone. He said he's got multiple security cams with visibility of the alleys on either side of the building, as well as his entrance in back. He said he'll get us the footage."

"Good." She took a swig of beer, letting the cold liquid soothe her throat. Talking about the attack was putting a knot in her stomach. "What else?"

"I wanted to ask again if you remember anything from before."

"Before what?"

"Before you went inside the office. Did you notice any suspicious vehicles when you pulled up, or any people hanging around?"

"I answered all this already."

"I know."

She just looked at him.

"Sometimes people remember details later," he said. "Things that seemed like nothing at the time."

She focused on the gurgling fountain and tried to think. She'd been on the phone and distracted when she pulled up. And she knew that was a mistake. She should have paid more attention while walking around alone at night, especially in the middle of downtown.

"Skateboarders," she said. "That's all I got."

His eyebrows arched.

"There were a couple kids on the sidewalk when I showed up."

"How old?"

"I don't know. Thirteen? Fourteen? They were probably headed to the parking garage on the corner to use the ramps."

"Did they look at you? Make eye contact?"

"No."

Her phone chimed from inside, and she looked through the glass door to see it glowing on her kitchen table.

"Just a sec." She went inside to check the caller. Javi. If she didn't answer, he'd worry.

"Hey," she said. "Can I talk to you later?"

"Just wanted to see how you are."

"Pretty good."

"You want me to come by?"

"Thanks, but I'm fine. Just having a beer."

"God. Have several."

"I might. And I'll probably take a bubble bath."

"Okay, well call me if you need anything."

"I will. Thanks. And thanks for showing up tonight."

"Please."

"You didn't have to do that. I know you were out, and I ruined your evening."

"I'm going to pretend you didn't say that. *Ciao.*"

"*Ciao.*"

She set the phone down and went outside, where Brandon was now standing by the fountain, examining the gate leading to her driveway.

She stepped over and looked up at him in the dimness. "Still critiquing my security?"

"Yeah."

"How is it?"

"Fair."

She nodded at the gate. "I keep it locked."

"Good."

She stepped closer, heart thudding as she drew near enough to feel his body heat. The air between them felt charged, and a confusing array of emotions swirled inside her—nervousness, stress, relief to finally be home.

Relief that she wasn't in the ER right now. Or worse.

"Thanks for coming over," she said, and her voice sounded raspier than she'd expected. She cleared her throat. "Weird day."

He took her hand, shocking her as he gently turned it over. He traced his thumb over her wrist, setting off a ripple of nerves. His fingers were thick and strong, but his touch was featherlight. He released her hand, and she looked up. He gazed down at her, his brow furrowed with concern.

To Leigh's horror, her eyes filled with tears.

He wrapped his arm around her and pulled her against him. She rested her head on his chest, and it felt like the most natural thing in the world.

She closed her eyes and took a deep breath. He smelled good, like male body heat and a trace of cologne, or aftershave, or some kind of masculine soap. His arms around her were solid and comforting, and she couldn't believe she was getting all weepy in front of him. She was supposed to be a tough-as-nails trial lawyer.

"Sorry," she said, her voice muffled against his shirt.

"Why?"

"I'm not like this."

"What?"

She sighed. "Weepy." She swiped at her cheeks as he eased back.

He stared down at her, his face shadowed in the dim light. Her heart started to thud, and her stomach tightened—but not from fear now. Attraction.

His gaze dropped to her mouth.

A low buzz startled her, and she jerked back.

Muttering a curse, he pulled his phone from his pocket and checked a text message.

"Work." He looked at her. "I have to go."

She nodded. "Sure."

He was a homicide detective on call. Of course he had to go. But he didn't move. Instead, he stood there, gazing down at her with those dark eyes.

He bent and kissed the top of her head, sending a flurry of sparks through her.

"Will you be okay tonight?" he asked.

"Yeah."

She turned and led him back inside and to the front door, dismayed by all the memories of the day swirling through her mind—her routine morning, her drive out to the lake, the attack at her office.

Brandon on her patio, pulling her into his arms.

She opened the front door for him.

"Be sure to—"

"I know. I'll set it," she said.

He looked down at her. Before she could lose her nerve, she stood up on tiptoes and kissed him on the cheek.

"Thank you for coming by," she said.

Regret flickered in his eyes. Because he had to leave? She sure as hell hoped so.

CHAPTER TWELVE

ANTONIO PULLED INTO A reserved space in front of the station and hung their parking pass from the rearview mirror.

"Yo. Food truck," he said. "Perfect timing."

Brandon scowled. Nothing about this morning had been perfect, starting with being called out of bed at four-fucking-thirty to respond to a convenience store holdup on the east side. Two people shot—including the elderly clerk—as the perpetrator fled the scene with thirty-six dollars and a carton of smokes.

Thirty-six dollars.

And now an elderly veteran was in the ICU with a punctured lung.

The kid who shot him was in the hospital, too, after being tracked down through a tip. And why the kid had decided to mess with a store clerk whose arms were covered in military tats and was practically guaranteed to have a gun behind the counter, Brandon would never know.

Another unanswered question from his shitty morning.

Brandon got out of the car, and Antonio was already digging out his wallet.

"You coming?" Antonio asked.

"No."

"Sure? Two-for-one Fridays, bro."

"I'm not hungry."

Antonio turned to leave but stopped short as a woman stepped into his path.

Brandon's heart gave a kick. How had he missed her? He looked over Leigh's shoulder and spotted her blue Mustang at a meter down the street. They'd driven right past it.

He shifted his attention back to Leigh. She wore another silky white blouse today, along with tight black pants and black ankle boots with skinny heels. Her hair was in a ponytail instead of the usual bun. Mirrored sunglasses covered her eyes, making him wonder if she'd had a restless night.

She stopped in front of Antonio. "Morning."

"Morning." Antonio darted a look at Brandon. "I heard about what happened. How's the arm?"

Leigh's smile wavered. "Fine, thanks."

"Good to hear."

He glanced back at Brandon, probably wondering what Leigh was doing here and guessing it had something to do with him. "So . . . I'm going to grab breakfast. Catch you later, Leigh."

"Bye."

She watched him walk toward the taco truck on the corner, where a line of hungry cops had already formed.

She turned to Brandon.

"We had a shooting this morning," Brandon told her. "I don't have an update on your case yet, sorry. I haven't even been in."

"I figured it was too soon." She stepped closer, but he still couldn't see her eyes behind the sunglasses. "You have a minute? I wanted to talk."

He checked his watch.

"This won't take long." She nodded at the place across the street. "How about coffee?"

"Sure."

They waited for a break in traffic, then cut across the street. Brandon reached around her and opened the door to the coffee shop. It was empty of customers, which would speed things along. Leigh peeled off her sunglasses and strode up to the counter, and Brandon tried not to stare at her ass in those tight pants.

Leigh ordered a fancy blender drink and Brandon got plain coffee. She insisted on paying and then picked a table in the corner with impossibly small chairs.

He sat down and stretched out his legs.

Leigh drummed her glossy fingernails on the table and glanced around, looking impatient as the barista whipped up her drink.

She smelled good this morning. She looked good, too. He'd never seen her in anything besides a skirt before now, and he wondered if she'd picked her outfit today to hide the bruises he'd noticed on her knees last night.

Anger festered inside him. He sipped his piping-hot coffee, which did nothing to settle him down.

"So." She smiled. "Guess you've been working pretty much round the clock the last few days, huh? Does that ever get old?"

An interesting question coming from someone who practically lived at her office. And she took work home with her, too. He'd noticed the stack of files and legal pads on her coffee table.

"I'm used to it," he said.

"Yeah? Getting called out of bed in the middle of the night?"

He shrugged. "I'm kind of a night owl."

"Really? Me, too."

The barista placed her drink on the counter, and Leigh jumped up to get it. She seemed nervous today. More antsy than usual.

Brandon watched her doctor her coffee at the bar, adding sweetener and shaking cinnamon on top. He wished he knew more about her. What he *did* know only made him more curious.

He knew she was smart. She'd graduated law school at the top of her class at UT—no small feat—and gone to work for the public defender's office, which was a natural stop for someone wanting to rack up courtroom experience. From there, she'd taken a job with Thornton & Davis, a downtown law firm that represented some of Austin's top tech companies. Thornton & Davis occupied the top two floors of a sleek tower overlooking the lake, and Brandon happened to know they paid big bucks, even to young associates like Leigh. With some trial experience under her belt, Leigh had been on the fast track to become a litigator for some of the city's highest-profile companies.

But then she'd quit.

After less than a year making good money, she'd left to join Javier Mendez in a tiny practice focused on sexual harassment and revenge porn, with some workplace discrimination mixed in. By the looks of their offices, Leigh and Javier were getting by, but by no means raking in cash.

So, why the sudden change? Brandon didn't know, but he had his suspicions.

She returned to the table with her drink.

"So." She poked her straw into the whipped cream. "I was up late, thinking about what you said."

He waited for her to elaborate. At a glance, she looked normal this morning. But up close he noticed the puffiness around her eyes. Her lower lip was swollen, too, and the little cut there made his stomach clench.

I was pinned under him . . .

The fuckhead had tackled her to the floor. And split her lip open. And sprained her wrist. And it wasn't Brandon's case, but he'd made it his mission to oversee every last detail until they made an arrest.

"What I said about what?" he asked.

"Details." She poked at her drink and sucked foam off the end of her straw. "How they can seem like nothing but turn out to be important."

"Did you think of something about your assailant?"

"No. At least—I don't think so. I'm not sure, really. I remembered something from yesterday afternoon. You know how I went out to the lake to talk to you? When I got back to the office, I noticed a truck following me."

"Following?"

"It was behind me on I-35. He exited at Sixth Street, like I did. He was behind me all the way to my office, but then kept going when I found a parking space."

Brandon just looked at her.

"I know, I know. I should have mentioned it last night, but I didn't think about it. It just kind of popped into my head when I was trying to fall asleep."

"What kind of truck?" he asked.

She tugged a slip of paper from her back pocket. It was a three-by-five notecard with neatly printed words:

Pickup truck
Black
Ford F150 or similar
Tinted windows

"You're sure this truck was following you?"

"No. But he was behind me for, like, fifteen minutes. I was on the phone part of the way, so I didn't really tune in until he exited the freeway when I did. I thought it was a little strange, but then he kept going when I reached my office, so I blew it off. Anyway, now I'm thinking maybe it's relevant."

He took the notecard. "I'll pass it along."

"You think it's related?"

"Could be." He tucked the card into his pocket.

A look of relief washed over her face and her shoulders sagged. "Thank you." She sipped her coffee, and he noticed the worry line between her brows. "It might be nothing."

"We'll look into it."

She glanced up, her green eyes filled with concern. "I've worked with some sketchy people over the years."

"I know."

Surprise flickered across her face.

"Some of your cases have been in the news."

She sighed. "And I've definitely gone up against some real dirtbags in court. Some of the men I deal with—" She shook her head.

"What?"

"Some of them are volatile. The kind of guys who are allergic to rejection. Or who don't understand it as it relates to them. They can be very vindictive."

"You ever get threats?"

She snorted. "Uh, *yeah*. That's pretty much guaranteed."

"Anyone specific come to mind?"

"No." She poked at the foam again, and he noticed she'd hardly made a dent in the drink. She just seemed to be sort of stirring it around. "I plan to go through my office today to try to see if I can figure out what he was interested in, why he was there in the first place."

"What about the office next to yours? The associate?"

"Kyle. Yeah, it could have been his office that he went through. I couldn't really hear that well when I was barricaded behind the door. But I'll talk to Kyle later, see if he has anything missing or out of place."

"You two have any cases together?"

"Not yet. He's pretty new, and mostly he's worked with Javi and Samantha. We hired him to help with our appeals workload."

"Thanks for the tip."

Brandon watched her, wishing he could skip out on his workday and spend time with her. It was Friday, and for the first time in weeks, he wasn't on call all weekend. He had a shit-ton to do, though, starting with trying to persuade his lieutenant that his missing-person case needed to be upgraded to a homicide, ASAP. His lieutenant didn't want to put more detectives on it until and unless a body turned up or the lab work came back from the blood in the woods showing a match with the blood in Vanessa's car. And the lab work was dragging because the case wasn't a homicide. It was a catch-22 that he'd dealt with before. Meanwhile, the precious, never-to-be-recovered early days of the investigation were ticking by. So if and when the case ever *did* become a homicide, the trail would likely be stone cold.

Leigh leaned forward, and he caught her scent again, the same tantalizing scent he'd gotten a nose full of last night when he'd kissed her hair.

Why he'd done that, he had no idea.

Except that he did. Leigh got to him. And not just her looks—it was everything about her, from her pushy attitude to her stubborn refusal to butt out of his case. She'd come to her door last night with her hair all disheveled and her sexy bare feet, and all the fantasies Brandon had been trying to ignore for days had come flooding back. And when she'd stood on her patio and looked up at him with those watery green eyes, he hadn't been able to resist touching her.

"You seem upset," she said now.

"Yeah, well." He raked his hand through his hair. "It's been one of those days."

She made a face. "The day's barely started."

He checked his watch.

"Look, I know you need to go." She scooted her chair back. "So do I."

They stood up, and he grabbed the coffee she'd bought him that he didn't really want.

"Stay alert," he said.

"I will."

"Put your phone away and think about situational awareness."

"I will." She shouldered her purse.

"If you notice a black pickup again—"

"Oh, don't worry. I'll definitely call you."

LEIGH CHECKED HER surroundings as she neared her office. No loiterers. No suspicious black truck. She passed a yellow Mini Cooper and watched in her rearview mirror as it turned the corner. Much to her relief, Leigh found a free space in front, saving her from having to circle the block.

She got out and stood beside her car for a moment. Dread filled her stomach as she surveyed the building, which looked deceptively peaceful. Sunlight glinted off the dormer windows. The flower boxes brimmed with petunias. The freshly cut lawn was green and dewy from the sprinklers.

Leigh squared her shoulders and walked up the path, eyeing the fat gray cat on the porch swing. Watermelon had made himself scarce last night, probably hiding under the porch as police swarmed the building.

Leigh stepped into the office, and Bella glanced up from her computer.

"Oh my gosh." She stood up. "Are you *okay*?"

"I'm fine."

"What the heck are you doing here? I thought you'd be out today."

"Nope. Hey, was Tiffany Watson just here? I thought I passed her yellow car."

"You just missed her," Bella said. "She stopped in and talked to Javi."

Leigh glanced down the corridor as Javi leaned his head out of his office.

"You're here," he said.

"Yep."

Leigh pretended not to notice Bella's worried look as she strode into the corridor, passing the spot where she'd been pinned to the ground just a few hours before.

"What's up?" she asked Javi. Glancing over his shoulder, she was surprised to see someone at his desk. C.J. Foley.

"He's showing me the film," Javi said.

"What film?"

"You know—the surveillance footage from last night."

Javi frowned as he looked her over, no doubt noticing her pants. Miniskirts and heels were Leigh's trademark.

"I'm surprised you're in today," Javi said in a low voice.

"Why?"

He tipped his head to the side with a *get real* look.

Leigh ignored it and nodded at C.J. "What did he find?"

"Nothing useful."

Her heart sank. "Nothing at all?"

"Don't think so."

C.J. glanced up from Javi's computer. His longish brown hair was pulled back in a rubber band and he wore his typical black T-shirt and jeans.

Although it was hard to say what was "typical" for C.J. because Leigh so rarely saw him. The investigator kept odd hours and they communicated mostly by phone.

"Come take a look," C.J. said, pivoting the screen.

Leigh stepped around Javi and approached the desk. It seemed strange to see C.J. sitting in Javi's expensive Scandinavian desk chair—the crown jewel of his office décor—but Javi didn't seem to mind. As he had told Brandon last night, C.J. was a gadget geek. So, naturally whenever he showed anyone something on the computer, he wanted to drive.

Leigh leaned over his shoulder to look at the black-and-white video footage. The screen was divided into two rows, three frames per row, for a total of six separate camera angles. The shots included the alleys on either side of the

building, a second-floor view of the street behind the building, and three different shots of the building's back door,
which was the designated entrance for C.J.'s business.

The second-floor camera captured cars racing by in a
blur as the video played in super-fast motion. As the clock
at the bottom of the screen scrolled, ticking off minutes,
daylight faded and the shots became darker.

"This looks grainy," Leigh said.

"The light's crappy, I know," C.J. admitted. "But I've
been over it several times now. Only three people passed
through this alley between four and nine p.m. yesterday,
and none of them matches the description of the perp."

"Wait, go back." Leigh leaned forward and tapped the
screen. "There's that homeless guy."

C.J. rewound the footage of one of the alley views.

"That's Marvin," C.J. said. "He's not homeless. Just
spends a lot of time on the streets. He does odd jobs for me."

"He does?" Leigh looked at Javi, who shrugged.

C.J. glanced at her. "No criminal record, by the way.
He's just a little weird. Also, he doesn't fit the description
you gave police. Marvin's shorter than you are."

They resumed watching the footage.

"Okay, what about him?" Leigh asked as a bicycle
zipped into the alley.

C.J. paused the video again. "That's the delivery kid
from the pizza place around the corner. He cuts through
there a couple times." C.J. zoomed in on the image. The
person wore a dark hoodie and had an insulated box on the
back of his bike for transporting pizza.

The video sped up again. After a while, a man appeared
in the shot. He stopped beside the building.

Leigh leaned closer. "What's he—oh."

The man urinated against the wall and moved on. As the
man emerged from the alley, C.J. halted the video and
zoomed in.

"Too skinny." She cleared her throat. "Whoever broke in here was big. And heavy."

They continued watching. When the time stamp passed nine p.m., C.J. halted the video.

"I didn't see the first part," Leigh said. "Any sign of a black pickup truck?"

"No. Why?" Javi asked.

"I don't know. I thought one might have followed me back here yesterday afternoon."

Javi frowned. "Back from where?"

"I went out to the lake off Old Quarry Road. They had a team of divers there looking for a body."

The furrow in Javi's brow deepened.

"It might have been nothing." Leigh checked her watch. "I need to get to work." She nodded at C.J. "Thanks for your help with this. I assume you're going to share that footage with the police?"

"Already did."

"Thanks."

Leigh went to her office, hesitating only slightly before stepping through the door. She set her purse on the desk and looked around. Everything was slightly out of place, just as it had been last night. But if there was anything missing, she hadn't figured out what it was yet.

Her gaze landed on her top desk drawer, and she noticed the black smudges where the CSI had dusted for prints. Leigh's stomach clenched as she looked at the fingerprint powder. The man who'd attacked her had been wearing gloves, so whatever prints they'd lifted in here would probably turn out to be hers or from someone on the cleaning crew. Still, the smudges bothered her, and she had the sudden urge to wipe down every last surface with bleach.

"Hey."

She turned around as Javi stepped into the room, closing the door behind him.

"How's your wrist?" he asked.

"Fine. Good. I iced it last night."

He sat on the arm of her big leather chair, and she felt a lecture coming.

"Don't say it."

"Say what?" He pretended to be oblivious.

"You think I should take the day off." She sank into her chair and plugged her phone into the charger on her desk, clearly settling in.

"Don't you think that might be wise?"

"No. I think that might be catastrophic to my case. The Tannehill trial starts Wednesday—"

"The deadbeat dad thing."

"Yes, and I'm already days behind, plus I lost last night because I was stuck here talking to police."

He folded his arms over his chest, wrinkling his custom-tailored shirt. "So, if you're so behind, why'd you drive out to the lake yesterday to browbeat the investigators?"

"I didn't *browbeat* them."

"Oh good. So, you're *not* hounding them about Vanessa's case on a daily basis?"

"No." She leaned back in her chair. "I'm merely providing assistance. They don't know the victim like I do. I'm providing them with relevant information they wouldn't otherwise have."

"What do you mean, 'victim'? I thought it was a missing-person case?"

She huffed out a breath. "Why are you giving me crap about this? I'm trying to *help*."

"I know. But it's not your job. It's the cops'. And the more you butt in—"

"I'm not butting in! They came to *me*, remember? They want to know everything I know about Vanessa and any trouble she was having and what might have happened to her."

"And now you're being followed. And you've been attacked. And your office was broken into."

"Our office. We don't know that mine was targeted, and there's nothing missing. And we don't know that any of that is related to Vanessa Adams at all."

Javi just looked at her.

"What's that look? You know better than anyone the kind of assholes we deal with," she said. "I get threats all the time. Rape threats, death threats, threats to my nonexistent children. People are crazy. Anyone could be tailing me around town, trying to intimidate me."

"How do you explain the break-in?"

"I don't know. We don't even know what they were looking for. Maybe it has something to do with one of *your* cases, or Samantha's, or Kyle's, and I just happened to be in the wrong place at the wrong time. Did you consider that?"

Javi watched her silently, and she knew what he was thinking. They knew each other much too well, which was why he was sitting here in her office.

As much as she told herself that everything happening could be related to any number of cases they'd worked over the years, it simply *felt* like these disturbing events had to do with Vanessa. She was missing, possibly dead. And Leigh was openly helping the police.

Not to mention doing some digging on her own.

Javi stood and walked over, tucking his hands into his pockets. "I'm worried about you, Leigh."

She felt a pinch in her chest. Damn it, he knew just when to switch tactics on her.

"I'm fine. Really." She took a deep breath and forced a smile. "Anyway, what was Tiffany Watson doing here? Bella said she stopped by to talk to you?"

"She stopped by to talk to you, not me. She was on her way to work, and she wanted to pass some info along."

"About Vanessa?"

"I don't know why you're so determined to get mixed up in this case."

"Yeah, you do."

Javi sighed. "Tiffany said she's been chatting up some of Vanessa's friends at work, trying to find out more about some mystery man Vanessa was seeing over the summer. She said she mentioned it to you?"

Leigh's interest was piqued. "Yeah. She said Vanessa went on a date with some guy, but then wouldn't talk about him afterward. Tiffany had a hunch she was still seeing him."

"Well, she was seeing someone. Tiffany said a few of their friends saw her with some doctor over there."

"Saw them as in—"

"Leaving work together in his car, apparently."

"So what's the big deal? Is he married?"

"I don't know. She didn't really get into it. She was running late for work, and she wants you to call her."

"I will. Thanks for the message."

He was being dismissed, and he knew it. But he didn't move to leave.

"I still think you should take some time off," he said.

"Forget it. My trial starts Wednesday, and I'm not nearly ready."

"Look, I understand why this trial's important to you, but—"

"*Don't* go there. I don't need it today."

He just looked at her, and she tried to tamp down her frustration. This was a touchy subject for her, and he damn well knew it, and she could only take so much drama in one twenty-four-hour cycle.

"Fine." He stood up, holding up his hands in a gesture of surrender. "Do what you want. You're going to anyway. But we both know I'm right and you'd feel a lot better if you took a few days off and got some rest."

"I'd feel a lot better if I spent some time on my case so I can kick this deadbeat dad's ass in court."

A NTONIO STEPPED OUT of the interview room and closed the door behind him.

"He's in there?" Brandon asked.

"Yeah. Picked him up at his apartment. He said he was on his way to the gym."

"Is he dressed for it?"

"No. But he had a backpack with him, so maybe that's not bullshit."

"And how'd the pat-down go?"

"Wallet, cell phone, car keys," Antonio recited. "He's still got everything on him."

"How is he acting?"

Antonio shrugged. "Pissed. Claims I'm wasting his day off. But I guess not too pissed because he agreed to follow me here. His pickup truck is parked downstairs."

"Good. So he knows he's here voluntarily?"

"Yeah."

Brandon nodded. "Okay, watch for my signal."

"Roger that."

Antonio stepped away, and Brandon opened the door. The windowless room contained a small table and a pair of plastic chairs. In the chair closest to the door sat Jason Mandrapilias. Antonio was right—he wasn't dressed for a workout. He had on worn sneakers, yeah, but also jeans and a tight gray T-shirt that showed off his torso. Clearly, the man spent a lot of time lifting weights.

Brandon pulled out the chair across the table from him and sat, tossing down a thick manila file.

"Thanks for coming in," Brandon said.

Jason crossed his arms, making his biceps bulge, and Brandon pictured him in that hallway with Leigh. He was big enough to fit Leigh's description. But her attack might not even be connected to this case. And Jason was supposedly working last night when the assault happened.

Brandon watched his eyes closely. "You know why we asked you here, Jason?"

"No."

"Really? I'm surprised. Pruitt says you're smart."

He bristled at the mention of his probation officer.

"He also says you missed your drug test this morning."

Jason's jaw tightened.

"I would have thought you'd remember that. Especially after a pair of cops paid you a visit at your job yesterday."

Jason glanced at the camera mounted in the corner. Maybe he thought Pruitt was watching from another room. He wasn't, but Brandon didn't mind him thinking that.

Brandon leaned back in his chair. "You worried about the test?"

His slight shrug told Brandon everything he needed to know. "Why would I be worried about it?"

"I don't know. You tell me."

Jason glanced at the camera again, then looked at Brandon.

"What do you want me to do? Piss in a cup?"

"I want you to tell me the truth about Vanessa Adams."

His expression didn't change, which was just as telling as the too-slight shrug. He'd expected the question.

"When was the last time you saw her?" Brandon asked.

Jason uncrossed his arms and rested them on the table. "I told you before. I don't know."

"That's *not* what you told me before. Do you remember what you said?"

The guy's brow furrowed.

"You said, 'It's been a while.' You said you hadn't seen her since May." Brandon paused. "When was the last time you talked to her on the phone?"

"I don't know, man."

Brandon turned slightly and glanced up at the camera. "You sure? Think about it."

"Yeah. I mean, I talk to a lot of women. I work at a bar."

Brandon opened the folder in front of him and frowned down at some paperwork. It had nothing to do with the interview, but it helped to make the witness nervous.

After a full minute, he closed the folder and looked at Jason. "So . . . that's it? That's all you got? You're so popular with women, you can't remember them all?"

A buzz emanated from Jason's pocket. He slid his hand inside it.

"You need to get that? I'll wait."

Jason silenced the phone and recrossed his arms defiantly.

"Jason, here's the deal." Brandon leaned forward on his elbows. "We know you're lying. The only question is, why?"

The door opened and Antonio stepped into the room. He held up his cell phone.

Brandon watched Jason's face as awareness dawned. Antonio tucked his phone into his pocket and came to stand beside the table, propping his shoulder against the wall.

"The phone in your pocket called Vanessa Adams twice last weekend." Brandon let the words hang in the air. "We've got the records."

"So, what's a guy on probation for drug charges need with a burner phone?" Antonio asked.

"I don't—"

"That's a rhetorical question," Brandon said. "You don't need to answer it. What you *do* need to tell us is why you called Vanessa. And why your fingerprints are on the window of her car—right now, as we sit here today—if you haven't seen her since May."

Jason didn't speak. His Adam's apple moved up and down as he swallowed.

"I saw her for a couple minutes on Sunday."

"When Sunday?" Brandon asked.

"Sunday night. I don't know. After ten, I guess."

For the first time, Brandon felt like he was getting the truth. And the timing lined up with a call to Vanessa's phone at 9:40 p.m.

"Did you call her, or did she call you?" Antonio asked.

"First, she called me. It was, like, Wednesday I think. Wednesday of last week."

Antonio glanced at Brandon. That also lined up with Vanessa's phone records.

"So . . . she called you to meet her and what, hook up?" Brandon asked.

"No, she wanted . . ."

Brandon eased forward, waiting.

"What'd she want, Jason? No more bullshit," Antonio said. "We know when you're lying."

He gulped again. "She told me she wanted to buy a gun."

CHAPTER THIRTEEN

B RANDON WATCHED HIM. "A gun."

"Yeah."

Brandon leaned back in his chair, trying to cover his surprise. He didn't often get surprised in an interview. It was a point of pride for him.

"She didn't want drugs?" Antonio sounded caught off guard, too.

"No. She wanted a pistol."

"Why?" Brandon asked, his stomach filling with dread as he thought about all that blood in the woods.

"She didn't say." His gaze darted away. Brandon caught it, and he could tell Antonio did, too.

"She just randomly called you out of the blue and—"

"*Yes.* I swear." He looked at Brandon, desperate now as he started to internalize the depth of the shit he was in. Forget missing a drug test. Possession of a firearm, much less selling one, would put him in a world of hurt with the judge who'd given him probation.

Antonio looked at Brandon. "Sounds like we need to get Pruitt in here."

"Wait! Just wait, okay? I'll tell you whatever you want. There's no reason to call him."

"Oh, we'll definitely call him," Brandon said. "But it would be good if we could tell him you're cooperating with our investigation."

"I am. I will."

The door opened, and Brandon's lieutenant leaned his head in. He'd been watching the interview from the next room.

"Peña, a word?" he asked. Antonio stepped out, and the lieutenant gave Brandon a sharp look. "While we talk, you may want to advise Mr. Mandrapilias of his Miranda rights."

When the lieutenant stepped out, Brandon turned to Jason and recited the Miranda warning. The man wasn't in custody—they'd made it clear he was free to leave—but it was better to be safe than sorry.

"Do you understand?" he asked at the end.

Jason nodded.

"Respond yes or no. Look at the camera."

He looked up at the camera mounted on the wall. "Yes, I understand."

Antonio stepped back into the room and took his place leaning against the wall.

"Cooperating doesn't mean lying," Brandon said. "That makes it seem like you've got something to hide. Such as what you did to Vanessa."

"I didn't do anything to her! I swear. I met her for, like, five minutes—"

"Where?" Antonio cut in.

"Out by some lake. Off an old road on the edge of town."

"Why'd you meet there?" Brandon asked.

"I don't know. She wanted to meet up there. She said it was private."

Brandon watched Jason's expression. Again, what he was saying lined up with the evidence they had. He'd switched back to being truthful, and Brandon was getting better at spotting when he toggled back and forth.

"Back up," Brandon said now. "What did Vanessa say when she called you last Wednesday?"

Jason ran a hand through his hair, making it stick up in patches. He looked stressed now, and he had good reason to be.

"She was upset. I don't know why."

"She didn't say?" Brandon asked.

"Not really."

"What *did* she say?"

Another deep breath. "At first, it was just small talk. But I could tell she called me for a reason because she seemed distracted. Like she wasn't really listening to me. And then she told me she needed a favor, and could I help her out."

Brandon glanced at Antonio. His partner was still leaning casually against the wall, but he was on high alert.

"Okay, what else?" Brandon asked.

"She said her sister was having trouble with some guy and—"

"Wait. Her *sister*?" Antonio shot a look at Brandon.

"That's what she said. Her sister Kate was worried about herself and her kids and needed something for self-defense."

Antonio's gaze drilled into him, and Brandon could see Jason getting worried about revealing too much. Brandon wanted to keep him talking.

"So, what kind of trouble was her sister having with a guy, supposedly?" Brandon asked.

"I don't know. She didn't go into it. And I didn't really buy it, anyway, because when I met her out at the lake, it was pretty clear the gun was for her."

Brandon waited, wanting him to expand.

"Why was it clear?" Antonio asked.

Jason glanced at him. "I don't know. Just a feeling I got. Like she was really relieved to have it."

"What'd you sell her?" Brandon asked.

"A Ruger EC9."

"How much?"

He hesitated a beat. "Four hundred."

That was a rip-off, and everyone in the room knew it.

"Was it loaded?" Brandon asked.

"What?"

"The gun." Antonio leaned over him. "Did you sell it to her loaded?"

"No. Jesus. I'm not stupid, all right? You think I'm going to sell some crazy woman a loaded gun and then turn my back and walk away?"

"What makes you think she's crazy?" Brandon asked.

Jason clamped his mouth shut.

"Come on, Jason. Let's hear it. We need you to cooperate."

"Nothing, really. She just seemed . . . I don't know. Tense. I mean, she called me Wednesday in a panic, and then when I see her, she's all upset, and I just thought, I don't know, *she* was the one who needed the gun."

CHAPTER FOURTEEN

===|===

BRANDON DROVE DOWN THE narrow road, scanning the pine trees as he waited for the call to connect. This area got spotty reception—a detail that might or might not turn out to be important.

"Detective Tate."

"Hey, it's Reynolds. Anything new?"

"You're talking about the law firm thing? Not since this morning."

It was Sam Tate's not-so-subtle way of pointing out that this was Brandon's second call today horning in on a case that didn't belong to him.

"Any word on the labs?" Brandon asked. "The CSI lifted that partial from the windowsill."

Given that Leigh had said her attacker was wearing gloves, the print probably belonged to someone on the cleaning crew or the lawyer whose office it was. But they were short on leads and the print was still worth running.

"Nothing yet," Tate reported.

"What about the shoe print in the flower bed?"

"Nothing on that, either. And I hear they're pretty jammed up over there. A burglary's got to be low on their list."

"An *assault*. A woman was injured."

Tate went quiet, probably catching the edge in Brandon's voice.

"I'll follow up with the lab." Tate cleared his throat. "How is she, anyway? The lawyer? She sprained her wrist, right?"

"Yeah."

Tate knew Brandon was friends with Leigh because Brandon had shown up within minutes of her calling him from the crime scene.

"Well, we just brought a guy in for going after his wife with a baseball bat," Tate said. "So my afternoon's gotten pretty derailed. I'll call the lab and put a rush on that fingerprint, though."

"Appreciate it."

"What's up with her? Are you two—"

"No." Brandon thought about that kiss on her patio. It had lasted maybe a second, but he'd been thinking about it all day. "She's a friend."

"All right, well, I'll let you know what I hear."

They ended the call as Brandon spied the sign in the distance. RUSTLING PINES STATE PARK. He'd passed it a bunch of times but never actually stopped. He hung a left onto the entrance road and parked in a row of spaces outside the gatehouse.

Brandon got out and surveyed the area. The air smelled of pine and burning leaves. He walked over to a picnic area with a view of the water. The lake was surrounded by fir trees, scrub brush, and scattered campsites, a few of them occupied by trucks and RVs. On the far side of the lake was a rack of green canoes and a wooden pier. A man stood on the end casting a fishing line. Brandon did a slow 360, taking everything in. The park consisted of more than two hundred undeveloped acres, a rare pocket of tranquility on the outskirts of town.

Lot of places to dump a body. Too many to count, really.

A place like this was a killer's dream, and Vanessa Adams had disappeared less than a mile away.

Why had she wanted to meet an ex out here?

Or maybe Jason was lying, and he'd suggested the place.

So what did Vanessa's case have to do with what happened to Leigh? Maybe nothing. Maybe Brandon was paranoid. He could admit that he was on edge about Leigh's safety. It was possible Leigh's attack had nothing to do with the missing-person-probable-murder case he had in his lap. Leigh had crossed paths with plenty of lowlifes and criminals in the course of her work. But still he couldn't ditch the nagging feeling that Leigh had stumbled into something, and whatever—or whoever—it was, was related to the break-in at the law firm. Leigh had a way of pushing people. To him, it was a turn-on. But he could see how that same pushiness might piss someone off.

Brandon took a last look around, then trekked past the gatehouse, where an attendant was eyeing him curiously. No doubt he'd noticed Brandon's unmarked police car and probably drawn a connection with the law enforcement activity on the other side of the lake yesterday.

Park headquarters consisted of a small log cabin with a stack of firewood outside and a hand-painted sign: $10 BUNDLES. The months-long burn ban had recently been lifted, and people had resumed campfires and s'more roasting.

Brandon stepped inside the building, taking off his shades as he approached the counter where an attendant perched on a stool. The woman was thin, midforties, and had a long dark braid that hung down her back.

"Afternoon." She smiled. "What can I do for ya?"

Brandon flashed his badge and introduced himself.

"You guys book most of your reservations online, or do people just show up?" he asked.

"Some of both. But if they show up during the high season, they're probably out of luck. That's fall and spring, when the weather's milder."

Brandon nodded at her computer. "Can you look up a name for me?"

She pursed her lips.

"Vanessa Adams," he said. "I think she was here in the spring sometime, maybe February."

Without comment, she turned to her computer. "That's the girl who went missing." She glanced up. "We had divers on the lake yesterday."

Brandon nodded but didn't elaborate.

The attendant typed in the name. "No record found. But someone else could have booked it. You know what car she was in?"

Brandon took out his cell phone and pulled up a photo he'd snapped of the license plate on Vanessa's abandoned Toyota. He recited the plate, and the attendant tapped it in.

"No record found," she repeated. "Maybe her friend drove?"

Brandon had thought of this already and had the plates for both of Vanessa's exes ready to go. Jason's turned up nothing. Then he recited the license plate for Cooper Collins. The woman's face brightened.

"That one, we've got," she said. "February twenty-seventh of this year. A Mr. C. Collins."

"Just one night?"

"Yep. And he was here again . . . April twenty-first to twenty-third. That was a two-night stay. And then . . . let's see, two more times this fall." She shifted her computer screen to show him.

Brandon peered over the counter and read the dates.

Son of a bitch.

ANTONIO CUT THROUGH the crowded corridor, ignoring his buzzing phone as he sidestepped gurneys and harried hospital workers. He rushed to catch the elevator and slid through the door just in time.

His phone buzzed again, and he gave the nurses beside him an apologetic look before answering the call.

"Peña."

"Hey, it's me. Get this. I'm at Rustling Pines and—"

"Hang on."

The elevator opened. Antonio held the door for the nurses and then followed them into the busy corridor. The emergency department was packed today, and the weekend had barely begun.

Antonio pushed through a pair of doors into the waiting room and made a beeline for the exit.

"Okay, sorry. I'm just leaving the hospital," he told Brandon. "How'd it go at the campground?"

"No record of Vanessa. Or of Jason. But get this. Her other boyfriend, Cooper Collins, booked a campsite here five times in the last year."

Antonio stepped around a couple of paramedics standing around the ambulance bay taking a smoke break. They seemed oblivious to the irony.

"Well, that's not really surprising, right?" Antonio spotted his car at a meter. He'd gone over the time limit but didn't have a ticket yet. "I mean, didn't he tell us they'd gone camping there together?"

"Yeah, in February. He mentioned that. But he's been four times since then, including October ninth."

"The ninth."

"Yeah."

"That's the day after Vanessa went missing."

"Exactly."

Antonio's pulse sped up, like it did when a whole new path of investigation opened up.

"Weird coincidence," he said.

"No shit."

Brandon didn't think it was a coincidence at all. He didn't believe in coincidences. It was one of the first lessons he'd drilled into Antonio from his first day as his training officer. *Look hard. If you see something that looks like a coincidence, look harder.*

"So, I guess we'll follow up with him?"

"I'm working on it," Brandon said. "Tell me how it went at the hospital."

After transporting the convenience store shooter to jail, Antonio had returned to the hospital for a follow-up interview with the store clerk.

"Well, he's pretty doped up," Antonio said.

"The victim?"

"Yeah. He's been out of surgery for hours now, and it looks like everything went how they wanted, but he's still pretty out of it. I got a few details we didn't have, but I'm going to have to come by here again and talk to him."

"He have any family there?"

"Yeah, a daughter. I gave her my number."

"Okay, that's good. I can handle the follow-up if you don't want to."

"I thought you were off this weekend?"

"I am."

"Then take your own advice and take the time while you can."

"I will."

Antonio unlocked his car and slid behind the wheel, glad to be out of the damn hospital. And now he had to go back tomorrow. He was dreading it, but he wouldn't ask Brandon to cover the interview on one of his rare off-call days.

"So, where are you now?" Antonio asked.

"I've got something to wrap up, and then I'm heading out."

His answer was vague, and Antonio knew what that meant. Whatever the "something" was had to do with Leigh Larson. Brandon wasn't usually a fan of lawyers, but that didn't apply to Leigh, apparently. Antonio didn't know what was going on with the two of them, but he knew better than to ask.

"Call me if you need anything," Antonio told him.

"Same to you."

* * *

BRANDON WALKED DOWN the ramp, scanning the cars and pedestrians outside the garage. No sign of any black pickups. No skateboarders, either, although Brandon had spotted evidence of people hanging out and vaping at the top of the parking garage.

Exiting the garage, he looked at Leigh's building. The porch light glowed, along with a light on the second floor, where the accounting firm had offices.

As Brandon retraced his steps toward his truck, he noted the light spilling from a first-floor window on the side of the building. Leigh's office. It looked like she was working late. On a Friday night, no less. He should leave her to it.

Instead, he found himself walking up the sidewalk and mounting the steps.

The door swung open.

"Hi," she said with a smile.

"Let me guess. You're on your way to get dinner?"

"Nope." She nodded across the street. "I saw your truck from the window and then I noticed you walking around."

He watched her, wondering at his sudden inability to make small talk. Her hair was still up in a ponytail, but little strands had come loose around her neck.

"So." She tipped her head to the side, looking amused. "What brings you over here tonight?"

It was a softball, and he managed to catch it.

"I'm following up on the lead you gave us."

"The black truck?" She cast a worried look over his shoulder.

"The skateboarders."

"Oh. Any luck?"

"No."

She gazed up at him, and he tried to keep his focus on her eyes, and not the second button of her blouse, which had somehow come undone since he'd seen her that morning.

"Would you like to come in?" She moved back to usher him inside.

Brandon stepped into the dim lobby and looked around as Leigh tapped a code into the security system by the door. The only light came from the glow of a computer on the receptionist's desk. Last time he'd been in here, it had been a hive of activity. Now, the place was much quieter, but he picked up the faint sound of someone clacking away on a keyboard.

He turned to look at her. "You're working late again, I take it?"

"Yes, but not alone."

She turned and led him down the corridor, and he noticed she was barefoot again. For someone who obviously spent a lot of money on shoes, she seemed eager to get rid of them at the end of the day.

He followed her to her office and stopped short inside the doorway. The coffee table was completely buried with files and legal pads.

"You cleaned," he said.

She gave him a curious look. "No, I didn't."

"I smell bleach."

"Oh, that." She waved a hand. "I wiped down the surfaces. All that fingerprint powder was creeping me out." She gestured to the big leather armchair. "Sit down. Have you had dinner? We've got a pizza coming."

We, meaning whoever else was here tonight.

"I'm good," he said, taking a seat.

Actually, he was starving. But sharing another meal in her office was probably a bad idea, even with one of her colleagues working down the hall. Brandon didn't trust himself.

"I'm glad you stopped by," she said.

"Why?"

She sank onto the sofa right beside the armchair, and he noticed the excitement in her eyes. "I've had a breakthrough."

"A breakthrough."

"About Vanessa." She leaned forward, resting her elbow

on the sofa arm. "You remember Tiffany? Vanessa's co-worker at Pura Vida?"

Brandon just looked at her.

"Tiffany Watson. She said you and Antonio talked to her."

"No, I know who she is. I'm just wondering why you're still going around interviewing Vanessa's friends after I specifically told you—"

"She came to *me*, all right?" She huffed a breath. "This is a big lead. Do you want it or not?"

Good question. He definitely wanted and needed a "big" lead, or even a medium one, but he doubted he was about to get anything close.

"What is it?" he asked.

"I've got another POI for you."

"POI?"

"Person of interest? Isn't that what you call people when you don't want to label them a suspect?"

He felt a dart of frustration. "Who is it?"

"Mason Lloyd."

He frowned. "Who is that?"

"He's a doctor at the clinic where she works. Or so he says. I haven't vetted him yet."

"Are you saying you think he's a quack?"

"Not necessarily. I'm just, you know, covering the bases. I looked him up on LinkedIn, and his professional history is a little spotty. But listen to this—he and Vanessa started seeing each other over the summer. She didn't tell anyone about it because—of course—he's married. But one of her friends figured it out."

"How?"

"She saw them leaving work together several times. This was in June, which lines up with when Tiffany said she mentioned someone new but wouldn't tell her his name. I think maybe they broke up over the summer and that's when things went sideways."

"How do you know things went sideways?"

"According to Tiffany, one of their friends saw—"

"All this is hearsay, you know. Did you actually talk to any of these supposed witnesses?"

Irritation sparked in her eyes. "No, because I'm butting out, remember? But *you* can talk to them now that I'm giving you this lead."

He watched her, trying to tamp down his temper. She wasn't butting out at all—she was doing the exact opposite. After everything he'd said, and everything that had happened, she was still sniffing around his case.

"As I was saying, these two friends saw them arguing in his car once in the parking lot. This was on their lunch hour sometime in June." She waited a beat. "*June*. Which is interesting timing, don't you think?"

"Why?"

"Well . . . because that's the same month her car was broken into. And she moved and started subletting her apartment. And then she got a new phone number. And then—"

"Wait." He held up a hand. "You're saying you think this doctor was, what, harassing her all summer?"

"That's what it looks like to me."

"All based on some workplace gossip?"

She crossed her arms over her breasts. "What's wrong with workplace gossip? This is a solid lead." She reached for the laptop on the table. "You need to check into it. I mean, look at this guy. Look at his work history."

Brandon didn't move—he just looked at her. She turned the computer to face him, showing him a social media profile.

"*Look*."

Brandon leaned closer and scanned the screen, scrolling down to the part that showed the man's employment history. He skimmed the page and sighed.

"Okay, what about it?"

"He's jumped around. Tampa, then Dallas, and now Austin. He's worked for three different clinics in ten years. And he's been married multiple times, too."

"Where'd you get that?"

"Asking around."

Frustration swelled in his chest. "Leigh. I swear to God—"

"This is a *good lead*, Brandon. Stop focusing on the messenger and think about the message." She gestured toward her laptop. "I mean, look at this objectively. Vanessa was having an affair—"

"You don't know that for sure."

"Okay, *allegedly* she was having an affair with a married man. And then someone broke things off. And then, suddenly, she's being stalked and harassed and—"

"You don't know that for sure, either."

She took a deep breath, clearly exasperated. "Look. I do this for a living. This is the primary reason people hire me. Obsessive exes, stalkers, and revenge porn. I see this day in and day out, and I'm telling you there are red flags all over the place." She ticked them off on her slender fingers. "The new apartment, the new phone, the bogus lawsuit, the sudden change in mood and appearance. Talk to anyone who knows her—her sister, her friends, *me*—and everyone will tell you that she was under duress lately. The woman was dealing with major *stress*, and now suddenly she's disappeared without a trace."

She stared at him, waiting for his reaction to this supposed breakthrough.

"Can't you at least admit Mason Lloyd is a person of interest?" she asked.

"We've already got a person of interest. Two, in fact."

She frowned. "Who?"

He shook his head. He was done giving her crumbs to follow. It was his fault she was involved in this at all, and the guilt had been eating away at him for days.

"Really, Brandon. Who?"

"Not going there. This isn't your case."

"Don't even tell me you're looking at Cooper Collins or Jason Mandrapilias." She searched his face, obviously wanting him to confirm or deny that they were suspects. "Because neither of them fits the profile."

He laughed. "You're a profiler now?"

"In a way, yes. I am. I deal with these kinds of cases all the time, and I'm telling you Cooper and Jason are not the type."

"Why not?"

"They just aren't," she said. "I checked them out. By all accounts, they appear stable. Both have steady jobs and no history of violence."

"You know one of them has a criminal record?"

She shrugged. "So? That was a drug crime. Like I said, no history of violence. Mason, on the other hand, is on his third wife in ten years. I bet if we go dig up his divorce records, we'll find some interesting skeletons in his past."

Brandon tipped his head back and muttered a curse.

"What's that?"

He looked at her, struggling for calm. Why couldn't she let this go? The more he wanted her to drop it, the more determined she seemed to hang on.

"Don't look like that," she said.

"Like what?"

"You're pissed at me. I can tell."

"I'm not pissed."

That was a lie, and she knew it.

He changed tactics, because telling her what *not* to do wasn't getting him anywhere.

"Look, don't you have enough to do without meddling in my case?" He gestured to the files covering her coffee table. "Looks to me like you've got some other clients that could use your attention."

"Oh, I do. But that doesn't mean I'm going to just ignore a lead that's staring us right in the face."

Us. Like she was a detective now.

A buzzer sounded at the front door.

"That's the pizza." Leigh set her laptop on the table and jumped up, looking happy for the interruption.

Brandon stood, too. Time for him to go. The last thing he needed was to spend the evening in Leigh's office, debating with her and getting all worked up. With every argument, he was just feeding her interest in the case, and she needed to let it go.

Brandon followed her into the lobby and watched as she disabled the alarm and opened the door for the delivery guy. She gave him a big tip and an even bigger smile. When he was gone, she set the pizza box on the reception counter and opened it. The smell of garlic and oregano instantly filled the lobby.

"Oh, good. They remembered the extra jalapeños this time." She glanced up. "Will you stay? There's no way we can eat all this."

She was just being polite, but Brandon wanted to say yes anyway. He wanted to stay. He wanted to eat pizza on her sofa, and keep her company while she worked, and spar with her about anything and everything she wanted to talk about. This woman had his number. She was pushy and headstrong and frustrating as hell, and he couldn't think of a single place he'd rather be tonight than hanging out with her on that damn couch.

"I should go," he said.

"You sure?"

Temptation pulled at him. But the sooner he left, the sooner she could finish her work and get home safely. The idea of her walking to her car by herself later bothered him, even though her little blue Mustang was parked right out front.

She gazed up at him in the dim light of the screen saver. They'd stood in this same room together just last night, and she'd been shaken and wide-eyed. She'd been in shock. A full day had passed, and she had her composure back. Almost. He still detected some nerves underneath the surface.

Brandon stepped closer. Wariness flickered in her eyes, as if she knew he what he was thinking.

"What?" Her voice was quiet, almost a whisper.

He reached up and touched her lower lip, tracing his finger over the swollen spot. Her eyes went dark, and she eased closer, close enough for him to feel the warmth of her breath on his neck.

"Is that the pizza?"

Leigh jerked back as a man walked into the room. Average height, thin, wire-rimmed glasses. He wore black slacks and a dress shirt with the sleeves rolled up.

"Kyle, hey." Leigh cleared her throat. "Have you met Detective Reynolds?"

"No."

Brandon nodded. "Hi."

The guy looked fresh out of law school. As an appellate lawyer, he might be useful, but as a nighttime security guard, not so much.

"Brandon's helping with our case," Leigh said.

"Oh. Thanks." Kyle looked from Brandon to Leigh, obviously puzzling over walking in on them standing there in the dark. "I'll just . . . go grab a Coke."

He disappeared down the hallway, and Leigh looked at Brandon.

"That's one of our associates."

"I know."

She gazed up at him. "Sure I can't talk you into staying?"

"Yeah." He moved toward the door. "Lock up behind me. And set the alarm."

"Of course."

He turned to look at her and felt a surge of protectiveness. It was on the tip of his tongue to tell her to call him when she got home.

"How late are you staying?" he asked instead.

"Until my work's done."

He shot her a look. "Be careful going home tonight."

"I will."

CHAPTER FIFTEEN

A NTONIO CALLED BRANDON AS he left the police station. "Come on, come on," he muttered, merging into traffic. Downtown was packed tonight with tourists and weekend revelers.

His partner didn't pick up. Maybe he was out. That would be good, really. Brandon hadn't gone out much since his last breakup, and he was becoming a workaholic. Antonio kept telling him he needed to get out more, which seemed a little hypocritical tonight because *his* big plans included watching Ultimate Fighting and microwaving a Hot Pocket.

The call went to voicemail, and Antonio waited for the beep.

"Hey, I'm just taking off. I went back to the hospital tonight and our shooting victim was awake and alert. Got a good statement from him and just wrote everything up. Call me later, and I'll fill you in. . : . Unless you're out tonight, in which case, have fun."

The last part was interrupted as a call clicked in. Antonio didn't recognize the number.

"Peña," he said.

Silence.

"Hello?"

"Sorry to call so late."

"Kate?" There was a tremor in her voice. She sounded like she was crying or shaking or both.

"Yes, it's Kate Morris. Sorry. I'm just . . ."

"What's wrong? Where are you?"

"I'm at home," she said.

Antonio had been about to jump on the freeway to head back to his apartment. Instead, he stayed on the feeder road.

"Kate, what is it?"

"It's Kelly. My fifteen-year-old. A man . . . approached her tonight."

Antonio listened, waiting for more.

"The police were just here, but . . . I don't know. I'm sorry. I was hoping we could talk."

"I'll be right over."

"Thank you."

The relief in her voice was unmistakable. She needed him, and for some crazy reason, he didn't hesitate to pull a U-turn and head straight to her house.

As he drove, possibilities flooded his mind—none of them good.

Approached her . . .

What did that mean? Had she been assaulted? Flashed? Did someone try to sell her drugs? And if any of those had happened, why had Kate called him?

Twelve minutes later, he pulled onto her street. A text landed on his phone.

Girls in bed. Pls come around back.

Antonio pulled up to her house and parked discreetly under the shadow of a pecan tree. Yeah, it was dark, but he didn't want any nosy neighbors spotting his car in front of her house this time of night.

Antonio scanned the block as he walked up the driveway. The street was mostly one-story houses, most with porch lights on and moderately priced cars in the driveways. It was a nice neighborhood in a good school zone, and he wasn't sure how Kate afforded it as a single mom with four kids.

The kitchen window was dark. Ditto the utility room. He approached the back door off the driveway.

"Antonio?"

He looked over the gate as Kate opened the back door that faced the patio. The living room lamp was on, and he saw her curvy body silhouetted in the light as she stepped outside. She wore jeans and a tight white shirt, and she was pulling a cardigan sweater around herself.

"Hey," he said, matching her quiet volume as he opened the gate and joined her on the patio.

"Thank you for coming."

He stepped around a red wagon, the one he'd seen her kids in just the other day.

"You okay?" he asked.

"No." She pulled out a lawn chair and gestured for him to sit down.

Antonio took a seat, glancing over her shoulder at the house. The kitchen was dark, and the only light came from the living room. No TV on, and the other windows facing the yard were dark.

"They're asleep," Kate said. "Everyone but Kelly. She's on her phone. Took me forever to get Sylvie down. She can tell when I'm anxious."

Antonio leaned forward, resting his elbows on his knees so he could look her directly in the eye.

"How's Kelly?"

"Upset. I had to tell her about Vanessa tonight."

"She didn't know?"

"I didn't want to tell the girls yet. Not until we knew something definite. I didn't see the point, and it hasn't been on the news yet, so . . ." She cleared her throat. "But I knew the officer would ask about it."

"Back up," Antonio said. "Who was here?"

"Officer Meyers."

"I don't know him."

"He interviewed Kelly, and she told him everything."

"Tell me."

She took a deep breath, and he kept his attention on her face.

"I don't know where to start," she said.

"Start at the beginning."

"Okay." Another deep breath. "So, Kelly's on the drill team. They danced at halftime tonight."

He nodded.

"Her friends went out for burgers after. Most of them don't drive because they're freshmen, but one of them has a license. Kelly didn't want to go—she has cramps tonight— so they dropped her home right after the game." She paused. "After they drove off, this man approached her—"

"Here on your street?"

"Yeah. Right in front of the house." She ran her hand over her hair. It was in a ponytail again, and she tucked a strand behind her ear. "He approached her and said, 'Kelly, hi.' And she said at first she thought he was a neighbor, because he knew her name. She thought he was out walking his dog. And then he said, 'I like your boots.' She was in her dance uniform, and she wears these white ankle boots with fringe. He said, 'I bet you do good high kicks.' Kelly thought that was creepy, and that's when she realized he didn't have a dog with him. And then he said, 'I'm Mason, a friend of your aunt's. Have you seen her around?'"

"He referenced Vanessa?"

"Yes. Kelly shook her head, and he said, 'Do you happen to have her phone number? I need to get in touch with her.'"

Antonio studied her face, understanding now why Kate was so upset.

"What did she say?" he asked.

"She told him she didn't have it. Even though that's not true. She does have it, but by then she was suspicious."

"She's got good instincts."

"But he kept pressing. Then he walked closer and said, 'Oh, come on. I bet you have it on your phone.' She was holding her phone in her hand. She told him she had to go and stepped away, but he said, 'Wait. Give me your aunt's number. I'm a friend.' And that's when she got really creeped out and ran into the house and locked the door."

"What time was this?"

"A little after ten. I called 911 to report an attempted kidnapping, and they sent a car right over. They had someone in the area."

"A kidnapping?"

"I didn't know what to say. Some pervert comes up to my fifteen-year-old and starts talking about high kicks?"

"No, I get it," he said. "I just want to make sure I understand what happened. Did he touch her?"

"No. She said no."

"Did he ask her to get in is car? Or ask her to go with him anywhere?"

"No."

"Did he have a car nearby?"

She nodded. "She said there was a silver SUV on the street, but she didn't know whether or not it was his."

"All right." So far, they had a possible name and a possible vehicle. That was a good start. But without any physical contact or coercion, the incident wasn't likely to be written up as an attempted kidnapping.

She leaned forward. "Do you understand why I'm upset?"

"Yes."

"Do you really? I mean, some middle-aged man approaches my daughter—"

"I understand."

"And he *knows* Vanessa. That's the worst part. She works

with a doctor named Mason at Pura Vida. I'm beginning to think they had a relationship or something." She pressed her hand to her mouth. "And then . . . he did something to her."

Antonio scooted his chair closer. He looked her right in the eye.

"I understand why you're upset."

She shook her head. "I really don't think you do."

"I do. But you're making some assumptions here, okay? First, you're assuming he is who he said he was. He could have used a false name. Did Kelly give a description?"

"Yeah. She said he was tall. Dark hair. She couldn't tell his eye color because the streetlight was behind him, and his face was shadowed."

"Okay, but she got a description. That and the SUV will help us a lot."

He was trying to reassure her, and he couldn't tell whether it was working.

"Even if he isn't who he claimed—don't you think he has something to do with Vanessa's disappearance? Don't you think he did something to her?"

The raw desperation in her voice got to him, and she swiped a tear off her cheek.

"Okay. Let's go with that." He held her gaze. "If he had something to do with it, why would he need her phone number?"

She just stared at him, and he could tell that in her worried frenzy, she hadn't thought it through.

"If he hurt her or took her somewhere, why would he need her number and why would he want to draw attention to himself to get it? That would be a big risk for him. Why would he do that?"

"So . . . you *don't* think it's weird that some man who knows Vanessa is approaching my teenager and asking about her and—"

"No, it's definitely weird. I agree. We just don't know what it means yet."

"Well . . . can't you drag him in for questioning and figure it out?"

Anger was starting to replace the desperation in her voice, which was probably good. Anger, Antonio could handle. Desperate tears were much worse.

"We can, yeah."

"Well . . ." She trailed off, looking frustrated as she stared at him in the dimness.

"We'll definitely follow up. I promise. Okay?"

"Okay."

"I have another question for you." He watched her face, wishing there were more light out here so he could see her reaction. "Do you keep a gun in the house?"

She stiffened. "No. I hate guns."

"Have you ever thought of getting one? I'm not saying you should, I'm just asking if you've thought about it."

"No."

"Have you had any problems with anyone that might make you consider a home security weapon?"

She shook her head. "When Rick moved out, I got some Mace for my bedroom. But I keep it in the top of the armoire, so Sylvie doesn't find it."

"Rick's your ex-husband?"

She nodded.

"Where does he live?"

Her gaze narrowed. "Why?"

"Just wondering."

"He bought a condo in South Austin with his girlfriend." The look on her face made him feel like crap for asking. "Sorry."

"What does this have to do with Vanessa?"

"I'm just filling in details," he said. "You never know what might be important."

It was a lame answer, and he could tell she didn't buy it. But maybe she was too distracted to push the point.

She looked out over the yard. In the dimness, he saw the

outline of the swing set where her girls had been playing
the first time he'd come over here. Had the swing set come
with the house? Or had Rick installed it for his kids before
running off with his girlfriend? What a dickhead.

"Today's my birthday."

Kate's words were so soft, he barely heard her.

"Happy birthday," he said, and immediately felt like an
idiot.

"I'm thirty-three." She looked at him. "I know. Young to
have a fifteen-year-old, right? We started early." She looked
at the swings. "How old are you?"

He hesitated a beat. "Twenty-nine."

She nodded silently. "Vanessa never misses my birthday."

Antonio didn't know what to say to that.

"All day long, I've had this pit in my stomach." She
looked at him.

"We'll find her."

He regretted the words as soon as he said them. He was
talking about a body, and he could tell she knew it.

"I promise, Kate. We'll find out what happened."

LEIGH TURNED ONTO the dark street and searched for
numbers on the curbs, but if there were any, they were
blocked by cars. She passed a row of ramshackle houses
with chipping paint and slumping front porches. Five years
and a lifetime ago, she had had a client who lived in this
neighborhood. He'd been arrested for buying meth three
blocks from here. It had been one of Leigh's first cases for
Gertie in the public defender's office, and she'd been determined to do a good job. After days of painstaking prepara-
tion, Leigh and her client had participated in a ten-minute
hearing where the judge let him off with probation.

Leigh passed a boarded-up house tagged with graffiti.
Didn't look like the neighborhood had improved much since
Leigh's last visit. Most of East Austin was changing dramati-

cally, with young professionals and house-flippers buying up cottages and dumping money into them. But this little pocket had somehow missed the wave of gentrification.

She neared a row of attached brick homes, all with identical front stoops. The units might have once been cute, but the wooden siding was moldy and some of the shutters were hanging off the windows. One unit had an old sofa out front on a weedy patch of lawn. Leigh squinted at some numbers on the side of the building, then checked her phone.

"Three twenty-five Clark Street," she muttered.

Leigh pulled over and parked behind an old pickup. She leaned over and opened her glove box to retrieve her self-defense weapon of choice, which was a carryover from her public defender days. Her very first week on the job, Gertie had admonished Leigh about personal protection, extolling the virtues of her snub-nosed Smith & Wesson, which fit easily into a purse. But Leigh had no experience with guns, so instead she'd armed herself with a tube of pepper spray.

Leigh got out of her Mustang, locked it, and looked around. The air smelled foul, probably from the water treatment plant nearby, and she realized why the homes in this particular area weren't getting snatched up. The wind gusted, sending cold darts of air through her clothes. A fast-food bag cartwheeled down the street like a tumbleweed.

Leigh glanced up and down the block, wishing for more streetlights as Brandon's parting words came back to her. *Be careful going home.* Somehow she doubted this little errand was what he'd meant.

Stepping onto the sidewalk, she noticed a shadowy figure on one of the porches across the street. A chill snaked down her spine. The man slouched against the house, watching her from the shadows as he pulled a cigarette to his mouth.

Leigh strode up the paved path to unit 104. No interior lights visible from the front. The neighbor's place was livelier, and she noticed a flicker of light behind the blinds and heard the low drone of a television.

Leigh rapped on the door and waited. Nothing. She rapped again, and the volume of the TV next door went down.

Leigh glanced around the small concrete porch. In the corner was a shriveled fern in a chipped clay pot, and she spotted a package tucked behind it. She crouched down to examine the package. It was a padded bubble mailer from Amazon with a label addressed to COOPER COLLINS. She was in the right place at least.

Leigh stood up and looked at the silent door. There was something going on with Cooper, and she wanted to talk to him. She'd interviewed him twice now at the bookstore where he worked and both times she'd left with the distinct feeling there was something he wasn't telling her. She didn't know what, exactly, made her think that, but she'd been taking depositions long enough to know when someone was holding back. The fact that he'd dodged her last two phone calls only reinforced her suspicions.

Leigh rapped on the door again.

Maybe she should have told Brandon her suspicions.

No, she definitely *should* have told him. He was the lead detective on this case.

But Brandon had already wasted enough time with Cooper—who didn't fit the profile of a vindictive ex—when the person he really needed to be looking at was Mason Lloyd.

Leigh checked her watch, annoyed with herself for coming all the way out here and netting no new information whatsoever. She could be at home right now, slipping into her fuzzy bathrobe and pouring herself a glass of wine, but instead she was running down leads for an investigation that wasn't even hers.

"Screw it," she muttered, turning to leave. But as she stalked down the sidewalk, she felt a niggle of uncertainty. She had spent an hour online tracking down this address and she'd come all the way out here. The least she could do was make sure he wasn't really home, ducking her visit like he'd been ducking her phone calls.

She walked across the grass, cutting through the neighbor's lawn before looping around the building. Behind the row of homes was an alley and a string of carports, five in all, each with its own bright floodlight shining down onto the pavement. Every carport had a car in it with the exception of the second unit from the end, which would be Cooper's.

Leigh stomped her foot. Okay, so she'd officially wasted her trip.

"Looking for someone?"

She whirled around and saw a tall, lanky man walking toward her. Or rather, being pulled toward her by a very big and very eager black Lab.

The dog whined softly and strained against the leash, and Leigh took a step back.

"He's fine," the man said, stepping into the light from one of the floodlights.

The man wore jeans and a gray hoodie. He looked to be midtwenties, with shaggy dark hair and a goatee. He was taller than she'd first thought, and she took another step back as she gripped the pepper spray.

His gaze went to her hand. "Cooper's not here," he said, probably trying to put her at ease.

"You live nearby?"

"Across the street. I saw you drive up."

She caught a faint whiff of cigarette smoke and guessed he was the man in the shadows. So, he'd just happened to decide to walk his dog right now? Or did he have some other reason to want to approach her?

The dog whined and strained against the leash, and the man pulled him back a few inches.

"Hooch, *no.*"

She smiled at the dog, trying to appear calmer than she felt.

"I'm a friend of Cooper's," she lied. "You happen to know where he is?"

"Haven't seen him in a couple days. You try his work?"

"Yes, actually."

"Then I don't know. Could be at the lab."

"The lab?"

"The physics lab. Sometimes he gets in the zone and camps out there for days."

"Oh. Good point."

She felt her shoulders loosen a bit at the evidence that this guy did, in fact, know Cooper Collins at least enough to know that he was a graduate student.

She blew out a sigh, like she was merely inconvenienced and not frightened to be standing out here in the dark with a strange man. Usually, she wasn't so paranoid with people, but yesterday had made her skittish. "Guess I'll give him another call."

She walked around Hooch and his owner, giving them both plenty of space. She returned to her car, glancing over her shoulder to make sure she was wasn't being followed. She slid behind the wheel, locked the doors, and took a deep breath.

Well, that had been a waste of time.

Probably.

She'd learned that Cooper hadn't been seen in a few days, and also that he sometimes got immersed in his work and didn't come up for air.

So, maybe that explained why he was ducking her calls.

She should let it go. Or share her hunch with Brandon and *then* let it go. He was the detective, after all. But he'd probably give her a lecture for coming out here.

No, he'd definitely give her a lecture.

Leigh dropped her pepper spray into the cup holder and started the car. She was done playing detective, at least for now. She didn't need any more hunches to follow or mysteries to unravel. What she needed was a long, hot bath and a good night's sleep.

CHAPTER SIXTEEN

B RANDON FOLLOWED THE SOUND of slack key guitar music into the crime lab. No sign of Jane, but the CSI he'd seen earlier in the week was crouched beside a mangled black bicycle collecting something with tweezers.

"Hey, is Jane around?"

The guy looked up from his work. "In the fume room," he said, nodding toward a door behind him.

Brandon set down the cup of coffee he'd brought with him and took a minute to pull paper covers over his shoes so he wouldn't get an earful about tracking debris. Then he crossed the garage, pausing to watch the CSI.

"That looks bad," Brandon said.

"Bike versus SUV. Hit-and-run."

"I heard about it on the scanner yesterday. Didn't we get a license plate?"

"A partial one. But don't worry, we'll get him." The CSI held up his tweezers. "He left behind some good paint chips."

Brandon headed into the next room, where he found Jane hunched over a glass chamber. From the superglue smell, he could tell she was doing cyanoacrylate fuming.

"Good morning," he said.

She turned around and switched off the noisy vent above the fuming chamber. "Hey." She pushed a pair of goggles to her forehead, and her gaze went to the Starbucks cup in his hand.

He held it out to her. "Double shot caramel latte."

Her eyes narrowed. "How did you know?"

"I'm a detective."

Smirking, she walked over and took the coffee. "Uh-oh. A bribe." She took a big sip and closed her eyes. "Wow, I needed this. I skipped breakfast this morning." She gave him a suspicious look. "You must be here about the shoe print from the law firm break-in."

"How'd you guess?"

"Maybe because you've left me two messages since yesterday?"

"It's a priority case," he said. Which was why he'd decided not to wait around for a junior detective to follow up. The guy hadn't yet figured out how to light a fire under people.

"Yeah, I caught that," Jane said. "That's why I was here late last night working on it. Want to see what I found?"

"Yes."

"You heard the print from that windowsill belonged to someone at the law firm, right?"

"I heard." Brandon had expected it to be a dead end, but they had had to try. Now in terms of forensic evidence, they were down to a shoe print. He was hopeful, though, because the print had been found in a key location—the exact location Brandon would have chosen if he'd wanted to see people coming and going from the law firm while remaining concealed and avoiding the building's security cams.

Jane led him to the opposite side of the room and brought a computer workstation to life with the tap of the mouse. Not bothering to sit down, she clicked open a photograph of the shoe print that had been taken by the forensic photographer Thursday night. By shining a spotlight at an oblique angle, the photographer had managed to heighten the detailed ridges in the dirt.

"Normally, this would take a while, but I've got a friend at the Bureau who specializes in footwear evidence. I asked him to take a look for me."

"Thanks," Brandon said, grateful that she'd called in a personal favor.

"He came back with good news and bad."

"Let's hear the good."

"Okay, well the *good* is that he can definitely identify it as a Merrell Zion Peak hiking boot, size fourteen."

Brandon's gut clenched. "Fourteen?"

"Yep. The guy you're looking for isn't small."

Leigh had described her attacker as "big" but that was a relative term. Leigh was only five feet four, and abject fear had a way of messing with people's perceptions.

Now Brandon knew that her description was accurate.

"What's the bad news?" he asked.

"The bad news is that this is a new boot. Or at least, it hasn't been worn a lot. He didn't find much in the way of individual wear patterns. So, assuming you ever do find a suspect who has a pair of these boots, it could be hard to trace them back to this exact print."

Brandon refused to take this as bad news. When—not if—they tracked down Leigh's attacker, Brandon planned to have a lot more evidence lined up than a single shoe print. This guy was going down.

Jane tipped her head to the side. "Can I ask you something?"

He raised his eyebrows.

"Why is this one high priority? I thought you and Antonio were working that missing-person case."

"There's a possibility this is related."

Her eyebrows tipped up. "How?"

"The woman who was attacked is the missing woman's lawyer."

"Hmm. Well, in that case, you'll be glad to see what else we found. Come look."

She led him to the fuming chamber, which looked like a big aquarium. The lid had been removed, and Brandon's pulse picked up when he saw a pair of clear latex gloves inside.

"Where'd those come from?" he asked.

"Detective Tate sent them in. One of the CSIs recovered them from a dumpster about a block away from the crime scene."

Damn. Brandon had underestimated the guy. And now he wanted to know exactly where this dumpster was, because the attacker had probably parked his vehicle nearby.

"Tate didn't mention the gloves?" Jane asked.

"No."

She lifted an eyebrow. "Maybe he didn't want you hounding him for lab results all weekend."

She was probably right. He had a reputation for being demanding, but that was the only way to do this work. Every case was on a clock.

"I'll show you what I found," she said, reaching over to turn off the overhead light. Then she switched on a spotlight attached to a metal arm and directed it down at the gloves.

"It's hard to see right now, but I've developed a good set of prints."

"These are inside out?" he asked.

"Right."

"The other side of the gloves—"

"I found a trace of blood," she said, reading his mind. "I swabbed it and sent it to the DNA lab."

Leigh's blood.

He hated the thought of it. But in terms of forensic evidence, the gloves were a gold mine.

"As for the fingerprints," she said, "we should be able to see more detail when I dust them with fluorescent powder. Then I'll use an alternative light source to photograph them."

Brandon stared at the gloves, which had likely been discarded in a rush after Leigh's attack. Fury swelled inside him as he pictured some man's hand clamped over Leigh's mouth. He shouldn't let this case get personal. He knew better than that. But it was too late. Ever since he'd met Leigh, everything that touched her commanded his attention.

He looked at Jane. "How soon can we run the prints?"

"That all depends." She smiled sweetly. "How soon can you leave me alone so I can finish my work?"

LEIGH ATE THE last warm dumpling and slurped the very last drop of soup from her spoon. She'd meant to take her dinner to go, but she'd walked into Mei's famished, and the aroma of fresh spring rolls and wonton soup had been so tempting, she'd decided to stay and eat there, while it was hot. Now she glanced around the little restaurant that was packed with rain-dampened customers who'd come in from the cold.

Leigh tucked an extra spring roll into a white paper sack and dropped it into her computer bag for later. She tidied up her table and looked through the window at her building across the street. For the first time in days, she felt relaxed and sated—and decidedly unmotivated to go home and put in another three hours of work tonight. Maybe she'd do a yoga workout to reenergize. She had to get a second wind. She was too far behind to blow off the night.

Leigh threw away her trash and grabbed a fortune cookie from the big glass bowl on her way out the door. Stepping into the chilly air, she hitched her bag onto her shoulder and rubbed her arms, wishing she'd checked the weather before leaving the house. She was in a sweater and jeans, but she'd left her rain jacket at home. She eyed her car down the block and then glanced across the street at her building, thinking of Watermelon. She probably shouldn't worry about the old cat—he'd been there since long before they were, slinking around, eliciting food and sympathy from tenants up and down the block. Leigh hadn't seen him today, but she'd left some food on the porch, and it had disappeared while she and Kyle had been inside working.

"Leigh Larson?"

She turned around as a man stepped from the restaurant. Tall, golf visor, friendly smile. She'd glimpsed him in line behind her when she paid for her order.

He stepped closer, and she got a better look at his eyes under the visor.

Mason Lloyd. Her heart skittered and she stepped back, but he moved, too, trapping her between the building and a concrete planter. His smile vanished as he loomed over her.

"You've been talking about me," he said in a low voice.

Leigh tried to step around him, but he blocked her path.

"Better watch that sweet little ass of yours." He stepped closer. "Or I'll sue you for libel."

Her heart hammered and her throat felt dry. But she found her voice.

"Are you implying I *wrote* something about you?"

He frowned.

"Libel is defamation in printed form," she said. "I think you mean slander. I suggest you get some legal advice before you file a lawsuit."

She tried to go around him again, but he shifted.

"You have don't have a clue who you're dealing with, do you?" His lip twitched as he eased closer. "I could squash you like a bug."

Leigh kept her gaze on his, but her chest tightened with panic. Bile rose in the back of her throat. She tried to make her face neutral, and she desperately regretted that initial flash of fear. Men like him got off on it.

He reached out and traced the tip of his finger over her neckline. She forced herself not to wince as his finger grazed her skin.

"Nice sweater. Too bad it hides your tattoo."

Leigh bit the inside of her mouth. She shifted her weight to create more space between them.

"If you touch me again," she said calmly, "I'll have you charged with assault." She stared up at him. "Now, move out of my way."

He gave her a slow, smug smile. Several seconds ticked by before he stepped aside.

Leigh strode across the street to the sidewalk, grateful for the break in traffic, because she hadn't even looked. She walked quickly toward her car, praying she wasn't going to catch the heel of her boot or slip on the slick pavement. As she neared the Mustang, she dug the keys from her purse and popped the locks.

With a glance over her shoulder, she slid behind the wheel and tossed her bags in the passenger seat. She yanked the door shut and hit the locks.

Leigh's heart jackhammered as she looked at the rearview mirror. The raindrops created prisms on the back window, making it impossible to see. She checked the side mirrors.

He was gone. No sign of him, no sign of his vehicle. With trembling fingers, she started the engine and backed from the space. Usually, she drove past the Thai restaurant, but this time she turned the opposite way and circled the block, checking her surroundings for any sign of someone following her.

Holy shit.

Holy shit. Holy shit. Holy shit.

Her stomach did little flip-flops as she replayed the encounter. He'd been in the restaurant that whole time, probably watching her eat, and she hadn't even noticed. Where had he been sitting? She thought back, trying to remember if she'd read anything sensitive on her phone while she'd scarfed her meal. No, she'd gone through some emails and played a game of sudoku.

Leigh gripped the wheel as she drove through downtown, navigating the wet streets toward the Lamar Bridge. The rain had let up, but it was still misty out, and a layer of fog hung over the lake.

She felt shocked and shaky. The dumplings were like stones in her stomach. She wove through several neighborhoods, checking her mirrors compulsively as she took a circuitous route home. But when she reached her street she kept going. She couldn't pull into her driveway yet. She'd gone to great lengths to keep her address unlisted. She couldn't simply let someone follow her home.

Leigh checked the mirrors again. Was she being paranoid? Maybe. But she didn't want to risk it. Being careful was what gave her peace of mind. She wended through neighborhood after neighborhood until she reached South Congress and hung a left.

She took a deep breath as she drove north on the brightly lit avenue. Tourists and partygoers lined the sidewalks, undeterred by the damp weather as they hopped from bar to bar. Leigh passed her favorite Mexican dive, her favorite ice cream shop, a boot store. She passed the Continental Club, where a line of people stretched around the corner waiting for a chance to see whatever up-and-coming band was listed on the marquee. She passed a trendy movie saloon and several swanky loft apartment buildings before hanging a right onto a narrow side street. After passing a noodle shop and a karate studio, she neared a two-story brick walkup.

Leigh pulled up to a meter and parked. She cut the engine and stared at the building.

It definitely didn't look like much. The 1970s architecture wasn't pronounced enough to even be considered retro, really. The place merely looked old, with sagging gutters and ugly yellow light fixtures. But Brandon was right—you couldn't beat the location.

Leigh studied the building, counting the windows until she located—she guessed—number 208, Brandon's unit.

She had looked him up, and she didn't feel a shred of guilt over it. It was what she did now—she vetted people.

She knew what he paid in rent. She knew his salary range. She knew that he'd been married over a decade ago, and that it barely lasted a year. She knew he had a stellar credit rating and that he'd been the captain of his football team at Travis High School in San Antonio. She knew all this and more from just a couple hours online and a few handy tricks of the trade.

Leigh studied the nondescript building, not sure whether to be relieved or disappointed that his unit was dark. What had she expected? She didn't even know why she'd come here.

Mason Lloyd had seen the video.

Too bad it hides your tattoo.

Even if he hadn't said that, she would have known from the way he'd looked at her—aroused and taunting. He'd wielded his words like a whip, delivering a quick sting, and she knew he got off on that.

Tears slid down her cheeks, and she brushed them away. She should be past this now. Two long years later, she should be numb to this crap. Usually, she was. But then something would leap out of nowhere and slap her in the face.

Better watch that sweet little ass of yours. Leigh's stomach filled with acid as she pictured that leering, revolting grin.

A tap on the window made her jump.

Brandon peered down at her. She felt a flood of relief, quickly followed by embarrassment. She popped the locks and pushed open the door.

"You lost?" he asked with a wry smile.

"No. I was looking for you, actually."

He seemed amused. "You looked up my address?"

"Yep." She forced a smile. "I'm nosy."

He pulled the door open wider and she hesitated a moment before getting out. It was the only move that made sense. She couldn't very well tell him she'd come over here just to stare at his building.

Looking him over, Leigh realized she hadn't thought this through. Here she was in jeans and a faded sweater with her unwashed hair in a messy bun. He was in jeans, too, but his clean-shaven face and hint of cologne told her he was on his way out for the night.

Good lord, did he have a date? Her cheeks flushed at the prospect, and she scrambled for something to say.

A smile spread over his face as he gazed down at her. "You had dinner?"

"Yes. What about you? Are you on your way somewhere or—"

"I'm headed out for a drink. Want to come?"

She gazed up at him, weighing his words. He looked all cleaned up, and he was going out for a drink. By himself. Which probably meant he'd been planning to meet up with someone or pick someone up.

He leaned closer. "It's not a hard question," he whispered.

"Yes. I'd love to have a drink with you."

"Good." He smiled, once again looking amused by the situation, which she had to admit was strange—her showing up at his place out of the blue.

He nodded at her car. "That your computer? You probably want to put it in the trunk."

"Oh. Right."

She reached across the seat and grabbed her computer bag, then popped the trunk open. He stepped back and watched as she stashed the bag in the trunk between a pair of Banker's Boxes filled with case files and legal pads. Then she retrieved her purse from the front seat. On impulse, she grabbed a lipstick out of the console so she could sneak away for a minute and freshen up. She locked her car with a chirp and zipped the lipstick and keys into her purse.

"All good?" he asked.

"I think so. Am I okay to park here?"

"You're fine. Weekends are free."

"That case, I'm all set." She glanced around. "Where are we going?"

He gave her a sly smile that sent a ripple of nerves through her. "You'll see."

CHAPTER SEVENTEEN

LEIGH HAD NO TROUBLE keeping up with him as they walked along Congress, and she realized he was shortening his strides. He seemed to do it naturally, the same way he walked closest to traffic and steered her away from street hazards and sketchy-looking people. He scanned the area, his gaze relaxed but alert, as they made their way down the busy strip.

The chilly air seeped through her loose-knit sweater, and she wished she'd worn something warmer. Or at least sexier. If she was going to be cold, she should at least have some cleavage showing. She liked her shoes, though. The heeled black ankle boots did what heels always did for her—projected confidence and gave her ego a tiny boost, which she needed tonight.

Leigh couldn't help but notice the female heads turning as they walked down the strip. She snuck a glance at Brandon. His black T-shirt fit perfectly over his muscular torso—not too loose, and not too tight like some guy trying to look like the Incredible Hulk. He moved with comfortable athleticism and didn't seem the slightest bit cold, even without a jacket.

He glanced at her. "What?"

"Where's your weapon?"

"Come again?" He bent his head closer.

"Your gun. Usually, you wear a leather jacket when you're off-duty to conceal your Glock."

"Ankle holster," he told her.

She looked down, noticing his scuffed brown work boots. He'd had them on the other night, too, when he showed up at the law firm.

"This way," he said, settling his hand on her lower back and steering her around a line of people waiting outside a burger joint. They turned down a side street and his hand dropped away as they walked toward yet another line, this one outside a plain black door. Above the door was a neon-purple sign: LEONARD'S LOUNGE.

"You like jazz?" he asked.

"I don't know."

He shot her a scowl. "How can you not know?"

"I've never really listened to it." She surveyed the queue, which seemed like an endorsement. "I'm open minded, though."

"Good."

He took her hand, and she felt a flurry of anticipation as he tugged her past the line of people to the side of the building. They walked past a row of dumpsters, and she glanced over her shoulder at the crowded corner.

On the far side of the building, they came upon an open door with two men standing around smoking. Brandon nodded at both and walked straight between them, pulling Leigh behind him.

"What is this, a speakeasy?" she asked as he towed her through a crowded kitchen. The air was hot and humid, and dishes clanged.

They entered a dark corridor where Brandon passed a

huge Black man wearing a Saints jersey and a do-rag. He and Brandon exchanged words, and the man pointed out something in the main room.

The man flattened himself against the wall, making room for Leigh to squeeze past his stomach.

"Y'all be good, now," he told her.

She smiled, still clutching Brandon's hand as he pulled her into a dim room with a long bar along one side and an exposed brick wall along the other. Every bar stool was occupied, and the high-top tables were full, too. Brandon paused a moment and dropped her hand. He scanned the area and then motioned with his head for her to follow him through a throng of people. Way at the back, he found an empty stool near a narrow ledge that ran the length of the wall. The shelf was just big enough to rest a drink on, and many people had.

He tugged the stool forward. "Sit."

Leigh hitched herself onto the seat but kept her purse on her shoulder. "Do we order at the bar or—"

A server halted beside Brandon, propping her empty cocktail tray against her hip. "Hey." She smiled from Brandon to Leigh. "What can I get ya?"

He nodded at Leigh. She started to order a beer, but then thought better of it.

"Vodka tonic with a twist, please."

The server looked at Brandon.

"Shiner Bock."

She smiled and whisked away, and Brandon leaned his head close to Leigh. "They just wrapped up a set," he said over the din of voices.

She nodded. "I didn't see a restroom when we came in. Do you know—"

"Left of the bar."

She followed his gaze and spotted the sign.

"Be right back," she said, slipping off the stool.

She felt Brandon's gaze following her as she wove

through the clusters of people and made her way to the bathroom. No line for once. Leigh closed herself in the tiny room and cast a look in the mirror.

It wasn't as bad as she'd feared. Her hair was a mess, yes, but her cheeks had some color from their brisk walk over here. She washed her hands, then dug a tissue from her purse and fixed her eyeliner. She took out her lipstick but decided to skip it. Her cut was still healing, and she didn't want to draw attention to it.

Leigh looked in the mirror and adjusted her sweater, shuddering at the memory of Mason Lloyd's obnoxious finger. Her stomach roiled, but her nerves were calmer now. She'd stopped shaking. And her fear was quickly transforming into a healthy combination of outrage and determination. Obviously, he thought he could bully her into submission, but he was in for a surprise.

She made her way back through the crowd to find that Brandon had abandoned their lone stool for a high-top table with two chairs in the corner. He stood as she walked over, and she marveled at his manners as he pulled the stool out for her. She hitched herself onto it.

He sat down beside her, looking her over with those sharp eyes, his gaze lingering on the side of her lower lip. His attention always seemed to go there, lipstick or no.

She hung her purse on the back of the chair.

"You seem to know the people here," she said over the noise.

"I've been coming here for years."

"Neighborhood hangout?"

He shrugged. "Even before that." His gaze skimmed over the crowd, watching, assessing, taking in details that Leigh felt certain were lost on ninety-nine percent of people. Brandon was observant. Vigilant. And although his low-key demeanor covered it well, she could see him taking note of every aspect of their surroundings. Once again, just being in his presence made her feel safe. The odds of some rando approaching her with a crude comment or grabby hands were zero.

The server returned with a full tray and a warm smile as she set their drinks on the table.

"Let me know if y'all need anything else," she said, giving Brandon a wink.

Leigh watched his reaction, but he pretended not to notice. He kept his attention on Leigh as she picked up her glass and took her first sip. The drink was tart and cold, and the fizz felt wonderful on her tight throat.

Leigh looked out at the room, enjoying the low lighting and the hum of lively conversation. She'd always liked people-watching, trying to imagine the little dramas playing out between strangers. In law school, she'd taken a body-language class that focused on jury selection, and she'd discovered she had a knack for reading people. Four summers of waiting tables had probably helped. She could spot the good tippers a mile away, as well as the cheapskates, the posers, and the sexist pigs.

Brandon sipped his beer, and she leaned closer.

"What time do they start?" she asked.

"Soon."

Leigh stirred her ice cubes and sipped her drink. Her shoulders loosened, and she felt a warm buzz spreading through her as the vodka kicked in. The feeling was good, and she chose to focus on it instead of the strange fact that she was out at a jazz club with Brandon. It was a bad idea for many reasons—not the least of which was that he was the lead detective on her client's case. And Leigh had very intentionally *not* told him everything he wanted to know about it.

She hadn't lied. She just hadn't been completely forthcoming. She doubted he'd see the difference. Withholding information wouldn't go over well with him. But at the moment, she had no choice.

Leigh took another sip and surveyed the room full of

people. She couldn't remember the last time she'd been in a nightclub. It had been with Javi, but she couldn't think of a specific time. They'd been so slammed with work lately, weekdays and weekends seemed to blur together.

At least, for her they did. Javi had been out Thursday night, so he seemed to be keeping at least some semblance of a social life.

Brandon tipped his beer back, watching her. He set the bottle down carefully.

"What?" she asked.

He leaned forward on his elbows. "What happened earlier?"

"Earlier?"

"You were crying."

Her pulse skittered and she looked away, searching for what to say. She was good at thinking on her feet. But Brandon didn't fall for her usual deflection and misdirection tactics.

She stirred her drink with the little red straw. "Rough day at the office." She glanced up at him with a smile.

He watched her patiently.

She could tell him to drop it, and he might. But that would just postpone the inevitable. The topic wasn't going to magically go away.

"I had a little run-in with Mason Lloyd."

His gaze sharpened. "A 'run-in'?"

"He approached me outside my office. Basically told me to stop gossiping about him."

His eyes narrowed. "Did he touch you?"

"No."

She thought of his finger on her sweater and stifled a shudder.

Brandon's jaw tightened. "Leigh . . ."

"We exchanged words." She shrugged. "He threatened to sue me for slander. He probably heard I was asking around about him, doing some background research."

She stirred her drink, debating how much to reveal about her research. She hadn't planned to get into this with Brandon—at least not yet. But she hadn't planned to go to a jazz club with him, either. He was watching her intently, and she felt pressure to at least hint at the newest development. He'd learn about it eventually, and she might as well tell him so that she could control the message.

"He may have also heard I'm representing Vanessa's sister," she said, trying to sound casual.

"You're talking about Kate?"

"Yeah. I'm sure Antonio told you that Mason showed up at her house and talked to her daughter Kelly, right? Kate said she told him about it."

"So, you're representing Vanessa *and* her sister now?" His eyes flashed with barely concealed frustration.

"Yep."

"Why?"

"She knows me, and she wanted a lawyer. She wants me to get a restraining order to keep Mason away from her daughter."

"And you agreed?"

"I agreed to look into it. A restraining order isn't likely to be in the cards, given the circumstances of what happened. But I can at least fire off a letter on firm stationery. That gets us on record and should make him think twice before he goes near Kelly again."

"I'm sure it will. It'll also piss him off."

"He's already pissed off. That's his default state. I've been trying to tell you—the guy's got anger management problems. He doesn't know how to take rejection. In fact, he *doesn't* take it. He blows up and makes threats and gets violent and controlling."

"Where are you getting this?"

"I talked to one of his ex-wives."

"You—"

"Her name's Christine and she lives in Tampa. You

should talk to her, too. I can give you her contact info, if you like."

Brandon leaned back in his chair and tipped his head back.

"What? I told you it was a lead worth pursuing." She paused to watch his reaction. He looked exasperated. But also genuinely surprised that she hadn't followed orders when he'd told her to drop the case.

She was more involved now than ever before, and that was just tough toenails for him. She wasn't going to turn down business because something made him uncomfortable. She and Javi were building a practice, and they needed all the work they could get.

"Why did Kate go to you with this?" he asked, clearly unhappy that she had yet another tie to his case. "There're a million other lawyers in town."

"Because. Kate's a worried mother, and the police won't do anything."

"It's not that simple."

"I know," she said.

"No. Really. We can't just arrest him over a conversation. At least, not the one she described to police."

"I'm not being glib, Brandon. I get it. Crappy laws are the reason I have clients. Women are harassed and stalked and bullied, and oftentimes the police can't do anything about it until it's too late."

She herself had been a case in point. But that was another thing she didn't plan to tell Brandon about.

Leigh stirred her drink again and took a sip. When she glanced up, Brandon was watching her. His dark brows were furrowed, and he looked concerned.

And pensive. Nerves flitted in her stomach as she felt him trying to read her.

"Why do you do this work?" he asked.

"I'm good at it."

"Besides that."

She blew out a sigh. He wanted more than her canned answer.

"Same reason you do," she told him. "I want justice." She leaned forward. "*You* get it when you put someone behind bars. They lose their freedom. I get it when I get a judgment or a settlement. They lose their money. Either way, it's about payback."

"Money doesn't cut it," he said. "I'm a cop. For me, it's also about getting dangerous people off the street."

She nodded. "That's important, too. But I'm a realist. Some of the guys I deal with will never go to jail, no matter how many lives they screw up. But they have to be held accountable. I'll take what I can get."

He watched her closely with those sharp brown eyes, as though he sensed there was more to it. Leigh looked out at the crowd. She didn't want to talk about it. She'd been feeling relaxed, shaking off what had happened earlier, but now her shoulders felt tight again.

The lights dimmed and a hush fell over the room. It was followed by claps and whistles as three shadowy figures took the stage.

The room went silent. A few seconds later, she heard the soft hiss of drums. Then there was a low staccato, followed by the hum of a saxophone as a blue light went up on stage.

Brandon leaned back in his chair. Leigh did, too, letting the music wash over her. The buzz came back as the first song ended with a winding sax solo.

Brandon's warm hand slid over hers and squeezed. The waitress was back. He lifted his eyebrows in question. Leigh nodded, and he ordered another round.

The next hour spun out in a decadent haze. The meandering, wordless music stirred something inside her. She listened, closing her eyes for long moments, transfixed by the bone-deep vibrations that seemed to reach into her core.

She liked the unpredictability of it, the looseness. She liked the sultry twists and turns and the heady feeling of connection that permeated the room.

She and Brandon didn't talk or touch, but somehow they shifted until she felt surrounded by him. His arm rested on the back of her chair, and she inhaled the tantalizing scent of him that she'd been noticing on and off for days. She wanted to turn her head and nuzzle against his neck. She wanted him to kiss her, right there in the bar. They weren't even touching, and yet she felt like they'd carved out their own private corner, suffused with sexual tension.

She needed to snap out of it. A week ago, she didn't even know this man, and now she felt inexorably drawn to him all the time. She kept seeking him out, wanting information and advice and—worst of all—reassurance, as though she couldn't make decisions for herself. She needed to put some space between them. Since they'd met, she hadn't gone a day without seeing him.

His knee touched hers beneath the table, and she felt the brief contact in every cell of her body. Still, she didn't look at him. She focused on the band and their instruments and the captivating movements of their hands as the music surrounded her.

Leigh closed her eyes. She liked being here. She liked this moment. She liked the air and the lighting and the total absence of words. So much of her life was about arguing and strategizing and persuasion. It was a relief to turn her mind off and simply absorb.

Brandon murmured something, his breath warm against her temple.

"What?" she asked.

"Another round?"

She glanced back to see the server there again, her teeth a white flash in the dim blue light.

Leigh turned to Brandon. His dark eyes held hers, and it was a loaded look. No way would she drive home after three vodkas. And he wouldn't let her try. But his place was only a few blocks away.

Nerves danced in her stomach as she gazed into those simmering brown eyes.

The server leaned in, breaking the spell. "Y'all want another drink?"

"No," Leigh said. "Thank you." She looked at Brandon. He turned to the server and asked for the check.

The set seemed to be wrapping up as they got the bill. Leigh took out her wallet, but Brandon insisted on paying.

They relinquished their corner table, and Brandon reached back for her hand as they squeezed through the horde of people. This time they went through the front door, stepping from the warm blue haze into the brisk air. A light rain pitter-pattered on the sidewalk, and the line of people now huddled against the building, sheltering under the eaves. Brandon dropped her hand as they moved toward the lights and traffic of South Congress.

Cold, damp air filled her lungs. Back to reality.

And to logic, which told her it was time to go home. Time to get back to her case files and her fuzzy bathrobe and the solitary plans she'd had for tonight before she'd turned up at Brandon's apartment like a stalker.

Even though they'd left the warm cocoon of the bar, her ears still seemed to vibrate from the music. It reminded her of riding home from the beach as a little girl, after spending hours playing in the waves, and still being able to feel the churning of the surf. Maybe it was the alcohol. She probably shouldn't have had that second drink, but she had wanted an excuse to stay.

They passed the burger joint again, where the air smelled of French fries, and Brandon glanced at her.

"Hungry?"

She tried to read him. Was he trying to prolong their evening?

She shook her head. "What about you?"

194   LAURA GRIFFIN

Thunder rumbled, and he glanced up.

"Nah, I'm good," he said. "We'd better hurry."

Leigh checked her watch. Almost ten. Peak bar hours, but the sidewalks were clearing as the light rain became a steady drizzle. In wordless agreement, they picked up their pace, stepping over rivulets of water and newly formed puddles. Taxis and Ubers stopped to pick up passengers, and pedestrians ducked indoors as the rain began to thrum.

"Come on," Brandon said, reaching for her.

She felt a little rush as his warm hand surrounded hers. They strode together, deftly weaving around people and obstacles. Looking north through the rain, she spotted the sign for his street two stoplights ahead.

Leigh's heel snagged, and she pitched forward. Brandon caught her arm, hauling her upright before she hit the ground.

"You okay?"

"Yeah."

A taxi sped by, hitting a pothole and sending up a spray of water. Brandon jerked Leigh against him, cursing as the taxi sailed through the intersection.

Leigh stared after it in shock as cold water seeped into her boots.

"He get you?" Brandon looked down at her legs. "Ah, shit."

She barked out a laugh. "Who cares? I'm soaked already."

She glanced down at her sodden jeans as Brandon tugged her forward. Wind whipped through her sweater, and she looked and felt like a wet street rat.

Brandon pulled her into a doorway, and she glanced up. "What—"

Her words vanished as he kissed her.

His mouth was warm and firm. After a moment of shock, she parted her lips and felt the hot glide of his tongue. Heat rippled through her as she got her first taste of him—sharp and male and musky, and she pulled his head closer and wanted to drink him in. His arms wrapped around her as she slid her fingers into the damp softness of his hair, and he pulled her against the solid wall of his body. His arms tightened again, and she felt herself being lifted off her feet and turned, then eased back against something hard and flat.

Desire coursed through her like a shot of vodka as she kissed him, curling her fingernails into his scalp. She wanted more. Him. This. She wanted him right now, right here in this doorway in the drumming rain. She kept kissing him, sliding her hands over his shoulders, and loving the feel of his firm muscles under the damp T-shirt. He felt deliciously warm and hard and determined as he leaned her against the wall and explored her mouth.

A car honked nearby, and she pulled away. She glanced back to see Brandon's big hand splayed behind her head like a cushion.

"Where are we?" she asked, dazed.

"Don't worry, it's closed."

"What is it?"

"A shop."

He took her mouth again, like he couldn't get enough of her, and she leaned back, tipping her hips against his, and he made a low sound deep in his chest.

His hands moved down her sides, shaping her body under her shapeless sweater and coming to rest on her hips. The tips of her breasts tingled, and she shivered, pulling him closer, pressing herself against his solid heat as his mouth moved over hers. His kiss alternated between hard and gentle, seeking and evasive, until she felt dizzy just trying to keep up. God, he could *kiss*. His avid mouth moved over hers, and she couldn't get enough of him. Slowly, he eased closer, sliding his thigh between hers and pinning her to the wall. She shifted for balance.

"Relax," he whispered, moving to support her weight with his strong thigh.

She closed her eyes and kissed him again, pressing her pelvis against him while his hands slid under her sweater. She gasped as his fingers moved over her ribs. His mouth trailed down her neck. She closed her eyes and shivered against him, loving the friction of their bodies through two layers of denim. His thumb rubbed over her nipple, and she let out a whimper.

He went still, and her eyes fluttered open.

"Come home with me."

She eased back, and chilly air wafted between them. She looked past his shoulder at the rain-drenched street. She felt disoriented, and suddenly unsure. The kissing and the rain and the booze had made her light-headed, and she knew the smart thing would be to say no.

"Leigh."

She looked at him, and the intensity in his eyes sent a jolt through her. No one had looked at her that way in a long, long time, and she'd forgotten how it felt.

Slowly, she slid her hand up the front of his T-shirt. She let it rest on his warm shoulder, where the muscles were bunched with tension.

She looked up, and he arched his eyebrows in question.

"Yes."

CHAPTER EIGHTEEN

———◆———

Leigh turned to look down at the wet courtyard through the veil of rain, trembling with a combination of nerves and cold as Brandon unlocked the door to his apartment. In two short blocks, the rain had become a downpour, and now they were completely soaked to the skin.

He opened the door, and she followed him inside, dripping water all over the Saltillo tile.

"We're getting your floor—"

He backed her against the door, kissing her even as she heard him click the lock into place. She wrapped her arms around him, pressing her breasts against him as his hand snaked under her wet sweater. He pulled the bra cup aside and cupped her breast in his warm palm. She tipped her head back as his lips slid from her mouth to her chin to her throat. He pushed up her sweater, and her wet skin instantly chilled, but then his hot mouth fastened on her nipple, making her shiver.

"Cold?" He looked up from her breast, and the heat in his gaze made her shiver again. "Take this off," he said.

She wrestled out of the wet sweater. He tossed it over the

back of a bar stool, and she peered over his shoulder at his apartment. They were standing in a small foyer beside a counter that wrapped around the kitchen. Beyond it was a living area with a big black couch and a low coffee table with a laptop computer on it.

He slid his arms around her again, and she relished the warmth of his body through the damp clothes. She pressed closer, wanting to absorb his heat as he kissed her neck and toyed with her breast, rubbing a lazy circle over the nipple with his thumb. Not breaking the kiss, he guided her back against the counter. They were still dripping water everywhere, and she pulled away to look down at the wet floor.

She glanced up, and he was watching her with an intent look that made her body tingle with anticipation. He touched her shoulder, tracing her collarbone and then the purple butterfly tattoo over her right breast. He leaned forward and kissed it softly as his fingers slid under her bra straps, and she felt a waft of cool air against her bare skin. Then he brought his mouth up to hers, leaning into her and pressing the cold dampness of his T-shirt against her breasts.

"That's *cold.*"

"You're hot," he said against her neck, as his hands slid down her sides and over her hips and then back up again. He clasped her waist and lifted her, and she made a little yelp of surprise as he set her on the counter. She rested her hands on his shoulders as he reached around and deftly unfastened her bra, then slid it from her arms and added it to the pile draped over the bar stool.

Standing between her thighs, he kissed her again, and she got lost in the taste of him. He dipped his head down, and his hot mouth on the tip of her breast sent a jolt of lust through her. He kissed her, warming her and teasing her and making her insides tighten, and then he moved to the other side. She tangled her fingers in his thick hair, loving the silky dampness of it. His mouth pulled and tugged, and she pressed against him, bringing him closer with the heels of her boots.

It felt so good, everything he was doing, and she couldn't believe they were here together in his dark kitchen. She glanced around the room and her gaze went to the computer again as his mouth moved to her neck.

"Let's go to your bedroom," she whispered.

He stopped and looked at her. The raw desire in his eyes was unmistakable. But he seemed to hesitate, and suddenly she felt a tug of doubt.

"Hold on to me," he said, sliding his hands over hers and moving them to his neck.

"You don't have to—"

He picked her up and walked her through the slick foyer.

"Oh my God. You're going to slip and break our *necks*," she yelped, clenching her legs around him.

He walked her into his bedroom, and she glanced around as he lowered her onto the firm expanse of his bed. It was covered with a navy bedspread, and a dim shaft of light came from the bathroom.

He rested his knee between her thighs. "This better?" he asked, stretching over her.

She nodded, anxious all over again because this was really happening. She slid her hands under his shirt, thrilled to touch the warm heat of his skin under the damp fabric. She tugged at it, and he pulled it over his head, then tossed it to the floor and eased down to kiss her again.

He settled between her thighs, and she squirmed instinctively against the hard ridge of him. He kissed her deeply, exploring her mouth again, as she ran her hands over his muscular back and lean hips. She slid her hands over his pockets and felt the outline of his phone. Her stomach knotted.

Brandon pulled back. Propping his weight on an elbow, he looked down at her.

"What's wrong?" he asked.

"Could you put your phone in the other room?"

He stared down at her.

"Sorry, I just—"

He kissed her forehead. "It's okay," he said, pushing up from the bed. He disappeared into the hallway, and she sighed and stared up at the ceiling. She hated that she was like this, but she couldn't help it, and she wouldn't be able to relax if there was a phone in the room.

He came back and sat on the edge of the bed to take off his boots. She leaned back on her elbows to watch as he removed his ankle holster. He walked over to set the holster and the gun on the dresser and then stepped to the end of the bed.

He stood there, silhouetted in the light of the bathroom, all wide, muscular shoulders and narrow hips, and she felt a tingly rush as he reached for her boot. He lifted it, slid down the zipper at the side. He slipped it off, along with the sock, and cupped her heel in his hand as he set the boot on the floor. Then he rested her bare foot on the bed and did the other boot with painstaking slowness, as if he enjoyed drawing the process out and making her wait.

His knee sank onto the bed, and the mattress shifted as he leaned over and rested his weight on his palm beside her hip. He slid his other hand over her damp jeans. Holding her gaze, he undid the button and slowly eased down the zipper. Leigh's heart hammered as he stood again and pulled the cuffs. She arched her hips to help him as he stripped the jeans away.

He stretched out beside her, leaning on his elbow as he traced his finger down her front, grazing her navel and her silky white underwear before tracing back up again. His finger trailed down again, over her thighs, carefully avoiding the bruises on her knees. They were a hideous shade of purple today, and she was glad for the dim light in here.

"I didn't mean to pin you earlier," he said. "I wasn't thinking about it."

Her chest squeezed. He was referring to the attacker pinning her the other night. She was surprised he'd brought it up and that he was tuned in to her feelings enough to think about it.

"It's okay," she said.

She turned on her side, sliding her thigh to rest on his hip. She kissed him and pressed against him, wanting to banish all the distractions that seemed to be everywhere. She wanted that look of desire back, and she rocked her hips against him. He kissed her, gently this time, drawing it out until the air between them grew warm and humid and the only thing she could focus on was his mouth.

Slowly, he rolled her onto her back again and eased on top of her, right where she wanted him, and she made a low moan of approval. She ran her fingers into his hair, kissing him deeply as he moved over her, pressing against her and making her body throb. Keeping her mouth locked on his, she slid her hand between them and unsnapped his jeans. He rolled away from her and quickly got rid of the rest of his clothes, and then he settled between her legs again, and the only thing between them was a thin scrap of fabric.

His skin felt warm and wonderful, and she ran her hands over the smooth muscles of his arms and his back, tracing her fingers up the valley of his spine. He slid kisses down her neck, then eased lower, kissing her sternum and spending time on each breast before sliding south again to settle over her belly button. He lingered there, making her flushed and impatient as she waited for him to move lower, and finally he did, sliding down her thighs and taking her panties with him. He dropped them to the floor and then moved up, settling kisses on her breast again as his warm hand slid between her legs. Kissing her deeply, he explored her body with his knowing hands, stroking and teasing her until every last cell felt like it was on fire. Over and over, he took her to the edge and eased her back, and then took her to the edge again, until she felt like she would lose her mind. She arched against him, kissing him harder, trying to make him hurry, but he wouldn't.

"Brandon . . ."

He leaned across her to open the nightstand. She watched as he tore open a condom and quickly put it on.

She closed her eyes as he moved over her and pressed her legs apart.

"Hold on," he said, sliding her thigh over his hip.

He pushed into her, and she gasped at the pleasure of it.

Leigh wrapped her legs around him, pulling him close and struggling against his strength as he drew back again. He shifted her hips, and then he found a rhythm, guiding their bodies to move together as the tension built and built. She clutched his shoulders, straining to hang on, desperate to absorb the raw power of him.

"Damn, you feel good," he said tightly.

She bit his shoulder and pulled him closer, as close as she possibly could as they moved together.

"Brandon."

"Yeah?"

"Hurry."

He made a sound somewhere between a laugh and a groan. "Just hold on."

"I *can't*."

She came in a white-hot flash that went on and on and on until every cell of her body seemed to sparkle and glow. At last, he gave a final, mind-numbing thrust, and she held on to him as they shuddered through the aftershocks.

Leigh opened her eyes. He was staring down at her, still supporting his weight as though he didn't want to crush her, even now. She slid her hand up his side and back down again before loosening her legs.

He rolled onto his back and dropped his forearm over his eyes, and she watched him, heart hammering. He turned to look at her, those dark eyes intense. Then he rolled off the bed and stepped into the bathroom.

Leigh gazed up at the ceiling, trying to catch her breath. Her body felt lax and utterly immobilized. She didn't want to move a muscle, or even try. She couldn't remember the last time she'd felt this way.

Brandon came back and stood over her for a moment, and she caught the heat in his eyes as his gaze roamed over her.

She turned onto her side as he stretched out on the bed. His skin was warm and slick, and not just from rain anymore. Resting her fingers against his chest, she felt his heart pounding steadily. His torso was a work of art—his entire body—and she trailed her fingertip over his chest. She glanced up. He was watching her with a look she couldn't read, and she felt a rush of self-consciousness. She'd never expected to be in Brandon's bed tonight, with her clothes strewn all over his apartment.

She scooted closer and tucked her head against his chest, hopefully cutting off conversation. She didn't want to talk now. She just wanted to lie here and be. Her body felt warm and glowy, and the rain thrummed outside the window. Leigh closed her eyes. It was a good moment, the first one she'd had with anyone in a long time, and she didn't want to ruin it by talking.

He wrapped his arm around her shoulder and pulled her close.

CHAPTER NINETEEN

═══╪═══

LEIGH CREPT DOWN THE dark hallway, feeling her way along the wall without making a sound. She reached the living room, where bands of gray light seeped through the gaps in the blinds.

Pausing in the foyer, she squeezed her eyes shut as the vicious headache oozed over her skull. She took a deep breath. Opening her eyes, she moved through the dimness to the pile of discarded clothes. With a furtive look over her shoulder, she collected her things. Her bra was dry, but her sweater was still damp, and her head throbbed as she pulled everything on. Glancing down the hall again, her stomach filled with nerves and she felt like a teenager sneaking out of the house. She grabbed her purse off the bar, and her gaze landed on a square yellow notepad by a stack of mail.

Leigh bit her lip. Then she unzipped her purse and rummaged for a pen. Stepping over to the notepad she debated what to write. Her thoughts were all jumbled. Finally, she decided on something short and sweet.

"Taking off?"

She jumped and whirled around. Brandon loomed behind her in the darkness, naked except for black boxer briefs. He looked like an underwear model, and she was struck speechless.

He stepped closer and lifted an eyebrow. "Early meeting?"

It was Sunday. He was being sarcastic.

"I have a headache." Her voice sounded hoarse. "A migraine, actually. I need to get home."

Frowning, he eased closer, and she caught the warm scent of his skin. He stepped around her and into the kitchen, where he opened an upper cabinet and took out a bottle. He shook out a few white tablets and placed them on the counter beside her, then took down a glass and filled it with water.

Her stomach tightened at the sweetness of the gesture.

"Thanks." She popped the pills into her mouth, even though she knew they'd have little effect.

"Gimme a sec." He walked around her and disappeared into the bedroom.

She took a gulp of water and set the glass down. Noticing the pad on the counter, she peeled off her scribbled note and stuffed it into her purse.

Brandon emerged from the bedroom in jeans, still bare chested.

"You should go back to bed," she told him.

"I'll walk you down," he said, zipping up.

"You don't need to—"

"Humor me." He brushed past her and grabbed a black hoodie off the armchair in the living room. He shrugged into it and stepped around her to open the front door.

The morning was cold and damp, but the rain had stopped. The sky was just beginning to lighten, and tall streetlamps still shone down on the parking lot beside his building. Without talking, they trudged down the stairs and crossed the wet lot. Almost no one was out this early—just a man walking blearily up the sidewalk and a woman in pajamas who stood in a patch of grass with a Schnauzer.

Leigh glanced at Brandon. He was scanning the area, taking in everything—like the cop that he was—as he walked her to her car.

Guilt needled her, but she ignored it as she dug her keys from her purse and popped her locks. She opened the door, and Brandon rested his hand on the top of it, the same way he'd done last night when she'd shown up here out of the blue.

He gazed down at her, his dark eyes unreadable, and her stomach tensed. This was the part she'd wanted to avoid when she'd slipped out of his bed.

"Try chocolate," he said. "My sister gets migraines. She says it helps."

Nothing would help except twenty-five milligrams of sumatriptan and a pitch-black room, but Leigh forced a smile.

"Thanks."

He pressed a soft kiss to her forehead and stepped back. No *text me later* or *I'll call you*, and she felt a wave of relief as she slid into the car.

And that was it. She pulled away, resisting the urge to watch him in the mirrors.

She turned onto Congress and grabbed her sunglasses from the console. Even the wan daylight was excruciating. She rolled to a stop at a deserted intersection. In the rearview mirror the capitol dome was warm and rosy with the first glint of morning.

She took a deep breath, unsettled for more reasons than she could stand to think about right now. Wending her way home through near-empty streets, she fought off the thoughts as well as the steadily blooming pain. She didn't regret last night. At least, not all of it. But she'd awakened in Brandon's bed with a bourgeoning headache and a tidal wave of insecurity crashing over her, and she'd had to get out of there. Everything was off. Brandon didn't feel like a one-night stand. But he didn't fit into any other category, either.

Nerves flitted through her already queasy stomach. She didn't have time for a man in her life right now. She had to focus on her career, on getting her practice established and paying back a mountain of loans.

There was no room for a relationship. Relationships were costly, not just timewise, but emotionally, and her last one had knocked her flat on her ass. It had taken months of relentless effort on the part of Javi and her mom to help her back up again.

Starting the law firm with Javi had pulled Leigh out of her depression and given her a productive focus. All that work had been a salve for her wounded and demoralized heart. It had restored her confidence in herself and given her a motive to get out of bed in the morning instead of wallowing in mortification and self-pity.

"So everyone's seen your tits. So what?" Javi had said when he'd dropped by one night after her world imploded. A week had elapsed since she'd discovered that her ex-boyfriend had uploaded a video of her to a porn site.

"It's not just my tits, Javi. I'm performing *oral sex*."

He'd waved her off. "There's so much sex on the Web, it's a drop in the ocean. You need to stop hiding in your house and get your shit together. If you spend another week at home, they're going to fire you."

"They can't. I already quit."

She would never forget the look on his face.

"You *quit* Thornton and Davis," he'd said with utter disbelief. "*Why* would you do that? They're paying you a fucking fortune. Anyone would kill for a job there."

"Someone sent the video around. All the partners saw it. At least all the male ones did."

"How do you know?"

"Because I can tell by the way they look at me. And they're friends with other lawyers. And judges. And practically everyone I work with every single day."

"So a bunch of horny old men saw you naked. So what?"

"So, now I have to sit in meetings with them, and stand in front of them in court, and I never want to see them again. I never want to see anyone!"

After patiently watching her lose her shit, Javi had curled up with her on the sofa and helped her polish off a pint of Ben & Jerry's. The next day, he'd shown up at her house again, all business this time, and made her an offer to join his new practice.

Saying yes had been the best—and riskiest—decision Leigh had ever made. From an economic perspective, it put her in a deep hole. But slowly, surely, they were digging their way out and building a practice. Their five-year business plan was starting to take effect, and the flow of work was becoming steadier. They had begun handing off more cases to their associates and talking about renewing their lease.

Leigh had worked incessantly for two years, forgoing vacations and weekends and dating. Now wasn't the time to let her foot off the gas and get entangled in a relationship, even *if* the mere idea didn't give her a migraine. Which it obviously did.

She turned onto her street and checked the mirrors before pulling into her driveway. For a moment she sat still, thinking of Brandon.

Come home with me.

It was his intensity that got to her—the fierce determination in his eyes when he wanted something. There was no way she could have said no to him. Even now, with the pain taking over, she didn't regret spending the night with him. But that was it. One and done. The next time it came up—if it ever did—she was going to resist.

CHAPTER TWENTY

Antonio walked into the bullpen and made a beeline for his desk. But then he spotted Brandon and changed course.

"Hey," he said, dropping a bakery bag on a stack of files.

Brandon responded with a grunt, focused on something on his computer screen.

Antonio popped the last bite of a chocolate glazed doughnut into his mouth and walked around to look at the screen.

"What's that?"

"An arrest report," Brandon muttered.

"I can see that. Whose is it?"

"Ross Collins."

"Who's that?"

"Cooper Collins's older brother. He was arrested on drug charges in Williamson County last January."

Antonio sucked a glob of icing off his thumb. "Why do we care?"

Brandon glanced up. His eyes were bloodshot and he needed a shave. "He's got a black Chevy pickup registered to his name." Brandon tapped the mouse, and the guy's mug shot appeared on the screen.

"Shit. He's big," Antonio said.

"Six-two, two-ten. Big enough to have a size fourteen shoe."

And with that, the reason for Brandon being at work on a Sunday became clear. He was still stuck on the law firm break-in. Because of Leigh. And he believed the break-in was linked to the Vanessa Adams case somehow.

Antonio looked at the mug shot again. Ross Collins was big and bulky with thick dark eyebrows. Antonio hadn't met Cooper Collins in person, but he'd seen his driver's license photo, and now he visualized the scrawny blond grad student who worked in a bookstore.

"Not a lot of family resemblance," Antonio said. "You sure they're related?"

"They lived at the same address four years ago. Maybe they're half brothers."

Brandon scrubbed a hand over his face, and Antonio watched him. He looked hungover.

Good. Maybe he'd gone out last night and had some fun for a change. Whatever he'd done, it didn't seem to have improved his mood, though.

Brandon sighed and looked at him. "So, what are *you* doing here?"

"Stopped by to check in with Meyers. He wrote up the report on the Kelly Morris thing."

Brandon frowned.

"Kate called me for an update about it this morning," Antonio said. "You know she hired Leigh to try and get a restraining order against Mason Lloyd?"

"I know."

"She thinks he had something to do with Vanessa's disappearance."

"I know."

Brandon didn't look convinced. He'd checked the man

out already, same as Antonio had as soon as his name came up in the investigation. But so far, they had nothing to link Mason Lloyd to Vanessa except some office gossip and speculation from Leigh.

Still, Antonio thought the man seemed like a more logical suspect than Cooper Collins. But Brandon was focused on Cooper, for some reason, and had been ever since he learned that he'd been at the Rustling Pines campground the night after Vanessa went missing.

Yeah, it was a weird coincidence—if that was what it was. But Antonio didn't view the guy as a viable suspect. And the idea that Cooper's brother or half brother was in on it seemed like even more of a stretch.

Brandon's effort to link Vanessa's disappearance to the break-in at Leigh's law firm seemed to be muddying the waters, but Antonio didn't say that. Instead, he tried to sound neutral.

"So, what's the connection you're working on?" he asked Brandon. "What does a drug arrest in January have to do with Vanessa going missing a week ago?"

"Maybe nothing. I just think that the guy's criminal record along with the black pickup and the physical description make it worth checking into. Also . . ." Brandon shook his head.

"Also, what?"

"There's something off about Cooper. I can't shake the feeling he's lying to me. I've interviewed him twice now, and the guy feels off."

"Hmm." Antonio didn't know what to say. He couldn't exactly argue with his partner's instincts. One, Brandon had been on the job longer. And two, he tended to be right about this shit. He had a knack for reading people, and Antonio didn't want to discount that.

Brandon turned to look at him. "You know, time's getting away from us on this thing. We can't ignore any leads."

Antonio could agree with that, at least. Tonight marked

one week since they'd first caught this case, and it felt like they were no closer to knowing what happened to Vanessa Adams than they had been that first night.

The difference was, the case seemed more urgent now, and not just because every day that ticked by meant less chance of finding Vanessa Adams alive. *That* Antonio had been fully aware of from the start. For him, the urgency had started the second he saw Kate walking toward him with her daughters in tow and that look of dread on her face.

Antonio tried not to let personal feelings affect him at work, but he couldn't help it with this one. He had four younger sisters and a soft spot for single moms, and the raw fear in Kate's eyes every damn time he saw her was getting to him.

Brandon combed his hand through his hair and looked at his computer, clearly frustrated.

"Have some doughnut holes." Antonio slid the bag toward him. "I just got them."

"No, thanks."

Antonio opened the bag and dug one out for himself. "How long you been doing this?"

"I don't know," Brandon said. "Couple hours."

"I thought you were off today. Why aren't you at a bar somewhere, having a beer and watching a game?"

The suggestion seemed to piss him off even more.

"What's wrong?" Antonio asked, because obviously something was eating at him, and knowing Brandon, it had to do with work.

"Nothing."

"Is it something about the case?"

Brandon's phone buzzed, and he looked relieved to dodge the question. He grabbed his phone, and his face tensed as he checked the number.

"It's Brie," Brandon told him.

"Who?"

"In the DNA lab." He connected the call. "Reynolds."

Brandon's gaze locked on his. "Yeah. . . . Okay. . . . Is that confirmed?"

Antonio gritted his teeth and waited.

"All right, thanks for the heads-up. I'll call the lieutenant." He hung up.

"What is it?"

"The DNA came back," Brandon said.

"And?"

"The blood in the woods matches the car."

"Is it—"

"It's Vanessa's."

Shit.

Brandon pushed back his chair and stood up. "Our missing-person case just became a homicide."

JAVI STEPPED INTO Leigh's office looking like he'd just come off the soccer field.

"You're here," he said with surprise. "I thought you worked yesterday."

"Yeah, well. I didn't get everything done." And her best-laid plans for the evening had gotten sidetracked.

Javi propped his shoulder against the wall, and Leigh moved her file aside because clearly he wanted to chat.

"You have a game today?" she asked.

"It's canceled. The field's too wet, so I'm headed to the gym instead. I just stopped by to let C.J. in."

"Why is C.J. here?"

"He's installing some security cams on our porch."

"He is?"

"It's part of our system upgrade. I told you about it Friday, remember?"

She didn't, probably because everything since Thursday had felt like a blur.

Javi's gaze narrowed, and he leaned over to shut her door. "What's up with you?" he asked.

"Nothing's up. Why?"

"Because you look like hell—no offense. Did you have a bad night?"

She tipped her head back and groaned.

"What happened?"

She blew out a sigh. "I spent the night at Brandon's."

"Oooh. This I need to hear." He sat on the arm of her leather chair. "How was it?"

"Good." Butterflies filled her stomach. "Mostly good, anyway."

"Mostly?"

She took a slug from the coffee mug beside her computer. The pill she'd taken this morning had knocked her out cold for three hours. She'd woken up groggy and had been guzzling coffee all afternoon just to be able to function.

She looked at Javi, who was eyeing her with a mix of worry and blatant curiosity.

"The sex part was *very* good. He's . . ." She trailed off, searching for a word. But for the life of her, she couldn't find one. Not that she wanted to, really. The kiss in the doorway and all that wet groping—it felt too private, even for Javi.

A slow smile spread across his face. "Damn."

She huffed out a breath. "Everything was fine, but then I woke up in his bed in the middle of the night and I couldn't stop analyzing."

He rolled his eyes. "Leigh. Seriously?"

"Yes."

"You think too much."

"What's wrong with analyzing something after it happens?"

He crossed his arms. "So, how'd you leave things?"

"I tried to sneak out. But he woke up, and I told him I had a headache."

He winced.

"What?"

"That's the best you could come up with?"

"It was true. I woke up with a screaming migraine, and I needed to get out of there before I threw up in his bathroom or something." She sighed. "And, also, I wanted to avoid an awkward scene."

"You wanted to avoid letting him know you like him," he corrected. "So, you had to make it seem like a casual hookup."

"It *was* casual."

Javi lifted an eyebrow, and she felt a twinge of annoyance.

"What?" she demanded.

"I was here Thursday. I saw how he looked at you."

"How did he look at me?"

He tipped his head to the side and seemed to be choosing his words. "With deep concern," he finally said. "And a dash of pent-up fury that someone had hurt you."

Leigh's stomach tightened. "He did?"

"Yes. It was very sexy, actually. I can see why you're hot for him."

She plunked her elbows on the desk and dropped her head into her hands. "Javi! What am I going to do?"

He laughed, and she looked up.

"Don't do anything," he said. "Just enjoy it."

"He's a cop."

"So?"

"So, he's investigating one of my clients." She'd been thinking about this fact all day. The more she thought about it, the more she realized it had potential to be a problem. "It feels a little—I don't know—fuzzy, ethically. What if he's manipulating me to get information about his case?"

Javi's face turned pitying. "Leigh, listen to yourself."

"What?"

"You sound paranoid."

"I can't help it."

"Not everyone has some hidden agenda."

"You know, you're not nearly cynical enough to be a lawyer."

Shaking his head, Javi stood up. "You have a hot man who's totally into you. Just enjoy the ride. Stop analyzing every damn thing." He opened the door and looked back at her. "Let yourself have fun, for once."

He walked out, leaving her frustrated and distracted. She'd been here for three hours, and she'd managed to accomplish almost nothing productive because she couldn't focus.

Her phone chimed from the desk and she snatched it up. Not Brandon.

She ignored the jab of disappointment as she tried to place the number. She didn't know it.

"Leigh Larson," she said, turning back to her computer.

"Hi."

It was a male voice, but she didn't recognize it. The caller cleared his throat.

"This is Cooper Collins. You gave me your business card?"

Leigh's pulse picked up. "Hey, Cooper, what's up?" *And why have you been dodging my calls?*

"I need to meet with you."

Something about his tone put her on edge.

"Okay . . . well, I can make room tomorrow morning if—"

"It needs to be today."

"Why?"

"It's about Vanessa."

Her heart skittered. She *knew* he'd been holding out on her.

"Cooper, if you have information about Vanessa, you need to give it to the police."

"I can't. They're the last people I can talk to about this."

Leigh's stomach clenched. "How come?"

"Look, you came to *me*, remember? And I talked to you

twice, even though I didn't want to," he said. "Can't you just meet up with me? It's important."

L EIGH AGREED TO meet him at a restaurant off I-35 on the south side of town. Maybell's Café. The place looked fine when she googled it, but she arrived to discover that it was adjacent to a giant truck stop crammed with eighteen-wheelers. She drove around to the back and pulled into a lot reserved for normal-size cars.

She got out and looked around, more than a little irritated by Cooper's choice of venue. There were plenty of places they could have met that weren't surrounded by roaring diesel engines and exhaust fumes. She held her breath as she crossed the lot and entered the diner.

A glass case filled with pies greeted her. Chocolate pies, cherry pies, banana pies, all missing a few wedges and all piled high with whipped cream. Leigh passed the dessert case and squeezed through the crowd of Levi's-and-flannel-clad men milling near the register. As they looked her over, she regretted her outfit today—yoga pants and a loose top that showed off her sports bra. Not her usual client-meeting attire, but this wasn't a usual meeting, and Cooper Collins wasn't even a client.

She scanned the restaurant and had no trouble spotting him in a booth in the back. The bespectacled grad student stood out in the room filled with long-haul truckers.

Plus, he was sporting a nasty shiner.

She crossed the restaurant, and the little warning bell that had been going off in her head since his phone call became a full-blown siren.

She slid into the booth across from him. The table was sticky with syrup, and she tucked her purse onto the seat beside her. Cooper had a half-empty mug of coffee in front of him. The bridge of his glasses was taped, and he had a bad case of bed head.

"What happened to you?" she asked.

"I got mugged in the parking lot next door."

"When?"

"Couple nights ago."

Leigh's mind raced as she tried to plug that bit of info into what she already knew about his activities this week.

"So, you're staying at the motel?" she asked.

"For now." He gazed down at his coffee mug, shaking his head. "People won't leave me alone. They keep coming by my work and my home."

"Oh yeah?"

He gave her a sharp look. "Robert saw you, by the way."

"Robert?"

"When he was walking his dog."

Robert would be Hooch's dad.

"The police have been by, too. Twice." He looked over Leigh's shoulder. "Do you think you were followed here?"

"Who would follow me?"

"That detective guy. Reynolds." He paused. "I saw the two of you talking on the porch of your office."

So, he'd been to her office. She was getting more and more uneasy with this conversation. Brandon believed Cooper was a suspect. Leigh had told him that was unlikely, but now she was starting to rethink her assumptions. Just because she was skilled at reading people didn't mean she could identify every whacko. Some people defied type.

"No one followed me here," she told him. "And I'd like you to explain what you're so worried about."

"I will, but we should go next door to the motel. It's safer."

A waitress stopped by. The sixtyish woman looked tired and hassled as she flipped open her notepad. "What can I get y'all?" she asked without eye contact.

"Just a check," Cooper said.

"I'll have coffee," Leigh said.

"Anything else?"

"That should do it."

The woman walked off, and Leigh leveled her gaze at Cooper. "I don't take meetings in motel rooms. Whatever you want to talk about, do it here."

Frustration flared in his eyes, and he darted a look at the door. "I *really* don't want—"

"Talk. Now. Or I'm leaving."

Leigh wouldn't really leave until she got some information out of him. But she didn't like his theatrics, and she definitely didn't like the black eye and the secrecy and the avoidance of police.

He raked his hand through his hair, making it stick up even more.

"I don't know where to start," he complained.

"You said this is about Vanessa. Start with that."

He took a deep breath. "I met her in February. We dated. I told you about all that."

"Okay."

"And I told you I hadn't heard from her in a while, but actually I had." He paused, watching her reaction to the admission. "She called me in June. She was really upset. Distraught. Her ex-boyfriend—"

"Mason Lloyd."

His gaze narrowed. "You know about Mason?"

"I know some."

"Well, he was harassing her. Calling her, texting her, showing up at her place after she broke up with him. He wouldn't let up, and it was getting to her. He kept escalating, and she thought he might be violent."

"She thought?"

"Yeah. I guess he'd mentioned something once about someone having a restraining order on him or something. She was worried, and she wanted help."

"Why did she go to you?"

He looked annoyed by the question. "I don't know. Because I'm nice?"

"And what did you do?"

"I advised her to get a new phone, or at least a new number, and she did. But then he started showing up more, and she would hide in her bathroom and pretend not to be home, but she was scared. She started keeping a journal of everything he did. Finally, it got so bad she decided to move out and sublet her place. But then she still had to see him at work, so she had to be careful driving home, and she was always worried he'd follow her and find out where she lived, so sometimes she'd end up at my place. This was in the summer, like late June." He turned his coffee mug. "Then everything died down, and I didn't hear from her for a while. I thought she was okay, and he'd backed off. But then she called me Sunday and said someone was following her again—"

"*When* Sunday?"

"I don't know. Late. She woke me up."

"You mean—"

A woman stopped at the table. Short black hair, blue eyes, baseball cap.

Leigh's jaw dropped. The woman slid into the booth beside Cooper, and Leigh's mind swirled with a mix of shock and disbelief.

"*Vanessa*. Do you have any idea—"

"Yes." She leaned forward, resting her hands on the table. They were clenched in tight little fists. "I do. Now can we *please* get out of here? It's not safe."

CHAPTER TWENTY-ONE

THE ROADHOUSE MOTEL WAS a two-story establishment that advertised low rates and free Wi-Fi. The crime scene van pulling out of the lot as they walked over wasn't much of an endorsement, and Leigh wondered how on earth they'd selected this place.

Still holding her breath against the diesel fumes, Leigh followed them past an open-air stairwell, and Cooper dug a key card from his pocket as they stopped in front of room 119, which had a DO NOT DISTURB sign hooked on the door.

Cooper slid the card into the lock and pushed open the door.

"I need to talk to Vanessa alone," Leigh told him.

He sent Vanessa a worried look.

"She's my client." Leigh dug a twenty out of her purse and held it out, figuring that if he really *had* been mugged, he could probably use it. "Is your car here? Why don't you go get some gas or some snacks or something and give us a few minutes."

He ignored the money and leaned around Leigh. "Van?"

"That's fine."

"I'll be back in half an hour." He gave Leigh a warning look. "Don't open the door for anyone."

Leigh stepped into the room, noticing the mildewy smell as she locked and latched the door.

The queen-size bed was a tangle of sheets and blankets, and beer bottles filled the top of the nightstand. A pizza box sat on the floor beside an overflowing trash can. Evidently, the housekeeping staff had been diligently heeding the sign on the door.

Leigh glanced around for a place to sit. She dragged a chair from beside the dresser and positioned it near the door. She didn't like being here, and she wanted an easy out if she decided to leave.

Vanessa walked to a cooler near the closet and combed through some ice.

"You want water?" she asked.

"No."

Something moved beneath the sheets. Leigh froze. A brown blur shot across the pillow and darted behind the bed.

Leigh backed against the door. "There's a *rat* in here!"

"It's a ferret." Vanessa sat on the end of the bed. "His name's Mobi."

Leigh stared at her.

"He's Cooper's. He won't bother you."

Leigh lowered herself into the chair and set her purse on the table beside her. She took a deep breath, trying to calm herself. She had something in common with Cooper—she didn't know where to begin. Part of her wanted to walk up to Vanessa and slap her. Which was an all-new feeling with a client. Another part of her wanted to give her a shake and ask *What the hell were you thinking??* That urge was much more familiar.

"Vanessa." Leigh leaned her elbows on her knees and looked at her client. Vanessa swilled from a bottle of Evian. "Do you have *any* idea what your sister is going through right now?"

"I know."

"Really? You do? Because I've been to see her three times since you disappeared, and she gave me the impression you two were close. Close enough that you'd give a damn that she's been *sick* with worry."

"I know."

"Kate thinks you're dead. So do the police. So did I." She paused, waiting for a reaction, but Vanessa just sat there.

Leigh looked her over, taking in every detail and trying to construe what each one meant. She'd chopped her hair and dyed it a near-black shade of brown that drew more attention to her appearance rather than less. She had wan skin and dark circles under her eyes, and Leigh realized she wasn't the only one whose life had been turned upside down by the events of the past week. Vanessa looked down at her water bottle. Her eyes were glistening, and Leigh felt a pang of sympathy for her.

"Tell me what happened with Mason," Leigh said.

She took a deep breath and removed the baseball cap to reveal a nasty red bump and scab at the top of her forehead.

Anger swelled in Leigh's chest. "He hit you?"

She shook her head.

"Vanessa, I don't have time for guessing games. Tell me what happened."

Another deep breath. "Everything started in June when I broke up with him. He didn't take it well."

How many clients' stories began just this way? Too many to count.

"Why did you break up with him?" Leigh asked.

"He . . . I don't know, changed. At first when we started seeing each other he was sweet and charming and always complimenting me. It was good. But then I started to have doubts." She glanced at her. "For one thing, he's married." She looked down. "Kate's ex cheated on her, and I felt really guilty about being with someone's husband. I mean, their marriage was a mess before me, but still."

"Okay, so he changed . . . ?" Leigh could guess where this was going, but she needed to hear it from Vanessa.

"He became controlling. He started grilling me about my plans all the time, and my friends. I caught him going through my phone. Stuff like that. I didn't like the way he was acting, and the guilt was getting to me, and I decided I needed to break things off, so I did. At first, he was nice. You know—relatively speaking. He tried to talk me out of it and told me he was in love with me." She rolled her eyes. "I didn't really believe that, but I knew he wanted to change my mind. But when I wouldn't, it was like he, I don't know, became a different person. We had this big fight in the parking lot at work and he started calling me names and threatening me."

"Threatening what?"

"He said he'd tell everyone at work what a whore I was." She shuddered. "By 'everyone' he meant his doctor friends, which would have been humiliating. At the time, I thought him bad-mouthing me to them would be the worst thing he could do." Her face contorted as she fought back tears. "Little did I know . . ."

She took a sip of water and glanced at the window. Leigh looked over her shoulder, wondering if Cooper was back. But she didn't see him in the parking lot.

"It got worse," Vanessa said. "He started calling me at all hours. Showing up at my apartment. Sometimes he'd be drunk. I blocked his number, but then he just started using other phones to call me, so finally I got a new number. But that backfired, too, and he showed up at my apartment even more, and every time he did it, I had to sit inside and wait for him to go away. One time he cornered me in the parking lot at Pura Vida when I was getting into my car, and I told him if he didn't leave me alone, I'd call the police."

"Did you?" Leigh asked hopefully, even though C.J. hadn't turned up any record of it.

"No. That night a cop showed up at my door and told me

Mason had filed a complaint against *me*. He said I'd slashed the tires on his Porsche. He'd told the police that I was crazy and obsessed with him and I'd threatened to tell his wife we were having an affair—"

"Wait." Leigh held up a hand. "Back up. A police officer came to your apartment?"

"Yes!"

"Did he show you a badge?"

"Yes. I wouldn't open the door until he held it up. His name was Detective Akins."

"So, was he wearing a uniform or—"

"No. Street clothes. But he had a badge and a gun, and he was definitely a cop. I mean, I could tell by everything he did and said."

Somehow C.J. had missed this. Maybe Brandon knew about it.

"He even had pictures of the slashed tires on his phone, and he said Mason was planning to press charges unless I agreed to leave him alone." She took a deep breath. "After the detective left, I was shaken. And confused. And I felt powerless, because everything had gotten all twisted around, and now *I* was the crazy one. That's when I decided to move apartments. And I thought that helped. I moved at the end of June, and didn't hear from him for almost two months, just caught a few glimpses of him at work, but he pretended to ignore me. I thought maybe everything had come to a head, but it was over. But then all that blew up in my face."

She drained her bottle of Evian and set it among the other empties on the nightstand.

"One of my high school friends reached out to me on Instagram and told me there was a video of me going around."

Leigh's stomach filled with dread. "On social media?"

"He saw it on a porn site. I thought he had to be mistaken, but he sent me a screenshot." She closed her eyes. "It was horrible. I wanted to die."

Leigh looked at Vanessa, trying to ignore the ache in her chest so she could be objective.

"All those weeks, I thought my problem was solved," Vanessa said. "But really, he'd just gone from threatening me to taking revenge. I was so clueless."

"The video he posted, I assume it was the two of you having sex?"

She nodded, not making eye contact.

"Was it consensual or—"

"Yeah, for *him* to watch. I didn't consent to him posting it online!"

"I'm just trying to understand the facts. So, what did you do?"

She blew out a breath. "I confronted him. I did it in the parking lot at Pura Vida so there would be people around and he couldn't do something dangerous. I told him to remove the video or I was going to take him to court. It wasn't an idle threat, either. The next day I went to see you."

Leigh got up and peered through the curtains to check the parking lot. Still no Cooper. She crossed the room and fished a bottle of water from the cooler. Twisting the cap off, she looked at Vanessa.

"Why didn't you tell me about this then?"

She looked down. "It's hard to talk about. I wanted to start with something easier, so I asked about your rates and told you about the landlord thing."

"That was bogus, you know."

Vanessa nodded, not looking surprised. "Mason, right?"

"I'm still not sure. But your landlord doesn't know anything about it, and neither does the law firm that supposedly sent you the letter."

She shook her head. "As soon as I reengaged with Mason, everything went downhill. I was careful leaving work, always taking a different route home and checking to see if I was being followed to my new apartment, but I could never really be sure. And then Wednesday of last week, I *knew* I saw his car behind me at a stoplight. And something inside me just snapped. No matter what I did—I blocked him, I got a new number, I freaking *moved*—he was still tormenting me. I decided, screw it, that's it. I'm getting a gun."

Leigh closed her eyes and muttered a curse. Her hopes of getting Vanessa out of this mess were fading fast.

"I called up this guy I know—"

"Who?" Leigh asked.

"His name's Jason."

"Jason Mandrapilias."

She looked startled. "How do you know him?"

"His name came up in the investigation. What happened?"

"He agreed to meet me on Sunday night out by Rustling Pines State Park. It was quick. I paid him the money, he gave me the gun, and it was done. A few minutes later, I pulled over to look at the pistol I'd just bought when this big black pickup came up behind me."

Leigh's blood chilled.

"As soon as it stopped, I knew it was him."

"What did you do?"

"What else? I ran."

CHAPTER TWENTY-TWO

════╍════

L EIGH'S PULSE POUNDED AS she envisioned Vanessa, frightened and alone, out on that road.

"He chased me," Vanessa said. "And I thought I was dead. I was scared out of my mind, either that he would kill me, or I would have to kill *him*. And then *I* was going to end up on trial and possibly in jail for something that was all his fault. I made it to the woods and hid, and that's when I figured out the gun I'd bought wasn't even loaded. I ran deeper into the trees and tripped on a rock and conked my head." She rubbed her forehead near the bruise. "By then I was a mess. I was bleeding and disoriented. But I was also terrified, so I just kept moving through the trees toward the park where I saw a campfire flame. I'd been there before with Cooper, and I knew I could hide there and call for help."

She pictured Vanessa stumbling through the woods, frightened and bleeding, and anger welled inside her.

"When I made it to the restrooms, I was shaking and bawling. I was cleaning myself up, and this woman came in, so I asked to use her phone. I was going to call the police, but then I realized I didn't trust them. I wanted to call my sister, but it was the middle of the night, and she has little ones at home." A tear slid down Vanessa's cheek and she brushed it away. "So, I called Cooper, and he came to get me."

Leigh looked at her, trying to absorb it all. She imagined Brandon's face if he could see her having this conversation right now. Just the thought of his reaction put a knot in her stomach.

"By the time Cooper picked me up at the campground, it was like three a.m. My car had been towed, and I didn't know what to do. So Cooper took me to the police station but as we pulled up, I started to freak out and second-guess my plan to talk to the police. I started to think maybe there was another way."

Her voice had turned wistful, putting Leigh on edge. Now she knew where this was going.

"What other way?" she asked.

"For weeks, I'd been wishing I could just disappear. You know, hit reset on everything."

Leigh gritted her teeth. "So, you decided to fake your own death? And—let me guess—make Mason take the blame?"

She sent her a sharp look. "I haven't faked anything. All I've done is abandon my car on the highway. That's not a capital offense."

"You knowingly misled your sister, who's been completely *frantic* for a week. You knowingly misled the police." Leigh pictured Brandon again and those sharp brown eyes that saw through everything. "And you knowingly misled *me* after I've spent untold hours talking to your friends and sister and trying to figure out what happened to you."

Vanessa looked guilty, but not nearly guilty enough. "I'll work it out with Katie. She'll understand when I explain everything. Eventually."

The *eventually* got Leigh's back up.

"Let me be clear, Vanessa. I will not help you commit a crime."

"I didn't ask you to."

"I could get disbarred."

She started to say something, then bit her lip.

Leigh felt another surge of anger, but this time it was directed at her client. Through a long series of events, Vanessa had become mired in a deep morass of lies, deceptions, and half-truths. And now she wanted to pull Leigh into the muck with her.

"What about Cooper?" Leigh asked.

Vanessa looked startled. "What about him? He's been amazing."

Leigh sighed. "Are you guys back together?" she asked, even though the answer seemed obvious from the rumpled state of the bed.

"For now."

"Does he know you're using him?"

Her cheeks flushed. "I'm not using him. I just needed his help, and he agreed."

"Because he cares about you."

"Yes. And I care about him."

She nodded. "Well, in that case I'm sure you wouldn't want to ask him to do anything illegal for you."

"He hasn't."

Leigh lifted her eyebrow at her choice of words. Saying he hadn't done anything illegal wasn't the same as saying she hadn't asked. Leigh got the sense that Cooper's feelings for Vanessa were much stronger than hers for him. She also got the sense that Vanessa knew it.

Leigh turned to look out the window and spotted Cooper getting out of his little blue hatchback. He had a fast-food bag in his hand. A pair of sunglasses concealed his black eye.

"I know you don't approve of me."

She looked at Vanessa.

"Approval has nothing to do with it," Leigh told her. "You're in a mess, and I'm your lawyer. I want to help you, but you're not going to like my advice."

Fear came into her eyes then. "You don't understand. These last few days and weeks and *months* have been a living hell for me. All because of Mason. He's not reasonable. He's vindictive and cruel and he doesn't have boundaries like other people. He wants to kill me—I know it— probably even more now that the police are looking at him."

"Vanessa—"

"Don't say no. Just hear me out." She leaned forward, watching Leigh intently. "I need help, and you're the only one I can ask."

Leigh stared at Vanessa, ninety percent certain she was going to ask her to do something illegal. *One hundred* percent certain she was going to ask her to do something that would pour a bucket of cold water on whatever tiny ember of a relationship she had with Brandon right now.

She pictured him in his kitchen this morning, filling a glass with water for her and then walking her to her car. Since the day she'd met him, he'd been concerned and protective and *nice* to her, and just being in this room right now felt like a betrayal.

But she couldn't think that way. This was business, not personal, and this entire situation showed why she never should have mixed the two.

Leigh studied her client, trying to be objective. Vanessa's cool blue eyes swam with tears, but tears usually didn't work on Leigh. She was too used to them. Something in Vanessa's expression pulled at her, though—that combination of desperation and hopelessness that had been the center of Leigh's own life two years ago.

A sharp rap sounded at the door, and they both turned to look. That would be Cooper.

"Just hear me out," Vanessa said. "Please? There's no one else I can turn to right now, and you're my only lifeline."

CHAPTER TWENTY-THREE

L EIGH STOOD BENEATH THE hot spray, letting the water sluice over her tense shoulders. The pain was returning, slowly but surely taking over her skull.

A boomerang headache. Just what she needed tonight. She had hours of work to do, and she couldn't take anything that would make her groggy.

Stepping out of the shower, she wrapped herself in a fluffy white towel and wiped the mirror with the side of her hand. She looked tired. And hungover, although she wasn't. Leaning closer, she examined the raspberry-colored mark at the top of her right breast.

A hickey.

Leigh's stomach fluttered as she remembered Brandon's warm mouth lingering there. Throughout the night, he'd seemed drawn to that tender spot just above her tattoo.

Nerves filled her stomach as she thought of his mouth and his hands and his powerful body. And then she thought of him walking her down to her car without even a hint of resentment. She would have expected him to be sullen or cold when he caught her sneaking out at the crack of dawn.

But apparently, he had more maturity than that, and she didn't know why she was surprised.

Maybe because she'd dealt with so many jerks over the years, she'd developed low expectations when it came to men. It was a defense mechanism—she knew that—and the less she expected of people the less often she ended up disappointed. Brandon was different, though. More self-assured. And his basic *decency* permeated everything he did.

Which was one reason Leigh felt guilty over her meeting with Vanessa today. She couldn't tell Brandon about it, and not just because of attorney-client privilege. Vanessa had specifically asked her not to, and Leigh had agreed. What she hadn't agreed to do was help her set up a fake identity.

I can't go to the police. I won't.

Vanessa's words came back to her, along with the faintly queasy feeling Leigh had been battling all day. She didn't like this situation one bit. She understood, probably better than anyone, Vanessa's fervent desire to hit reset on her life and create a clean slate. How many times had Leigh wished for that exact thing? But it was a fantasy. It couldn't happen. Unfortunately, her attempts to persuade Vanessa of that fact had failed miserably. It had been like giving legal counsel to a brick wall.

Leigh towel-dried her hair and ran a wide-tooth comb through it, all the while racking her brain for that magic argument that had eluded her while she was sitting around the Roadhouse Motel with Vanessa and Cooper and a hyperactive ferret that kept burrowing in the sheets. Why couldn't she have normal clients, like other lawyers? Clients who came in with straightforward problems and wanted straightforward solutions? Over her five-year career, Leigh had had precious few clients like that—mostly when she'd been working for Thornton & Davis. They were the exception. Much more often, Leigh attracted people who had an uncanny knack for making their problems worse, not better. Clients who seemed intent on acting as their own worst enemy.

She'd somehow known Vanessa was going to be one of those from the very first day. She'd had a feeling about it, a strong one. And now, lo and behold, exactly *two* meetings into the attorney-client relationship, she and Vanessa were neck deep in a quagmire of lies and deceptions.

Leigh smoothed lotion on her arms and legs and then rubbed a few drops of lavender oil onto her temples, hoping against hope to nip her headache in the bud.

The sound of her doorbell made her freeze.

She checked her watch. It was 4:40. She wasn't expecting anyone, and her shoulders tensed as she threw on a sweatshirt and jeans and hurried to check the peephole.

Brandon.

Leigh closed her eyes and cursed softly. She'd known. The instant she'd heard the bell she'd somehow known it was him. Who else would it be besides the one person in the universe she needed to avoid having a conversation with right now?

She took a deep breath and squared her shoulders before opening the door.

"Hi." She forced a smile.

"Hey. I left you a message."

"I got it. Sorry." She stepped back to let him in. "I was planning to call you, but my afternoon got sidetracked."

He rested a hand on her shoulder and kissed her softly on the forehead. The sweetness of the gesture made her chest hurt.

"How do you feel?" he asked.

"So-so. I got rid of my headache this morning, but it seems to be coming back." Guilt needled her as he gazed down at her with concern. "How are *you*?"

"Fine. I won't keep you." He checked his watch. "I came by because I wanted to tell you in person."

"Tell me what?"

"Vanessa's case."

Dread filled her stomach, but she made her face blank.

"The DNA came back," he said.

An icy trickle of fear slid down her spine. "What DNA?"

"Some of the forensic evidence. We found a blood smear on her car door, as well as a large puddle of blood in the woods southeast of the vehicle." He paused to look at her, and Leigh's heart pounded against her rib cage. "The blood is Vanessa's. It's conclusive. We're working the case as a homicide now."

Leigh's throat tightened.

"I'm sorry to have to tell you." Brandon's hand felt impossibly heavy on her shoulder, and the sympathy in his eyes made her want to sink through the floor.

"What—" She cleared her throat. "What does this mean, exactly?"

"The case is getting higher priority. And we've got another detective on it now."

"I mean . . . has anyone notified the family of anything?"

"Antonio was just at Vanessa's sister's."

Leigh's heart sank. "So, he—"

"He gave her the update." Brandon checked his watch again. "I'm on my way to meet him now, out at the quarry. We've lined up a cadaver dog from the sheriff's office to search the woods." He eased closer and frowned down at her. "You all right?"

"I'm—I just . . ." She was at a loss for words. Completely. Whatever right words there were seemed to hover somewhere over her head but completely out of reach.

"I'm sorry to bring you bad news on top of everything else." He looked down at her with those bottomless brown eyes. "You sure you're okay?"

The sympathy in his voice made her feel sick.

"Yeah," she said.

He squeezed her shoulder. "I have to go. We're losing daylight out there." He reached for the door. "I'll call you if there's any more news tonight, all right?"

She nodded.

"Lock up behind me."

CHAPTER TWENTY-FOUR

═══╪═══

M ONDAY CRAWLED BY IN a series of leads that went nowhere.

The canine search in the woods had turned up nothing but a few drops of blood on some leaves. No body. No drag marks to the lake. No recently disturbed ground.

After meeting with his team and making calls from his desk, Brandon spent the better part of his afternoon in his car, trying to track down Ross Collins, who wasn't at his apartment or at the hardware store where his neighbor told Brandon he worked. Brandon had mixed feelings about Ross Collins. On one hand, there was the rap sheet and the black pickup truck. On the other hand, there was nothing at all directly tying him to Vanessa. But Brandon wanted a face-to-face with the guy. Until Brandon talked to him and ruled him out, he considered him a person of interest.

After striking out with Ross Collins, Brandon went looking for Vanessa's two confirmed ex-boyfriends. But Cooper and Jason weren't at work or at home, and if anyone knew where to find them, they weren't talking.

Finally, Brandon drove out to the West Lake Hills home

of Dr. Mason Lloyd. The house was a pink-brick colonial with a three-car garage and a pile of pumpkins on the doorstep. The door was answered by the third Mrs. Lloyd, who turned out to be blond and beautiful and about nine months pregnant. With her perfectly toned arms and flawless skin, Hannah Lloyd looked like an advertisement for Pura Vida. After glancing at Brandon's police ID, she told him her husband was at their lake house in Marble Falls.

"When do you expect him back?" Brandon asked, noticing the rock on her finger as she fidgeted with the end of her ponytail.

"Sometime today. Tonight, actually." She scrunched her brows together, somehow without showing a single wrinkle. "Is there a message I can give him?"

"No, thanks."

On the way to his car, Brandon spied Hannah's white Mercedes parked inside the open garage, but not Mason's silver Porsche 911, so that lent credence to her story. Who knew where her husband was—maybe she didn't even know—but it didn't look like the man was at home. Marble Falls was more than an hour away. Brandon wondered if Mason Lloyd really was at his lake house, or if that was just an excuse he used when he wanted to spend the night away from his wife.

Brandon returned to the police station frustrated and hungry. It was after five, and he wanted to call Leigh to see if she had plans for dinner. She probably needed to work tonight, like he did, but maybe he could talk her into taking a break. He'd been thinking about her all day, about her lush body and her sweet mouth. And he'd been thinking about the gnawing certainty that she hadn't wanted to see him last night. Something was wrong. Brandon wanted to figure out what it was, but to do that he needed to get her away from work, where she could loosen up and let her guard down.

Leigh had secrets. He got that. He didn't need to know

all of them, but he needed at least some level of trust if they were going to keep seeing each other.

Was that what he wanted?

A week ago, a relationship was the dead last thing on his mind. His breakup with Erika was too recent, and even though their split had been mutual, it had left a sour taste in his mouth. He didn't want to start something new. Or at least, he hadn't.

But from the second he saw Leigh in that crowded courthouse, he hadn't been able to get his mind off her. The moment they'd met, Leigh had given him the brush-off. Maybe if she'd been a little less prickly and a little more cooperative, he would have simply asked her some questions and moved on. But her stubborn refusal to let her guard down made him determined to get past it. He'd broken through Saturday, but now the walls were back up again.

Or so it seemed. Who the hell knew what was really going on? Brandon prided himself on being good at reading people and situations, but that was on the job. He didn't exactly have a stellar track record when it came to his personal life.

Brandon grabbed a Gatorade in the break room and went into the bullpen. Some people had cleared out already, but not Antonio. He and several other detectives huddled around a computer.

Antonio looked up. "Yo, we were just about to call you."

Brandon walked over. "What's up?"

"I don't know yet."

Brandon glanced at the other two, Sam Tate and Joe Harper. It was Tate's desk, making Brandon wonder if something had come up with the law firm break-in.

He looked over Tate's shoulder to see grainy black-and-white video footage of a gas station in a downtown area. Brandon didn't recognize the buildings.

"What's this?" Brandon asked.

"You know Detective Luzardo down in San Marcos?" Harper asked.

"No."

"He's in property crimes. Pulled the weekend shift." Harper nodded at the screen. "He sent this along, thought we might want to take a look."

Brandon watched the footage as someone in jeans, a baseball cap, and sunglasses crossed the parking lot and entered the store. Thin build, short hair, unisex clothes. Brandon leaned closer.

"Where is this?" Antonio asked.

"About forty miles south of here, at a Shell station west of the interstate," Tate said. "Just watch."

Brandon glanced at Antonio. His partner shrugged.

Two minutes later, the figure walked out, crossed the parking lot, and moved out of view.

"Now check this." Tate tapped the keyboard, and a new camera angle popped up. This camera showed the interior of the store from a ceiling-mounted view behind the cash register. Two customers were in line to pay—both heavyset men with beards. Brandon spotted the baseball cap figure at the ATM at the back of the store.

The hair on the back of Brandon's neck stood up.

"Watch," Tate said.

It was definitely a woman. Brandon could tell by the way she tapped in the PIN. Brandon shot a look at Antonio, who was frowning at the screen now.

Antonio leaned forward. "Is that—"

"Vanessa." Brandon looked at Tate. "When was this?"

Tate looked up. "It's Vanessa Adams? You're sure?"

"Yes. When was this filmed?"

"Two days ago in San Marcos," Tate said, zooming in on the figure. He looked at Brandon. "This doesn't look like her at all, though. You sure it's her and not someone who stole her ATM card?"

Brandon gritted his teeth as he watched the woman exit

the store. "She cut her hair and dyed it, but that's her." He looked at Antonio, who was gripping the top of his head with both hands.

"Holy fuck." He looked at Brandon. "What's she doing at some gas station in San Marcos?"

"Getting money," Brandon said. "Whose account is she tapping?"

"Hers," Harper said. "That's how we got this. We put a flag on her accounts, and this hit came in, and I followed up with a cop I know down there to get us the video footage."

"Is that really Vanessa?" Antonio asked. "I just told Kate—*shit*."

"It's her." Brandon looked at him. "I'm sure of it."

L EIGH LOOPED HER grocery bags over her arms and closed the car door with her hip. She glanced up and down the block, on the lookout for anyone suspicious, as she made her way to her door. After letting herself into the house, she dropped her bags on the kitchen counter and hurried back to lock the door and reset the alarm.

Home at last.

After a long and frustrating day, her headache was back—no surprise—and she was in for a late night of work. What she really wanted to do was soak in a hot bath and go to bed, but after her distraction-packed weekend, that definitely wasn't happening.

Leigh kicked off her heels and unpacked the groceries. Then she filled a kettle with water, hoping a steaming cup of tea would take the edge off her headache and settle her nerves. She switched the stove to high and leaned back against the counter, rubbing her temples as she waited for the water to heat.

Vanessa was ghosting her. Again. She was now officially in the lead for Leigh's biggest pain-in-the-ass client of all time.

Leigh was tempted to tell Vanessa to get another lawyer. But every time she thought about dumping her, she pictured her sitting on that rumpled motel bed, with that terrible dye job and that pleading look in her eyes.

I don't know where else to turn. I need help.

Leigh had agreed to help her. But now she felt like she was walking on a tightrope and the slightest wobble would send her plunging into the abyss.

And what was the abyss? Professional humiliation, for one. The things Vanessa had asked Leigh to do were either illegal or unethical or both and could get her disbarred. And the things Leigh had *agreed* to do weren't a whole lot better. Leigh had to watch her step. But it wasn't just professional ethics she was worried about.

The kettle whistled, and Leigh snatched it off the stovetop before it made her head explode. She took down her favorite Snoopy mug and poured water over the tea bag, then gazed at the selection of groceries arrayed on the counter. She was making her mom's chicken noodle soup tonight, in a determined effort to get rid of the headache and queasy stomach that had been plaguing her since Sunday when she'd left Brandon's house.

Don't think about him.

She couldn't go there. Not yet. Until she got this thing with Vanessa sorted out, she couldn't even think about Brandon or how he was going to react when he learned about all this. But of course, that was all she *could* think about, and she'd tossed and turned all last night worrying about it.

Leigh grabbed some kitchen shears and went to the patio, switching on the fountain for light as she stepped outside. The air felt cool and crisp, and the waxing moon overhead cast her rosebushes in a silver light.

Leigh crouched beside the trio of clay pots and clipped a few springs of rosemary for the soup. Her mint was growing like crazy because of all the rain, and she clipped some of that, too, to add to her tea.

A flash of movement caught her eye, and she jumped back, losing her balance and falling on her butt.

Sherlock.

The skinny black cat perched atop the brick wall and gazed down at her, swishing his tail back and forth. He seemed cranky with her, and she realized it had been days since she'd lounged on her patio and fed him a sandwich scrap.

Leigh stood and brushed the dust off the back of her skirt.

The low rumble of a truck made Leigh's shoulders tense. She listened closely as the truck stopped in front of her house and the engine cut off.

"Damn it," she muttered, heading back inside.

She dropped the shears and herbs on the counter as the doorbell rang. Heart thudding, she washed her hands and glimpsed her reflection in the window over the sink. She looked about like she felt—crappy. She pulled the pins from her hair and ran her fingers through it, but that only made her look like she'd just rolled out of bed. Cursing her insecurity, she twisted her hair into a knot again and padded barefoot toward the door. She was still in her work clothes—a gray silk blouse and black pencil skirt—and she wiped her damp palms on the front of her skirt before checking the peephole.

Brandon stood on her doorstep, looking amazingly tall and broad-shouldered in his dress shirt with the sleeves rolled up. He'd just gotten off work, and he still had his gun and his badge clipped to his hip.

Or maybe this *was* work. Just the thought put a swarm of butterflies in her stomach.

Leigh disabled the alarm and opened the door.

"Hey there," she said, trying to sound relaxed.

His gaze met hers, and she felt an instant chill. Something was wrong.

"Can I come in?"

"Of course," she said, stepping back.

He glanced around her dim living room. The only light came from the kitchen.

"Are you just getting off or—"

"Yeah." He stepped closer, gazing down at her with a look that made all the butterflies dance. "I came to give you an update."

"An update?"

"About the case."

"Oh." She gazed up at him, trying to read his face. She turned and led him into the kitchen. "Would you like a beer or anything?"

"No."

"I'm making some tea."

He followed her into the kitchen. Her tea had steeped, and she removed the tea bag and set it on the spoon rest. Then she turned to look at him, crossing her arms so he wouldn't see the tremor in her hands.

"What is it?" she asked, leaning back against the counter.

"It's about Vanessa."

She waited.

"She's alive."

Leigh looked at him, resisting the urge to bite her lip. Brandon eased closer. He didn't touch her, but his intense gaze seemed to pin her against the counter.

"You knew."

She stayed silent.

Disbelief flared in his eyes. But then it was gone.

He stepped back, leaning against the counter. "Wow." He rubbed the back of his neck.

"I just found out."

"Just?" The edge in his voice sent a chill through her.

"Sunday afternoon."

His eyebrows shot up. "So . . . when I came over here and told you I was headed out to the lake with a fucking canine team you thought, what, that you didn't need to mention it?"

"I couldn't—"

"And when I spent all day long working leads and tracking down suspects in Vanessa's *homicide* you thought, hey, he's probably got nothing better to do? There aren't any armed robberies or sexual assaults or abused kids that might warrant his attention?"

"Brandon, I couldn't—"

"You *could*, but you *didn't*! We're over here chasing our tails trying to solve a homicide and you're hiding the victim." He paused. "Is she being kept somewhere against her will?"

"No."

"Where is she?"

"I don't know."

He rolled his eyes and shook his head.

"Really, I don't. She's avoiding my calls."

He stared at her, clenching his jaw. "Don't lie to me again."

"I'm not! And I didn't *lie* to you yesterday, either. I just didn't tell you—"

"A lie of omission. Same thing."

"No, it is not."

"Oh, really? They didn't teach you about perjury in law school? You tell the truth, the whole truth, and nothing but the truth, or else it's lying."

Her stomach clenched as they stood there, watching each other. His jaw tensed and the veins on the side of his neck stood out, and she remembered the way he'd looked when he'd come to help her after the law firm break-in. *A dash of pent-up fury*, Javi had said. Only this time, the fury was directed at her.

Guilt churned inside her.

"What? No defense, counselor?"

"I have professional ethics to consider," she countered.

"So do you. That's why you didn't tell me about every lead you've been working on, because it's none of my business. And anyway, why are we making this about me? This is about Vanessa, and she has a very good reason for not going to the police after someone accosted her on a highway and made her fear for her life."

He nodded. "I want to hear it. Where is she?"

Leigh went quiet. She'd walked right into that—the thing she still couldn't tell him, even if she wanted to.

"Where is she, Leigh?" He stepped closer. "My department spent the past eight days looking for her, wasting time and resources, but you seem to know."

"I don't. I told you, she's avoiding me. But she has a good reason."

He shook his head and looked away.

"I'm trying to persuade her to go in and explain everything," she said. "When you hear what she's been through, you'll understand that she's the victim in all this."

He looked at her. "You know, yesterday we told her sister about the blood evidence and the canine team. Kate Morris thinks her sister is dead now." He paused. "Or is that bullshit, too?"

"What do you mean?"

"I mean, is Kate, your new client, in on this? Did she know her sister was alive when she filed a missing-person report?"

"No. Kate was in the dark—is in the dark—just like I was."

"Well, not anymore. Antonio is on his way over there to tell her Vanessa is alive." He rested his hands on his hips. "So, I guess Vanessa was fine letting her sister suffer all this time."

Leigh gritted her teeth. Vanessa's blithe attitude toward Kate was one of the main reasons she was on Leigh's shit list right now. A simple text or phone call could have saved Kate from eight solid days of heart-wrenching stress.

"That's between them," Leigh said. "I've told Vanessa—

in no uncertain terms—that she needs to come forward. When she sits down with you and explains what happened, I think you'll see that you haven't wasted your time."

Brandon's gaze narrowed.

"There is, in fact, a crime here. It just happens to be a lot more complicated than you thought. She has valid reasons for not trusting the police."

"Such as?"

Leigh weighed how much to reveal. If she wanted to help Vanessa, she needed law enforcement on her side. Or at least not against her. Right now Brandon had every reason to be pissed off, but he didn't know all the circumstances.

"Vanessa is scared. Scared enough to abandon her car and go into hiding. She was harassed and stalked for months—"

"You're talking about Mason Lloyd."

"Yes. He made her life hell, and when she threatened to go to the police, he sent them to *her* door with some made-up story about her slashing his tires and being crazy with jealousy after he dumped her."

Brandon's brow furrowed. "A cop went to her house?"

"Yes. Detective Akins."

"Never heard of him. Is this APD?"

"I don't know. He had a badge and a gun, supposedly. He threatened to charge her with felony mischief if she didn't leave Mason alone."

Brandon shook his head. "All the more reason I need to interview Vanessa. You need to bring her in."

"I can't."

"If you want to help her—"

"It's not a matter of want. I don't know where she is. She's not responding to my calls."

He watched her closely, and she could tell he didn't believe her.

Leigh's heart squeezed as she looked at him. Something

between them was different now. Broken. The man who'd walked her to her car Sunday morning and kissed her gently on the forehead was gone.

She let her hands fall to her sides. "I understand you're upset."

He laughed. " 'Upset'?"

"I really had no idea what was going on until she contacted me." She eased closer, and he stiffened. "You need to believe me."

He gazed down at her, and the disappointment in his eyes made her stomach ache.

He stepped around her.

"Where are you going?" she asked.

"Work." He glanced over his shoulder. "I still have a big mess to sort out."

She followed him to the door, panicking as it dawned on her that once he walked out, she might not see him again.

He pulled the door open and turned to face her. "Vanessa needs to come in and talk to us."

"I told her that."

"Tell her again. Persuade her." His eyes were dark and serious. "If she's in the kind of trouble I think she's in, she needs our help. If she tries to take matters into her own hands, it's not going to work out well."

He turned to leave.

"Brandon."

He stepped onto the sidewalk, putting space between them before turning around. The cool look in his eyes made her throat tighten.

"I'm sorry about yesterday," she said.

"Yeah, me, too."

CHAPTER TWENTY-FIVE

VANESSA WATCHED THE WOMAN slide behind the wheel of her little white Honda. Kaitlin. Or was it Karlyn? Vanessa couldn't remember. She'd only met her once at a party hosted by their downstairs neighbor. Kaitlin-or-Karlyn backed out of her space and exited the parking lot, oblivious to the dinged hatchback parked in the shadows just a few rows away.

She looked at Cooper. "Let's hurry."

"I don't see why you have to be here."

"Because. You've taken enough risks for me." She pulled the hood of her borrowed sweatshirt over her hideous new hair and cinched the drawstring, just in case they encountered anyone else she knew.

They got out, and she led the way up the outdoor staircase, scanning the parking lot for familiar cars. She still hadn't met many of her neighbors, but the police had been here, and she figured they'd interviewed enough people that if someone saw her, they might take notice.

Reaching the second floor, they walked down the open breezeway to her apartment. Cooper stopped in front of her door and handed her his key chain. He still had her key on it. He'd never taken it off after they broke up, and Vanessa didn't want to dwell on what that said about their relationship. She felt guilty enough for everything she'd asked him to do for her over the past week.

He stepped into the apartment ahead of her. Vanessa stood by the door as Cooper closed and locked it.

"Smells like . . . spoiled milk," she said, looking around.

"There are dishes in the sink," Cooper said. "You told me not to touch anything when I was here."

"No, I know. I'm just . . ." She trailed off as she noticed the laundry basket beside her sofa. The clothes were clean. She'd just done a load of laundry on the night she went to meet Jason near the campground. Vanessa walked over and grabbed her favorite T-shirt from the pile. She'd been wearing Cooper's clothes for days. He had come by here earlier, but she hadn't wanted him to pack a bag for her out of fear that someone might notice things missing.

Vanessa unzipped Cooper's hoodie and took it off, then pulled the T-shirt over her head. It felt soft and cozy, and just being in her favorite shirt brought tears to her eyes. She tied the hoodie around her waist, then went to the desk where Cooper was going through a stack of papers.

"You have any other cards you want to grab while we're here?" he asked.

They'd been hard up for cash after Cooper was mugged, so he'd come here to get a credit card that Vanessa had left on her desk with a pile of bills. All her other cards had been in the purse she'd abandoned with her car.

"No, that's it," she said.

"What about cash?" Cooper looked at her, and she couldn't help but notice the stress in his eyes. They'd blown through a lot of money this week, almost all of it his.

"I don't think so. But I'll check a few places." She went into her bedroom, stopping suddenly at the sight of her unmade bed. It was like her life had come to a screeching halt.

When she'd left her apartment last Sunday, she'd been weepy and distraught, completely distracted—which was probably why she hadn't noticed anyone following her out to that meeting with Jason. If only she'd paid closer attention that night, everything might have turned out differently.

Vanessa's stomach churned with a familiar combination of regret and guilt. Shoving the feelings aside, she walked to her closet and reached for an old purse on the top shelf. She rummaged through it, but only managed to turn up a few quarters and a new pack of gum. She pocketed the gum.

"Anything?" Cooper asked from the doorway.

"I'm looking." She grabbed another purse. Poking through the pockets, she found some folded bills. "Hey, look! Twenty-two dollars."

"Awesome. That will cover about two meals."

Ignoring the sarcasm, she stuffed the money into her pocket and shifted her attention to the white music box on the shelf behind a pair of boots. The first twangy notes of "Clair de Lune" floated out as she lifted the lid. She removed the velvet-lined tray and found an old Swatch and a silver chain with a tarnished heart pendant. The necklace was cheap, but it was tangled with a fourteen-karat gold bracelet, and Vanessa grabbed them both and tucked them into her pocket. Then she spied what she'd come for—the diamond earrings that had belonged to her mother. Vanessa's throat tightened as she touched the studs.

Guilt, guilt, guilt—more guilt than she could stand. But she was all out of options.

"Van, we need to get moving."

"I know." She removed her cheap silver hoops and replaced them with the diamonds, figuring her ears were the safest place for them. Then she closed the box.

"You ready?"

"Almost." Vanessa walked around her bed. She crouched beside it and lifted the mattress. Sliding her hand between the mattress and box spring, she found the thin spiral note-book she'd been keeping since June.

"What's that?" Cooper asked.

"My log."

"I thought your lawyer had it."

"Nope."

Leigh Larson didn't even know about it. The log was her insurance policy just in case her plan went sideways.

She stuffed the notebook into the back of her jeans and pulled Cooper's hoodie on again.

He was waiting impatiently in the doorway, a deep fur-row between his eyebrows.

"Can we go now? I *really* don't like being here."

"Ready." Vanessa walked past him.

"Put on the hood, in case we see one of your neighbors," he said behind her.

Vanessa pulled the hood over her chopped hair.

"Van!" he hissed.

She turned around just as Cooper snagged her arm and yanked her back, pointing at the front door.

Someone was unlocking it. Someone with a key. Va-nessa's heart squeezed as she realized who it was.

Cooper pulled her toward the bathroom just as the door swung open and Kate stepped into the apartment.

Her sister looked up and gasped.

CHAPTER TWENTY-SIX

ANTONIO FINISHED OFF THE last of his hot dog and pitched the wrapper into the trash. He wiped his hands on his jeans and checked his watch as he strode down the sidewalk. The lunchtime line at the food truck had been longer than usual, and he was running late.

Antonio walked into the lobby and spotted Kate on a bench near the reception desk, right where he'd told her to meet him.

She was distracted with her phone, and he took a second to stare. She wore a loose pink sweater and black yoga pants, and her hair was down around her shoulders today. She looked better than he'd expected—a hell of a lot better than she'd looked yesterday afternoon when he'd gone to her house and informed her that a video had turned up, indicating that her sister was alive. Kate had dissolved into tears right there on her patio.

She'd pulled herself together since then, but she still looked like she could use about ten days of uninterrupted sleep.

Kate glanced up from her phone as he walked over.

"Hi," she said, jumping to her feet. "Thanks for meeting me."

"No problem. Sit down." He joined her on the bench. As noisy as the lobby was, he preferred talking to her here instead of taking her upstairs and parading her through the bullpen.

She took a deep breath and looked at her hands.

"What's up?" he asked casually, trying to get her to relax.

"First . . . I'm sorry about yesterday." She looked embarrassed. "It seems like I cry every time I see you. I'm not like that at all, usually. It's just been . . . a stressful week."

"No worries. I get it."

She cleared her throat. "Well, you asked me to let you know if I heard from Vanessa."

He eased closer.

"I talked to her last night. Unexpectedly."

"Did she show up at your house?"

"I'd prefer not to get into that." She gave him a pained smile. "Sorry. But she told me about everything that happened, and I have a better understanding now of why she did what she did."

"Oh yeah?"

"Yes. And I encouraged her to come here to the police station and explain everything herself. She's still hesitant, though."

"Why?" Antonio tried to keep the annoyance out of his voice, but he couldn't really do it. He was too pissed off. He'd spent a full week basically wasting his time.

"She's not ready."

Antonio tamped down his temper. Kate looked at her lap and he waited for her to glance up. Finally, she did.

"Is Vanessa at your house, Kate?"

"What? No." She looked confused.

"Where is she?"

"Still with Cooper. Why?"

"So . . . that means you got a babysitter for Sylvie so you could come all the way here to talk to me. It must be important."

"Sylvie's at my neighbor's."

"Okay." Even with the other girls in school, he knew it was a hassle for her to come here. "What's really on your mind?"

She took a deep breath. "I wanted to ask you to please not drop Vanessa's case."

He just looked at her.

"I know you think she misled you. And she did. I know you and the other detectives put a lot of time and effort into searching for her and—"

"Eight days."

"I know. It felt like an eternity. But the thing is, I truly believe she is still in danger. I believe Mason Lloyd intends to harm her, and he will as soon as he can find her."

"Why?"

"He's controlling and vengeful. And extremely manipulative. That's the weird part." She shook her head. "After everything that's happened, everything he's done to make her life miserable, he still has some kind of strange hold over her. I can tell by the way she talks about him. I think that's what worries me more than anything."

Antonio looked down at Kate's hands as she played with the sleeve of her sweater. She'd gone out of her way to come here and make this case for her sister—the same sister who had put her through torture for the past week. After all that, Kate was not only ready to forgive Vanessa, she wanted to help her out of the mess she was in.

"I want to help your sister, Kate. But she needs to talk to us. No more hiding. If she's got a problem with this boyfriend of hers—"

"Ex-boyfriend."

He nodded. "If she's got a problem, she needs to come

in and make a statement. Or we can go to her. But she needs to put forward credible information, so that we can follow up."

"She *is* credible. I know you probably don't trust what she has to say because she let people believe she was dead for a week, and I totally get that, but she was afraid for her safety and she still is. Mason Lloyd is dangerous, I'm telling you. He's harassed her and threatened her for months, and she has evidence. She kept a journal of everything he did—"

"Where?"

"She has it with her."

"Tell her to bring it in. We need that information, and we need to interview her for an investigation to ever get off the ground."

"I know." Kate shook her head and looked away. "I've told her all that. Unfortunately, she doesn't always take my advice."

Antonio felt a pang of sympathy as he looked at her. Sometimes families sucked, especially siblings. His had put him through the wringer more than a few times. But nothing that came close to what Kate had been through.

"We're keeping an eye on Lloyd," he said.

He had no idea why he told her that. It was true, but it wasn't the sort of thing he should be telling Kate.

The pure relief on her face made his pulse pick up, and he knew *that* was the reason. He had a soft spot for this woman. It made no sense whatsoever, but there it was.

"Thank you." She rested her hand on his—just for a second—and then pulled it away. "I *really, really* appreciate it."

"No problem. That's my job, protect and serve." He stood up, ready to get out of there before he said anything else that sounded corny.

She stood, too. "Thank you, Antonio. Your help with all this—it means a lot. You have no idea."

*   *   *

BRANDON ROLLED HIS windows down, letting in a cold blast of air as he drove over the bridge. Dusk was settling over the city, and the neon lights of South Congress glowed in the distance. It looked busy for a Tuesday, with the sidewalk cafés already full and people zipping through intersections on rented scooters. Typically, Brandon didn't mind living in a high-traffic neighborhood. He liked the ebb and flow of people, not to mention the convenience of all the food trucks and takeout options. But some nights—like tonight—he was in no mood for crowds, and all the partygoers and scooters got on his nerves.

Brandon's phone buzzed as he turned onto his street. His pulse quickened as he saw Leigh's number on the screen.

"Hey," he said.

"Hi. Are you home from work?"

He caught the edge in her voice.

"On my way. Why?"

"This may sound weird . . . but I was wondering if you came by today."

"By where? Your house?"

"Yeah," she said. "Around noon."

"No. Why?"

"Just a sec."

He heard muffled voices and what sounded like a truck driving by. Then it got quiet.

"Sorry," she said. "I was outside with my neighbor."

"What's wrong, Leigh?"

"I came home from my run, and she was standing in her driveway, and she mentioned that she saw a man lurking around my house earlier."

"Lurking?"

"He was near the gate to the patio. She didn't get a good look at him, but she said he was tall, so I thought maybe it was you."

"Are you inside?"

"Yeah."

Brandon pulled a U-turn. "Okay, lock your doors. I'll be there in a minute."

"You don't have to—"

"I'll be there in a minute. Set your alarm."

Brandon wove through traffic, somehow managing to catch every red light. Pulling onto Leigh's street, he scanned the block and the driveways for unfamiliar cars. Everything looked normal, and the cars parked along the street were ones he'd noticed before.

Brandon parked in front of her tiny front lawn and got out. He glanced around as he made his way up the sidewalk. Both of the neighbors' driveways were empty.

The front door opened as Brandon reached the step.

"Hi." Leigh attempted a smile. "You didn't have to come all the way here."

That irked him for some reason.

"Tell me what happened," he said.

She stepped back to let him in. She was dressed for a run in stretchy black pants and a sweatshirt, and the sheen of perspiration on her face told him she hadn't been home long.

She closed the door behind him and flipped the lock.

"Well, I bumped into my neighbor as she was leaving for dinner," she said.

"The Lexus or the Jeep?"

"The Lexus." She looked surprised. "How did you know that?"

"I pay attention. What did she say?"

"Just what I told you. That she saw someone near my gate around lunchtime. She had come home from her office to pick something up and she noticed him as she pulled in. She said she figured he was a repairman or something."

"She say how he was dressed?"

"Jeans. She only saw him from the back, but she described him as tall with dark hair. That's why I thought maybe it was you."

Brandon scanned her living room. It looked even messier than the last time he'd been here. The sofa was covered with stacks of laundry, and paperwork blanketed the coffee table.

"Nothing's missing or anything like that," Leigh said. "When I got home, the alarm was set and everything was locked up, tight as a drum."

"Mind if I look around?"

"No. Of course not."

Brandon went straight to the bedroom. Her king-size bed had a fluffy white comforter and a mountain of pillows and made him think of a luxury hotel. He walked to the window that faced the patio and pulled a mini flashlight from his pocket. Shining it on the plantation shutters covering the window, he noted the thin layer of dust on the sill. The lock was intact, no sign of damage.

"I always keep the shutters closed," she said. "Everything looks normal."

"You check your jewelry?"

"I don't have a lot, but yeah. It's in my dresser."

"What about underwear?"

She arched her eyebrows.

"Check it," he said.

She stepped over to the dresser, and he went into the adjacent bathroom. He was hit with the unmistakable scent of Leigh—something light and floral, probably her shampoo. Cosmetics were spread out across a white marble vanity. He pulled back the shower curtain and checked out the rectangular window about six feet off the ground.

"I already checked all the window locks," she said. "Everything seems fine. And no underwear missing, as far as I can tell."

Brandon systematically made his way through the rest of the house, checking windows and door locks and ending up on the patio.

"I keep the gate locked," she said. "And that's the weird part."

Brandon stepped over to the gate and saw what she meant by *weird*. The gate was closed but not locked. It had a sturdy metal slide bolt that operated from the inside, and the locking pin had been removed.

"The thing is, it's a seven-foot fence," she said, and he caught the anxiousness in her voice. "It's not like someone could reach over and open it."

Brandon studied the wooden slats. None were loose. The fence and gate spanned the gap between Leigh's house and the brick wall separating her property from her neighbor's. A skinny black cat sat atop the wall watching him.

He turned to Leigh, who stood beside her rosebushes, arms crossed and hands tucked into the sleeves of her sweatshirt. She was shivering in the chilly night air.

"You're sure it was locked when you left for work today?" he asked.

"It was. I'm sure. I always keep it locked. I only ever use it if I'm bringing plants or potting soil in here." She paused. "What do you think happened?"

"I don't know. Maybe someone jumped the fence, poked around, then let himself out."

"Poked around?"

He stepped over to her and rested his hands on his hips. "Maybe he was checking out your security setup. Or maybe he planned to break in and changed his mind."

She shivered again.

"I need to get a CSI out to see if there are any prints on the gate," he said.

"You really think that's necessary? I've got company coming tonight."

Jealousy darted through him.

"When?" he asked.

"Eight." She checked her watch. "Javi's bringing carryout, and we're supposed to go over my opening argument for court tomorrow."

"It won't take long to dust for prints." He doubted there would be any, but they had to at least check.

Leigh led him back into the house, and he paused for a moment in the living room, looking around again. She had a basic wall-mounted TV, but not a lot of electronics lying around. Certainly nothing obvious that would tempt a burglar.

Brandon glanced at her, and the worried look in her eyes got to him.

"Be right back."

He walked out to his truck. Reaching behind the front seat, he retrieved a long, narrow cardboard box.

"What's that?" Leigh asked as he returned to the house.

"A steel brace for your slider."

"When did you get it?"

"This morning."

He walked into the sunroom and crouched beside the door. In a couple of minutes, he had the brace installed in the door track.

"It's on a spring. See?" He glanced up at her, and she was watching him with a furrowed brow. "It pops right out when you want to use the door." He stood up and dusted his hands. "I know it's an eyesore, but this is your most vulnerable point of entry and it needs to be addressed."

She looked up at him. "You got that today."

"Yeah."

"I thought you were mad at me."

"I am."

She looked down at the door again, and a shiver moved through her.

Brandon reached out and pulled her into his arms. She went still for a moment, and then her arms came around his waist and she rested her head against his chest. She felt warm and soft, but the tension in her shoulders was unmistakable.

"Why would someone . . ." Her muffled voice trailed off.

Brandon eased back. "I don't know." He slid his hand to her shoulder and rested his thumb against the soft skin of her neck. "I'm going to try to find out."

His phone buzzed, and he cursed inwardly as Leigh pulled away from him. He took the phone from his pocket and checked the screen. Antonio.

"Hey," he said.

"Did you take off already?"

"Yeah."

"Tate's looking for you. You know the latex gloves from that dumpster? The one near Leigh's law firm?"

"Yeah?"

"We got a hit on the prints."

ANTONIO EXITED THE watch room and spotted Brandon cutting through the bullpen.

"Who's in there?" Brandon asked, nodding at the interview room. The door was closed, and several detectives stood in the room next door, observing the action on closed-circuit TV.

Antonio smiled. "You know the convenience store holdup from Friday? The lieutenant has the shooter's girlfriend in there. She just confessed to driving him to the scene."

"That's good."

"Yeah. Guess the week wasn't a total loss." Antonio looked Brandon over. "I didn't know you were coming back tonight."

"I want to see that report."

"It's on my desk. Here." Antonio led him to his cubicle and grabbed the lab report off the top of his inbox. He handed it to Brandon and then sat down to log in to his com-

puter. "It's a forensic hit. Those same prints turned up at a
crime scene in Florida. A five-year-old burglary case."

Brandon skimmed the report. "Home burglary?"

"No. A workplace."

"Where in Florida?"

"Tampa. And listen. I already reached out to the detective. They never made an arrest, but he remembers the case
because it involved a shit-ton of oxies stolen from a clinic.
More than twelve hundred pills, with a street value of almost forty thousand dollars. They got the DEA involved
but still they couldn't manage to crack the case. And get
this—"

"Mason Lloyd worked at the clinic." Brandon looked up.
"How did you know that?"

"He used to live in Tampa." Brandon looked at the computer screen. "At least, according to Leigh he did."

"Yeah, well, Leigh's right. By the way, did she ever figure out what someone was trying to steal at her law firm?"

"No."

"She has no idea at all?"

"No."

"What about you?"

He shook his head. "Not really."

Which meant he *had* an idea, but he wasn't talking.
Maybe he hadn't firmed it up yet. Brandon didn't like to
talk about random hunches.

"So, are you thinking these are Mason Lloyd's prints at
both crime scenes?" Brandon asked.

"That was my first thought, too, but no. The detective
said they took all the doctors' and staffers' prints for exclusionary purposes. Didn't get any hits. Whoever's prints
these are isn't in the system."

"Or if he is, we don't know it yet."

Brandon was right. Given the backlog of biometric data
waiting to be uploaded—everything from fingerprints to
DNA samples—there was always the chance the perp had

been arrested somewhere at some point, but the database was running behind. Backlogs were way too common, especially when it came to DNA evidence.

Antonio pulled up the website for a dermatology clinic. "Check this out."

Brandon propped his arm on top of the cubicle and frowned at the screen.

"Doesn't look like any doctor's office I've been to," Antonio said.

The two-story gray stone building had tall turrets, fancy iron balconies, and elaborate landscaping. The parking lot outside the office was filled with luxury cars, including a silver Lotus, a red Ferrari, and a black convertible Mercedes.

"Looks like a French chateau," Brandon said. "What does this clinic do?"

"All kinds of stuff. Botox injections, liposuction, cheek implants." Antonio winced. "Stuff that sounds painful and expensive. They've got six doctors working there."

Brandon folded his arms over his chest as he looked at the screen. "What's the Tampa detective say about it?"

"I caught him on the way to a crime scene, so he didn't have the file in front of him. But he remembers the case because all the doctors drove these sweet cars. And he told me he always thought it was an inside job."

"Why?"

"Something about the alarm system. Either someone had a password or somehow bypassed it."

Brandon stared at the screen, his face unreadable. But Antonio knew what he was thinking. Brandon wasn't happy. From the get-go he had thought that Leigh's break-in had something to do with Vanessa's disappearance, and now he had corroboration.

Antonio also knew that he really, *really* wanted to get his hands on the guy who had attacked Leigh.

"So, what now?" Antonio asked him.

"We're missing something."

"How do you mean?"

"We've got two crimes connected by one set of finger-prints. Both crimes are linked to Lloyd, but they're not his prints. So, whose are they?"

"That's the big question."

Brandon tapped his knuckles on the cubicle wall and stared down at the screen.

"Has Kate heard from Vanessa?" Brandon asked.

"She saw her last night. She said she's still staying with Cooper."

"Where?"

"No idea," Antonio said. "Not at his place, though. I went by there this morning, and no one's seen them. Has Leigh heard from her?"

"She told me Vanessa's ducking her calls."

"Do you believe her?"

He paused. "Yeah."

It was only a second of hesitation, but Antonio caught it. Looked like he still had trust issues with Leigh.

Brandon muttered a curse as he stared at the computer screen.

"So, what are you thinking?" Antonio asked.

Brandon looked at him. "I'm thinking it's time to get eyes on Dr. Lloyd."

CHAPTER TWENTY-SEVEN

THE DILAPIDATED WOODEN SHED occupied a tiny patch of grass with a sweeping view of the lake. Brandon pulled into the gravel lot and squeezed his pickup between two cars. Glancing in the side mirror, he spotted the unmarked black police unit parked beneath a cottonwood tree.

Brandon checked his watch. He was five minutes early for the two o'clock meeting. He got out and crossed the lot to a weathered wooden picnic table where a guy with a silver buzz cut sat scrolling through his phone. At the sound of Brandon's boots on the gravel, the man looked up.

"Detective Akins? Brandon Reynolds."

The detective stood, and they shook hands. Akins was tall and had the beginnings of a beer gut.

"Thanks for making time," Brandon told him.

"No problem," Akins said. "I just ordered some food. You eating?"

"No, thanks."

"Can't beat Rosa's pork tacos."

"So I've heard."

Brandon sat down across from the detective. Despite the silver hair, he was only thirty-nine. He'd been with the Marble Falls Police Department for twelve years. Prior to that, he'd worked in Houston, where he'd gone through the academy with one of Brandon's friends.

"Pete says hi," Brandon told him.

"Yeah, tell him hi." Akins smiled, and the corners of his eyes crinkled. With his suntanned skin, Akins looked like he spent a lot of time outdoors. "Haven't seen him in years. How's he doing?"

"Good. Got another baby on the way."

"Yeah, that'll happen. So, you're working a burglary?" he asked, getting past the small talk.

"It's complicated. We've got a burglary and looks like it might be connected to an unsolved cold case." Brandon was being intentionally vague. This entire meeting was based on a hunch he'd been developing when he learned there was a detective named Akins with Marble Falls PD. "I understand you know Mason Lloyd, who owns a house out here?"

Akins nodded toward the lake. "He's got ten acres on the water. Bought the place three years ago."

"Sounds nice. He get out there much?"

"Almost every weekend. He plays a lot of golf at the club."

And according to Brandon's friend, Akins sometimes played with him.

Brandon pulled a piece of paper from his pocket and unfolded it. It was a printout showing the driver's license photo of Vanessa Adams.

"I wanted to see if you recognize this woman." He handed Akins the paper. "I understand she and Lloyd used to have a thing."

He smirked. "Yeah, I know. Is she a suspect?"

"Not yet. But we heard she might have had a conflict with Lloyd, so we're taking a look."

Akins shook his head. "Yeah, she's definitely got a screw loose."

"Oh yeah?"

"He broke things off with her over the summer and she flipped out, slashed all his tires and threatened to go to his wife." He handed the paper back. "Mason asked me to talk to her."

"Did you?"

He shrugged. "I dropped by her place. Kept it low key. I told her she needed to leave him alone or she was going to be looking at a criminal mischief charge."

"Was this an official visit or—"

"It was a favor." Akins lowered his voice. "The girl's obsessed with him. She sent him about a million nude pictures of herself." He smirked. "Not that that's bad or anything—she's definitely hot. But then when he broke it off, she had a meltdown."

"He showed you the pictures?"

"Yeah. Hang on." Akins got up and went to the shed, where he picked up a red plastic basket filled with foil-wrapped tacos.

"Sure you're not hungry?" Akins asked as he came back to the table.

"I'm good."

Brandon folded the picture of Vanessa and slid it back into his pocket.

"So far, this thing's shaping up like a he-said, she-said," Brandon told him. "Vanessa flatly denies touching the car."

Akins rolled his eyes. "Yeah, well I saw it for myself." He unwrapped the foil from his taco.

"Any chance Lloyd slashed his own tires?"

He snorted. "On a Porsche 911? Not a chance. That's four Pirelli tires at five hundred bucks a pop." He dipped his taco in hot sauce. "Look, the girl's crazy. She freaked out when Mason broke up with her, and he asked me to help him out before she blew up his marriage." He chomped into the taco, taking down half of it in one bite. "Trust me," he said around a mouthful of food. "He's the victim, not her."

Brandon's phone vibrated as a text landed from Antonio: Call me ASAP.

He looked at Akins. "I need to call in."

"Sure."

He got up and walked away from the table, leaving Akins to his tacos. He was glad to get a break from him. Brandon could only imagine Leigh's reaction if she knew that the guy who had used his badge to bully Vanessa had also seen pictures of her naked. It wasn't hard to understand where Leigh got the bottomless well of outrage that she needed to do her job.

Stepping under the shade of a cottonwood, Brandon called his partner.

"What's up?"

"I just got off the phone with that detective in Tampa. He retrieved the case file."

Brandon's pulse picked up. "What's he got?"

"You know how I told you they always thought the break-in at their office was an inside job and they took all the docs' prints but no matches?"

"Yeah?"

"Well, listen. This guy just read me their entire suspect list over the phone. They had fifteen persons of interest, but they never made an arrest."

"Who's on the list?"

"Guy by the name of Michael James Lloyd."

Brandon paused. "Mason's brother."

"Yep."

"What about his prints?"

"I'm assuming they're not in the system, or they would have arrested him. But get this—this guy left Florida a year ago, and you'll never guess where he moved."

Brandon already knew the answer. "Texas."

* * *

L'EIGH GLANCED UP and down the street and decided the coast was clear. Leaning into her back seat, she scooped up the pile of clothes and then shut the car door with her hip.

Her phone chimed as she hurried across the sidewalk and pulled open the door to the dry cleaner's. Damn it, there was a line.

Leigh stepped into the cramped little shop, which was unbearably warm and smelled like vanilla air freshener. Her phone chimed again as she squeezed into line behind a woman in a sorority T-shirt holding a flowered comforter.

Leigh dug her phone from her purse. Javi.

"Hi," she said.

"How'd your open go? Did you kill it?"

"No."

"What? Why not?" He sounded personally offended. He'd been at her house until midnight helping her craft the perfect argument.

"It didn't happen," Leigh told him.

The woman in front of her stepped up to the counter and proceeded to ask the clerk about pet urine.

"The judge's docket got shuffled at the last minute," Leigh said. "I heard from one of the paralegals that his brother-in-law died last night, so"—she glanced over her shoulder to peer out at her car, which was illegally parked near a fire hydrant—"the trial's been postponed, and suddenly my whole day is free."

"Well, *that* never happens. So, are you going to go shopping? Get your nails done?"

"No."

"Maybe invite your hot cop over for a little afternoon delight?"

"Ha ha. I'm catching up on my errands."

Leigh shifted her bundle of clothes, feeling dizzy suddenly in the humid little room.

"How are things going there?" she asked.

The pet pee lady left, and Leigh stepped up to the counter, muting her phone. "I'm dropping off for Leigh Larson," she told the clerk. "I may have a pickup back there, too."

The woman tapped the name into her computer, then disappeared into the back as Leigh dropped her load on the counter. Leigh shuffled through the blouses, only half listening to Javi talking as she counted her items.

"Leigh?"

"Yeah, sorry. What was that?"

"I said, what about Friday's hearing?"

Leigh's gaze landed on the white blouse she'd been wearing the night she was attacked.

She stared at the bloodstain, remembering the giant hand clamped over her mouth, the smell of latex, the coppery taste of blood. She'd bitten him. She'd bitten *him*. Her stomach clenched at the realization. The edges of her vision blurred, and she felt a weight on her chest. Her lungs constricted and she couldn't breathe, and suddenly she was back in her office, pinned beneath that impossible weight.

"Leigh?"

"Sorry. I—I'm at the dry cleaners. Let me call you back."

"Are you okay?"

"Yeah."

She hung up. The clerk was still in the back room, somewhere amid the endless rotating racks of clothes. The hangers zoomed by in a blur, and Leigh felt dizzy again.

She grabbed the stained blouse and walked out, her stomach heaving as she stumbled into the cold air. She returned to her car and slid behind the wheel, desperate to get into the safe haven of her private space. She popped the locks, then flung the stained blouse into the seat beside her and stared through the windshield.

Breathe.

She closed her eyes and inhaled deeply. Exhaled. Inhaled again.

Her heart raced a million miles an hour and her hands felt sweaty on the steering wheel. She opened her eyes and saw that her knuckles were white. Loosening her grip on the wheel, she forced herself to take another deep breath.

She stared through the windshield, trying to get control of her racing pulse and her swirling thoughts. Rush-hour traffic streamed past, the red taillights blurring in front of her as her eyes filled with hot tears.

Do. Not. Cry.

It was good that she'd remembered. It was a new detail, coming to her late, like Brandon had talked about. And now she had physical evidence that might be useful. The blood on her blouse might belong to her assailant.

Leigh's stomach flip-flopped and she forced the tears back, angry at herself for falling apart like this. She was alone. She was in her car, in a public place. She was perfectly safe.

Her phone vibrated, making her jump. She took a deep breath. It was a text message, probably Javi checking in on her because she was acting like a freak today.

She dug the phone from her purse. It was a number she didn't recognize and whoever it was had sent her a video. Leigh tapped the screen.

A line of girls moved in sync. They wore purple leotards and carried shimmery silver pom-poms. They punched at the air in unison—up, down, left, right. Up again, down again.

Leigh's phone chimed, and she answered distractedly.

"Hello?"

"Did you get it?"

Leigh looked at the screen. "Who is this?"

"It's *Vanessa*. Did you get the video?"

An icy trickle slid down Leigh's spine as she studied the line of girls. "The dancers?"

"It's Kelly. That's *her*!" Vanessa sounded panicked. "He's threatening her. You have to help me."

"Wait. Who—"

"Mason! He just sent me this. It's a *threat*."

"Vanessa, calm down." She took a deep breath. "Where is Kelly now?"

"I don't know. I can get a hold of Kate and—"

"In this video she's at dance practice, right? Was this taken today?" Leigh studied the line of girls as they kicked and twisted and twirled, their slender bodies as bendy as rubber bands.

"I don't know, but it's a *threat*," Vanessa insisted. "I need to go talk to him. He can't keep doing this."

"Vanessa, listen. Do not go anywhere near him. I'll contact the police and—"

"No! What if he does something to hurt Kelly?" Her voice was shrill. "That's what this video's about. He's taunting me and threatening to hurt her. Don't you get it?"

"Vanessa, calm down."

"No! You don't know him like I do. I need to see him. I have to end this. I can't stand that he's controlling my life from a distance, like I'm on some kind of leash or . . . or . . . some kind of—"

"Vanessa, do not go near him. Do you understand me?"

"He's at his lake house right now. I need to go see him."

"How do you know he's at his lake house?" Leigh dug out her car keys.

"Because it's Wednesday. He plays golf at his course there every Wednesday and spends the night away from his wife. We used to meet out there. I'll make a deal with him. I've got my stalker log. I'll tell him he can have it—he can burn it, destroy it, whatever—if he'll just get the fuck out of my life and leave me alone."

Leigh started up her car and glanced over her shoulder at the traffic whisking past.

"Vanessa, this is *not* a good idea. You're playing right into his hands."

"No, *I* have the stalker log. That's leverage. He knows

about it and he wants it because he thinks that without it, I don't have a case against him."

"Vanessa, you're not being rational. You need to calm down."

"Don't tell me to calm down when he's threatening my *niece*! She's freaking fifteen years old and he's taking videos of her!"

"He's bluffing. He's manipulating you, okay?"

"You don't know him like I do. He doesn't bluff."

Leigh took a deep breath. "Vanessa, where are you? Where's Cooper?"

Silence on the phone. Then sniffling.

"Vanessa?"

"He's at work. I'm in his car."

"Okay, let's meet somewhere."

"I'm sorry. I can't. I need to go."

"Vanessa, wait!"

"I'm sorry. I'll be fine. But I have to put an end to this."

W HAT'S YOUR PLAN?" Brandon asked Tate over the phone.

The detective was turning out to be more resourceful than Brandon had expected. An hour after getting the tip from Brandon that Michael Lloyd was potentially involved in the break-in at Leigh's law firm, he'd come up with not only the guy's home address but a social media profile that led Tate to the West Austin gym where the guy worked as a personal trainer.

"I talked to his manager, and he's off today," Tate reported. "So, I was thinking I'd go sit on his apartment and see if he shows up."

"We need to get his fingerprints," Brandon said. "I don't want to question him until we have concrete proof he's involved."

"I could do it surreptitiously," Tate said. "Maybe he'll, I don't know, toss a cigarette butt or a water bottle or something."

"If he's a trainer, I doubt he smokes. You could put a flyer on his windshield and see if he tosses it. Then we'd have his prints on the paper. Or walk up and hand him an address and ask for directions."

"Not a bad idea," Tate said.

A text landed on Brandon's phone from Leigh.

Where RU?

He stared down at it for a moment before responding: At the station. Why?

Part of him was still pissed off at her for lying to him—very pissed off. She'd broken his trust.

Another part of him desperately wanted to see her tonight.

"Let me know if you get eyes on him," Brandon told Tate as a call came in from Leigh.

"Roger that."

Brandon disconnected with Tate and took Leigh's call.

"I've got a problem," she said, making Brandon's heart skip a beat. "Vanessa just contacted me. Someone sent her a video of her niece at dance practice. She thinks it's from Mason and it's a veiled threat."

"Where is the girl now?" Brandon asked.

"I don't know. Neither does Vanessa. I tried calling Kate, but she's got a *Driving, Do Not Disturb* message on her phone."

Brandon glanced around the bullpen for Antonio. Maybe he could get a hold of Kate.

"Vanessa's freaking out," Leigh said. "She thinks she can bargain with him and get him to leave her and her niece alone."

"What makes her think she can bargain with him now if he's been stalking her and obsessing over her for months?"

"She has something he wants. She's been keeping a stalker log documenting everything he's done to her, and he's worried she'll use it against him in court."

Brandon didn't like the sound of any of this, and he especially didn't like the urgent note in Leigh's voice.

"Where is Vanessa now?" he asked.

"On her way to Mason's lake house. He has a standing golf game on Wednesdays, and they used to rendezvous there on Wednesday nights."

Brandon's pulse kicked up a notch. "Tell her not to go."

"I *did*."

"If he knows she knows where to find him, that means he's baiting her."

"I know that. But she won't listen to me! I'm on my way out there to try and intercept her."

"*You* stay out of it. The police should handle it."

"Yeah, no joke. That's exactly why I'm calling you."

Brandon stood up and looked around the bullpen. Where the hell was Antonio? He'd just been here a minute ago.

"Listen to me." He grabbed his keys and headed for the stairwell. "You need to keep away from Mason Lloyd. He's dangerous, and the situation could escalate." He waited for her to agree. "Leigh?"

"I know."

"You know Vanessa's got a gun, right?"

Silence.

Damn it, she was still hiding shit from him.

"She bought a pistol from Jason on the night she disappeared," he said.

"I'm aware of that."

"The whole thing could go sideways, fast, and I don't want you caught in the crossfire."

"You think she might shoot him?"

"More likely he'd disarm her in about two seconds flat. She doesn't know how to handle a gun, and Mason outweighs her by about eighty pounds. He's a danger to her and to you. So is his brother."

Brandon went down the stairs, passing a stream of patrol officers coming in for the late shift.

"Leigh? Are you listening?"

"Yeah, but what's his brother got to do with anything?"

Brandon crossed the lobby, still looking for Antonio. "We think he may have been the one who attacked you at your office. I think he may have gone there looking for this stalker log." He stepped outside into the chilly evening air. The streets were jammed with rush-hour traffic. "Do you understand what I'm saying, Leigh? Mason is dangerous. Investigators are closing in on him, and you and Vanessa don't need to be knocking on his door."

"I'm not going to. I'm going to intercept Vanessa and try to talk some sense into her."

"How the hell do you even know where this lake house is?"

"Simple Internet search. It pops right up."

Brandon cursed under his breath as he jogged across the street to the parking garage. He spotted Antonio crossing the intersection with a fast-food bag in hand. Brandon stopped to flag him down.

"You need to stay out of it," he told her. "I'm on my way. *Don't* get involved in a confrontation with them."

"I don't plan to," she said.

Which wasn't the same thing as saying she wouldn't, and she damn well knew it.

"Leigh, listen—"

"I have to go now, Brandon. I'll call you when I find her."

CHAPTER TWENTY-EIGHT

LEIGH BALANCED HER PHONE on her lap as she tried to follow the map and read the numbers on the mailboxes. It was a curvy dirt road, and some of the addresses weren't even in order, but she seemed to be getting closer. The multi-acre properties were spread out here. The road was surrounded by brush and a tall game fence on both sides, and it had been at least ten minutes since she'd caught a glimpse of the lake through the thick trees.

She checked the map on her phone again. At last she reached the blue beacon marking Mason's house. But there was not a road or a driveway or even a break in the fencing. Leigh kept going. The road dipped down. Curving around a bend she spotted a narrow drive, and her headlights illuminated a metal post with a keypad and a security camera mounted on top.

"Crap," she muttered, driving past it. She certainly didn't want to get caught on some camera out here. She looked around, searching for any sign of Vanessa or of Cooper's blue hatchback.

Vanessa had been here many times before. Would she

have simply let herself through the gate? Or would she have called Mason from whatever phone she was using—probably Cooper's—to let him know she was coming?

Leigh spotted a clump of juniper bushes and pulled onto the shoulder. She checked her watch. Then she checked her phone, but all her messages to Vanessa had been ignored.

Leigh's stomach clenched.

You know Vanessa's got a gun, right?

Leigh turned off her car and got out, glancing around. Wind whipped through the trees, slicing through the thin silk of her blouse. Regretting her high heels, she picked her way through some weeds to the game fence and peered through the wire mesh. Through the scrub brush, she saw the yellow glow of a house. At least, she thought it was a house. But she couldn't make out any parked cars or other details. Leigh followed the fence line, searching for a gap in the trees.

"Ouch!" she yelped.

Bending down, she plucked a pair of sticker-burrs from her ankle. Then she traipsed through the knee-high weeds and neared the game fence again. The yellow glow was brighter now, and through a gap in the foliage she had a clear line of sight to the house.

It was a sprawling two-story cabin made of dark-stained wood. The house perched atop a steep slope and had a deck jutting out toward the lake. A wooden staircase led from the lower level beneath the deck to a boathouse illuminated by floodlights. Two boats and a pair of Jet Skis occupied the slips.

At the sound of an approaching car, Leigh scampered behind a clump of bushes. The car slowed as it reached the bend, and Leigh tensed as the headlights flashed over her hiding spot. When the car was gone, she glanced back at the house. From this new vantage point, she had a partial view of the driveway.

Leigh's heart skittered at the sight of Cooper's car. She crept closer, peering through the branches, and spied the back end of something low and silver. Mason's Porsche, probably.

Cursing to herself, Leigh picked her way back to her car. She reached inside for her phone and texted Brandon.

Vanessa on property. Going to see if I can spot her.

Leigh tucked the phone into the pocket of her blouse and glanced around. She couldn't have picked worse shoes for this expedition. She popped her trunk and rummaged through the contents: file boxes, grocery bags, gardening tools. She located a pair of flip-flops and quickly slipped them on, then tossed her heels into the trunk. She wished, for the first time in her life, that she carried a pistol. But she didn't. She didn't even have a tube of pepper spray with her. She'd moved it from her car to her nightstand after the prowler yesterday.

Leigh glanced at the game fence again, then back at her trunk. On impulse, she grabbed a can of spray sunblock and a pair of gardening shears. She tucked the spray can into the waist of her skirt and quietly closed the trunk.

Her phone vibrated with a text from Brandon.

Wait for me. On my way.

Leigh's heart thrummed as she stared at the message. She looked at Cooper's little blue car. She needed to get the lay of the land so that when Brandon arrived, she could immediately tell him where to find Vanessa.

Leigh slipped the phone into her pocket again, then crept back toward the game fence, surveying the brush for a well-concealed spot. She squeezed behind a juniper bush and tentatively touched the metal shears to the wire mesh. Nothing. Satisfied that she wasn't about to electrocute herself, she clipped a vertical line.

Snip. Snip. Snip.

With every bite of the shears, Leigh's pulse quickened. She

cut a horizontal line, then tossed the shears to the ground and peeled back the mesh. Crouching low, she ducked through.

A shiver of excitement went through her as she stood up. She was officially trespassing on Mason Lloyd's property, and it was exhilarating. She crept behind a clump of trees and peered through the branches, studying the house. She zeroed in on a wall of windows near the deck. A big chimney rose from the roof there, and she figured it was the main room. Staying concealed behind the tree cover, she crept closer to the house, searching for any sign of people.

A light went on in the lower level. Leigh jumped behind a tree and watched beneath the deck as a pair of long shadows appeared in the rectangle of light on the concrete. A sliding glass door opened.

Vanessa stepped out, and Leigh's breath caught. She turned around, arguing with someone, and Leigh wasn't surprised when Mason stepped out behind her. He jabbed Vanessa in the shoulder, and she stumbled forward.

Leigh's blood turned cold. He had a gun.

Vanessa said something over her shoulder as he prodded her forward toward the narrow wooden steps leading down to the boathouse.

Leigh's throat went dry. She took her phone out, and her fingers trembled as she texted Brandon.

She—

Snick.

Leigh spun around as a big arm hooked around her neck.

W HERE, DAMN IT?" Brandon looked at Antonio.

"I don't know. It looks like"—he squinted at the map on his phone—"we should have passed it by now."

Brandon sped down the narrow road, glancing around

for any sign of a gate or a driveway. The road dipped down, then curved, and he barely touched the brakes.

"There! Up ahead there's a gate." Antonio braced a hand against the dashboard as Brandon tapped the brakes. "You just passed it."

Brand slowed, swerving to avoid a car on the shoulder. Leigh's Mustang.

"Fuck." Brandon pulled over and jammed to a stop, throwing his truck into park.

"That's Leigh, right?" Antonio looked over his shoulder. "Car's empty."

Brandon checked the phone in his lap. Nothing from her. Im here where RU? he texted quickly.

"Fuck," he said again, cutting the engine and getting out. He looked up and down the dark road.

"Do you think she went in there?" Antonio asked.

"Yes."

Brandon shoved his way through thorns and branches to the game fence. He took the mini-flashlight from his pocket and studied the eight-foot barrier. She wouldn't have climbed it. Which meant she'd probably walked right up to the gate and tried to get in.

"The gate has a security camera," Antonio said, walking around the back of the pickup.

"I saw."

Brandon strode back toward the gate, hugging the fence line. What the hell was she thinking coming out here and jumping in the middle of a confrontation?

Antonio had finally reached Kate and learned that her daughter had come home from dance practice today without incident—which reinforced Brandon's belief that Mason had drummed up a threat against the girl as a way to manipulate Vanessa into contacting him.

"Brandon, look."

He turned around. Antonio was kneeling about twenty yards away, shining his flashlight at the base of the fence.

A sour ball of dread filled Brandon's stomach as he saw the curl of wire mesh.

Antonio stood up. "You think she—"

"Yes." Brandon crouched down and squeezed through the opening, snagging his shirt on the wire.

"Dude. Maybe we should—"

"Stay here and wait for backup if you want."

Brandon ducked behind a clump of trees and tried to orient himself. The house was due west of him, on the steep slope facing the lake. A private driveway accessed the property from the east. Brandon unholstered his weapon as he surveyed the house.

"See that?"

Brandon turned around as Antonio walked up beside him, brushing leaves off his pants.

"No," Brandon said. "What?"

"The boathouse," Antonio said. "I thought I saw a shadow move down there."

Brandon stepped closer to the trees and spied the boathouse at the edge of the water. No lights around it.

"Let me see if I can get a better look," Antonio said, slipping into the trees.

Brandon watched the boathouse. The building was completely dark, and he saw no sign of movement.

An engine growled to life. It sounded like a boat.

"You! Drop your weapon!"

Brandon whirled around.

L EIGH HELD HER hands in the air, heart racing, as she tried to think of what do. The man behind her had a gun at her back and seemed to be going through her phone, probably reading her texts.

"Move. Let's go."

The voice was low and menacing, and Leigh's stomach filled with bile as she recognized it. It was the man in the ski mask who'd attacked her. Mason's brother, according to Brandon.

"*Now.*"

She started moving. "I'm here to talk to Mason. I—"

"Shut the fuck up."

Fear gripped her as she stumbled through the woods, veering around shrubs and trees as she strained to see a path in the dark.

"If you'll just let me—"

Pain exploded above her eye as he smacked her with the gun. She staggered forward, reeling with shock.

"Now *go.*" He prodded her lower back, sending her tripping forward through the trees. Pain pulsated through her head and she felt a warm trickle down the side of her face.

Leigh's heart pounded wildly. Where was he taking her? As she walked down the slope, she saw that the boathouse was dark now, no more floodlights.

She heard the low grumble of a boat engine.

Vanessa. She was down there with Mason. He was taking her out on the lake in the dark, no witnesses.

Was that where she was going, too?

Leigh's stomach clenched and her limbs felt leaden. She grasped for a plan, a weapon, something she could do to get away from him. She remembered the can of sunblock tucked into her waistband.

"Oops!" She pretended to trip, catching herself just before her knee hit the dirt. She grabbed the can and whirled around, spraying it directly at his eyes.

He staggered back with a curse, then lunged forward. She threw the can at him and made a dash for the trees.

"WE'RE AUSTIN PD," Brandon said as he slowly knelt down and set his Glock on the ground. He didn't want any misunderstandings.

The cop approached him, gun raised. As he stepped out of the shadows, Brandon got a better look at his face.

"Akins, it's me. Detective Reynolds." Brandon grabbed his weapon and straightened.

Antonio walked out from the trees, holding up his badge. "We're APD."

The Marble Falls detective looked from Antonio to Brandon, seeming confused.

"We got a call about a domestic disturbance," Akins said, holstering his weapon.

"Yeah, *we* called it in," Antonio told him. "We think we've got a potential hostage situation going down."

LEIGH RACED FOR the trees, not daring to look over her shoulder to see if she was being chased. Adrenaline spurted through her veins, and she ran flat-out, arms and legs pumping, until she felt like her lungs would burst.

She darted behind a flimsy mesquite bush that would do nothing to shield her from a bullet.

Pop!

Brandon's head whipped around at the sound.

"Gunshot," Antonio said. "Sounded like near the lake."

Brandon sprinted down the slope toward the boathouse, gun in hand. His heart jumped into his throat as he saw the shadowy shape of a boat backing out of one of the slips.

Was Leigh on that boat?

Was Vanessa?

He raced for the dock. The boathouse was dark, but he made out the form of a person at the back of the boat.

No, *two* people, locked in a struggle. A high-pitched scream turned Brandon's blood cold, and then one of the two people went over the side.

"Police!" he yelled. "Freeze!"

The taller figure leaped from the boat onto the dock and darted around the far side of the boathouse.

"I got him!" Antonio shouted behind him.

Brandon ran onto the dock, searching the water's surface. Nothing. Holstering his weapon, he rushed to the very end, scouring the inky water near the boat.

He spied a faint trail of bubbles and jumped in.

Cold water swallowed him. He groped through the blackness, and his hand encountered a limb. He grabbed on. Was it Leigh? Vanessa? She thrashed and flailed, trying to fight him off as he put her into a lifesaving hold and kicked to the surface. She came up choking and gasping, and Brandon got a look at her face.

"Vanessa, I got you!"

She punched and flailed.

"It's okay, I'm a cop. *Breathe.*"

But she continued to fight. Brandon kept her head above water as he scissor-kicked his way to the dock, scanning the shoreline with a tight knot in his chest. Where was Leigh?

Akins rushed to the end of the dock as Brandon moved toward it with a panicked Vanessa still struggling against him.

"Get her arms," Brandon ordered.

Akins reached down to take her arms, and Brandon helped lift her. She gasped and choked as she rolled onto her side on the wooden slats.

Brandon grabbed the edge of the dock. He tried to lever himself up, but his waterlogged clothes and shoes weighted him down. He tried again and managed to heave himself out. Wiping the water from his face, he looked down.

His white shirt was streaked with blood.

"She's hit," Brandon said, looking at Vanessa.

She was on her side now, coughing up water as blood gushed from a hole in her jeans.

Akins dropped to his knees and started pulling off his shirt. "I got this." He looked at Brandon. "Go help your partner."

Brandon surged to his feet.

Something in the water caught his eye. A head, bobbing above the surface.

Leigh.

The head went under. Brandon's heart seemed to stop.

"Leigh!"

He sprinted to the end of the dock, scouring the water's surface.

Her head bobbed up.

"Brandon."

He reached down and grabbed her under her arms, lifting her from the water and pulling her onto the dock. He ran his hands over her arms, her shoulders, her face. "Are you hit?"

"No."

"What happened? Are you injured?"

"I'm—" She sat up and leaned against him. "Someone chased me. I think it was Mason's brother. I hid in the trees, but I could still hear him looking for me." Her voice trembled as she gripped his arm. "So I snuck into the water and tried to swim to the neighbor's boat dock, but then I saw you and—"

"Where is he now?"

"He—" She glanced around dazedly. "I don't know. He was with me in the woods. Oh my *God*, you're bleeding!"

"Not me. Vanessa."

She gripped his shirt. "Are you sure?"

"Yes. Stay here." He cupped the side of her face with his hand. "Okay?"

She nodded, and Brandon jumped to his feet.

"Be careful," she said. "He has a gun."

CHAPTER TWENTY-NINE

BRANDON RACED UP THE hill, watching the house with razor-sharp focus. The yellow windows glowed, but he detected no movement inside. Where was Mason? Where was his brother? They were going to make a run for it, no question. It was the only move that made sense. Three cops were already on the scene and they had to know more were coming. The only other option would be to grab a hostage, but Vanessa and Leigh were both down by the water.

Brandon ran toward the house, scanning the driveway and listening for an engine. Would they leave together in one vehicle, or try to divide cops' attention?

A shadow moved in Brandon's peripheral vision. He pivoted just as something crashed into him like a charging bull. The force pummeled him to the ground, and a giant weight smashed down on him. All the air went out of Brandon's lungs. He tried to heave the man off, but he wouldn't budge. *Michael Lloyd.* Brandon somehow knew this was the size-fourteen scumbag who pumped iron for a living and had attacked Leigh.

A sharp jab to his ribs sent pain rocketing through Brandon's body as he struggled to push the guy off. Brandon kicked his leg back, trying to shift the weight and gain leverage. He managed to get an arm loose and landed an elbow blow, and his attacker grunted. The weight shifted, and a huge fist smacked into Brandon's temple. Everything went black as Brandon clamped his eyes shut and pain reverberated through his skull. When he opened his eyes again, the world felt off-balance. His ears were ringing and he realized the weight had disappeared.

Brandon rolled to his back, gasping for air as he yanked his Glock from the holster. He sat up and aimed . . . but there was nothing to aim at, no shot—only the blurry yellow glow of the house at the top of the hill.

Cursing, Brandon staggered to his feet.

ANTONIO FLATTENED HIS back against the side of the house. From beneath the deck a few moments ago, he'd seen Mason Lloyd run inside, and now he heard muffled voices in the kitchen.

Staying in the shadows, Antonio eased along the side of the house toward the garage. He reached a wall of windows and ducked under them as he rushed past the kitchen toward the driveway.

A powerful diesel engine roared to life. That would be the black pickup Antonio had seen parked in the garage.

Shit, they were taking off. He needed help to stop them. He didn't know where Brandon was, but Akins was still down on the dock with Vanessa.

Suddenly, the pickup shot from the garage like a torpedo. It sped backward down the driveway, heading straight for the wrought-iron gate, not even waiting for it to open. As the truck burst through the gate, the tail of another truck—Brandon's—moved into its path. Antonio heard an ear-piercing crunch of metal as the trucks collided.

Antonio ran for the black truck. It was completely blocked in by the bed of Brandon's pickup.

Antonio halted and aimed his gun at the windshield. "Police!"

The truck shot forward. The big silver grille lunged straight at him, and Antonio dove out of the way, hitting the ground. He rolled and popped to his feet, somehow managing to hang on to his gun.

The truck skidded, nearly hitting a tree. Then it accelerated, sending dust and gravel spewing backward as it raced across the grassy yard and careened into the brush, mowing down shrubs.

Another engine caught Antonio's attention, and he spun toward the garage. The silver Porsche shot backward, but Brandon sped up the driveway and made a sharp turn, blocking it in with his now-dented pickup.

Antonio ran to the Porsche and flung the door open. Mason tried to flee the other side, but Brandon was already there.

"Police! Show me your hands!" Brandon reached in and dragged him from the car as Antonio slid across the hood.

Brandon flipped Mason onto his stomach on the ground as he tried to wrestle free.

"Get the fuck off me!"

Instead, Brandon wrenched his arms behind his back. Heart thundering, Antonio managed to keep his arms steady as he aimed his weapon at Mason. Brandon slapped on the handcuffs and patted him down. He had a gun in the back of his jeans, and Brandon jerked it out and tucked it into his waistband.

Sirens sounded in the distance, getting closer and closer. That would be the backup they could have used ten minutes ago.

Above the sirens, he heard splintering wood and the screech of metal.

Brandon looked at him.

"You hear that? He blew through the freaking fence," Antonio said. "He's getting away."

Brandon glanced in the direction of the sound. "He won't get far."

CHAPTER THIRTY

THE REGIONAL HOSPITAL WAS busy for a Wednesday night, and Antonio watched people stream in and out of the waiting room. They'd had a broken arm, a heart attack, and a gunshot wound, all in the past two hours.

A priest strode through the double doors, Bible in hand, and headed straight for the nurses' station. They immediately buzzed him in, and Antonio's stomach knotted as the priest disappeared into the back, probably to go administer last rites. Antonio pictured the heart attack guy and imagined his tearful wife and grown kids gathered around him.

Antonio leaned against the wall, popping his knuckles as his attention alternated between the waiting room chairs and the clock on the wall.

The door beside the nurses' station swung open, and Brandon stepped out. He spied Antonio and walked over. The grim look on his partner's face didn't give him much confidence.

"How's Leigh?" Antonio asked.

"Three stitches. Mild concussion."

"She going home tonight?"

"Yeah." Brandon's jaw clenched as he looked back at the door he'd just come through. His shirt was streaked with blood, and Antonio didn't know whether it was his or Leigh's or Vanessa's.

After Mason had forced Vanessa onto his boat, she had tried to get his gun away from him and ended up getting shot during the struggle. Even with the gunshot wound, she'd been smart to put up a fight. Antonio had no doubt Mason had planned to kill her and dump her body in the lake. Antonio still wasn't sure what they would have done with Leigh—who'd taken them by surprise when she showed up—but it couldn't have been good.

"How's the head?" Antonio asked, eyeing the nasty bump at Brandon's temple.

"Fine."

"Did you need to—"

"How did it go with Vanessa?" Brandon interrupted. He didn't want to talk about his injury.

"Still going. The doctor just came out, said it's a shattered femur and they need to put pins in her leg."

Brandon glanced across the waiting room. "And Kate?"

Antonio turned to look at her. "She's on the phone with their brother, giving him an update. The doctor thinks the surgery is going to take a couple hours. She'll be groggy after, so we won't be getting her statement tonight."

"We can get it tomorrow. Leigh already filled in a lot of the details." Brandon rested his hands on his hips. "So, are you taking off soon?"

He looked at Kate, surrounded by a sea of empty chairs as she talked to her brother, who was on an oil rig somewhere.

"I'll probably stick around for a while."

Brandon's gaze narrowed. "You hate hospitals."

"Yeah, well." Antonio didn't know what else to say, so he left it at that.

Brandon pulled a set of keys from his pocket and held them out. "Use my truck. I can get it from you tomorrow."

Antonio took the keys. "What about you?"

"I'll take Leigh's car. The doctor doesn't want her driving tonight. I told her I'd take her home."

Antonio nodded and slid the keys into his pocket. "Any word on Michael Lloyd?"

"No."

The one syllable was packed with frustration. He couldn't imagine how Brandon felt knowing that the man who'd put Leigh in the hospital was still out there right now, evading police.

"They've got a statewide BOLO," Antonio said. "Shouldn't be long."

Brandon's jaw tightened, and he didn't look convinced. He started to say something, then shook his head.

"We got Mason, at least," Antonio said. "He's looking at a boatload of charges. Wouldn't be surprised if he sells out his own brother just to help himself."

Antonio glanced back at the waiting room as Kate set her phone on the chair beside her. She leaned her elbow on the armrest and rubbed her forehead.

He turned back, and Brandon was watching him.

"You should go talk to her," his partner said.

"Yeah." Antonio sighed. "Thanks for lending me your truck."

"Sure. Good work tonight."

He nodded. "I hope Leigh feels better."

"Me, too."

"Tell her thanks for helping us nail him."

LEIGH WAS SILENT on the drive back, and Brandon didn't blame her. She'd spent an hour perched on a gurney, giving a detailed statement to a Marble Falls cop while she waited for a doctor to stitch her up.

Michael Lloyd had pistol-whipped her. And every time Brandon looked at the bandage on her forehead, he felt his blood start to boil.

It had been five hours, and police still hadn't managed to locate the son of a bitch. He could be out of the state by now.

Leigh stared out the car window at the passing buildings, and the blank expression on her face made his stomach clench. He'd given her his blue APD jacket to cover her torn clothes. It was too big for her, and the sleeves swallowed her hands.

Brandon neared the exit to her house. He glanced at her. "You know, Leigh—"

"You don't have to convince me." She looked at him. "I agree."

"Agree what?"

"I shouldn't stay alone at my house tonight. Michael Lloyd is still at large."

Brandon's grip tightened on the wheel.

"That's what you were going to say, right?"

"Yeah."

"I don't want to be there right now anyway. The idea of him prowling around my patio . . ." She shuddered.

"Do you want to come to my place?"

She hesitated for a moment and then nodded.

They finished the drive in silence. Brandon pulled into a front-row space in the lot beside his building. Leigh walked up the stairs in front of him, and he noticed the scratches on her ankles, probably from traipsing around Mason's property.

Brandon unlocked the door and ushered her inside. The last time they'd done this, he'd been dripping wet and out of his mind with lust. This time, he was consumed by a different emotion. Leigh had been brutalized tonight, and the man who'd done it had slipped through Brandon's grasp. He'd been right there. If Brandon had just landed one good punch, he could have wrestled him into submission, but he'd gotten away. A smoldering anger filled Brandon's chest and made it hard for him to breathe.

He turned and locked the door.

Leigh looked at him in the dimness. He pulled her into his arms, and for a long moment, they just stood there.

"You're shivering," he said against the top of her head.

"It's cold in here."

It wasn't, but her clothes were probably still damp under his jacket. And she could be still in shock.

He eased away. "How about a hot shower?"

She arched her eyebrows.

"Not with me. You can relax and get rid of the chill."

She pulled back and nodded. "That sounds really good."

Brandon followed her to his bathroom and switched on the light. It was messy, but at least he hadn't left any dirty clothes on the floor. He opened the glass door to the shower and turned the water to hot but not scalding.

"Be right back."

He left her alone to go hunt up a clean towel. He found some in the dryer and grabbed his first-aid kit from the hall closet in case she had any more injuries he hadn't seen yet.

Returning to the steamy bathroom, he found her standing in front of the sink in her torn white blouse, her skirt and his jacket in a heap at her feet. She leaned toward the mirror, studying the purple bump on her forehead. She peeled the tape back and slowly lifted her bandage to examine the stitches that looked like three black spiders.

"So ugly." She sighed and replaced the bandage. "I hope that resident knew what he was doing."

Brandon stepped around her and hung a clean towel on the hook by the shower.

"Baylor med school, UT undergrad," he said.

She turned around. The corner of her mouth curved up in the first hint of emotion he'd seen in hours. "Don't tell me you interviewed him?"

He reached up and rested his hand on her shoulder. "I did, yeah."

Her green eyes softened, and Brandon's chest filled with some other feeling, something he couldn't put a label on.

She went up on tiptoes and kissed him, just a soft brush of her mouth. He slid his arms around her, and she kissed him again. He wanted to take it easy. But then she nibbled his lip, and he pulled her in tight, licking into her warm mouth and drinking in that sweetly erotic taste he'd been craving. Her hands slid up around his neck. He held her against him, as tightly as he could without hurting her, while he kissed her with all the pent-up need and frustration that had been building for days.

Finally, she pulled back and gazed up at him, resting her fingers on his sternum.

"Shower with me," she whispered. "I think you need to relax, too."

BRANDON AWOKE TO a noise in the kitchen. He listened for a moment, then got out of bed and pulled on some jeans.

Leigh stood in the light of the open refrigerator, surveying the contents. She wore one of his black T-shirts that hit her at midthigh.

"Hungry?" he asked.

She jumped and whirled around.

"God, you scared me."

He walked over and switched on the light above the microwave.

"I'm starving." She closed the fridge. "How about you?"

His stomach growled as he opened the fridge again.

"I could eat. You like grilled cheese?"

"You don't have any bread."

"Hmm." He opened the freezer. "Hot Pocket?"

She made a face.

"Ben and Jerry's?"

"*Oooh.* Yes!"

He looked at her, surprised that her reaction to ice cream could turn him on. He grabbed the pint of Cherry Garcia and took a pair of spoons from a drawer.

"You want bowls?" he asked.

She scowled and plucked the carton from his hand. "Please. Bowls are for amateurs."

She walked into the living room and sank onto the couch. He sat beside her and pulled her legs into his lap.

"I like your place." She peeled the lid off the ice cream, and he handed her a spoon. "Did I tell you that before?"

"No." He waited for her to take a bite and then scooped up a spoonful. "I think you were distracted."

She smiled slightly as she pulled the spoon from her mouth. He was glad to see her smiling again, and it almost made it possible to ignore the bandage on her forehead.

Almost.

Brandon watched her in the dimness. Her sleep-mussed hair fell in waves around her shoulders. He rested his hand on her smooth thigh.

"Brandon . . . I owe you an apology."

"For?"

"Leaving so abruptly. Without saying good-bye." She gave him a guilty look as she took a bite and slid the spoon from her mouth. "That was pretty crappy."

"I'm a grown-up. I can take it."

She watched him. "You weren't pissed off?"

"No. What pissed me off was the lying."

She sighed and dug her spoon in again.

"Okay, but admit it was a lie of *omission*. And it had more to do with attorney-client privilege than me trying to proactively deceive you." She dug up another spoonful. "You have stuff like that, too. It's not like you go around telling me all the details of the cases you're working."

He made a noncommittal sound as he ate another bite.

"Can you at least admit that it's not the same as *lying* lying?"

He leaned over the ice cream and kissed her nose.

"What is it with lawyers? You always want an admission out of people."

"Questioning should always have an objective," she said.

He sighed. "I will admit, it is a little different. But lying is a thing for me."

She squirmed closer. "Why?"

"I don't know. It's a hang-up I have."

"Yes, but why?

He didn't answer, and she gazed at him with those deep green eyes.

"Tell me about this hang-up you have."

LEIGH WATCHED HIM, wondering if he was going to open up to her finally, or say something evasive.

He reached over her and put his spoon on the end table, then rested his hand on her knee.

"Did I ever mention I was married once?"

"No. But I knew that," she said.

He lifted an eyebrow.

"I looked you up online."

He didn't react to that, probably because she'd told him as much when she showed up at his house like a stalker.

"What happened?" she asked.

He seemed uneasy talking about this, and she resisted the urge to do something soothing, like stroke the top of his hand. She had a feeling he wouldn't like that.

"Basically, we were really young and immature. Twenty-two." He gave her a sharp look, as if it were obvious no one should get married that young. "I was gone a lot with work. She got depressed for a while and then she slept with someone else. Lied to me about it." He paused. "We tried to work it out, but things weren't the same after. I didn't trust her."

Leigh watched him in the dimness. A dark layer of stubble covered his jaw, and she wanted to run her finger over it. But she didn't want to distract him, not when she was hanging on every word.

"Were you in love when you got married?"

"Yeah."

He said it without hesitation.

"*I* was." He looked at her suspiciously. "How did we get on this topic?"

"You were talking about your hang-up."

His hand slid up her thigh, and she knew he wanted to change the subject.

"Well . . . in the interest of full disclosure," she said, "I should probably tell you something else."

She turned and set the ice cream carton on the table behind her. When she looked at him again, he was watching her closely, and she felt a pang in her stomach. Was she really going to tell him about this?

"You asked me once why I do the work that I do." She cleared her throat. "You know, the stalkers, and the psychos, and the revenge porn."

He moved his hand to the top of her knee. She looked down at it and traced her finger over his knuckles.

"My last boyfriend posted a video of me." She looked at him. "On a porn site."

He watched her steadily, and she tried to read his expression. It didn't change, and her heart sank.

"You don't look surprised," she said.

"I'm not."

Her throat tightened. She had to force herself to speak. "Did you see it?"

"No."

"How did you—"

"I guessed." He held her gaze for a long moment. "I'm sorry that happened to you."

"How did you guess?"

"Different things." He reached up and brushed a lock of hair from her face, then tucked it behind her ear. "You're very passionate about your work, so I figured it was personal to you. And the first time we were together, you were uncomfortable with certain things."

"Your phone."

He nodded. "You had no problem with a loaded Glock in the room, but my cell phone freaked you out."

She blew out a sigh. "I know. I'm weird."

"No, you're not."

"Guess it's *my* hang-up."

He stroked her cheek with the back of his finger, and Leigh felt a familiar ache in her chest. She hated it. She *hated* knowing there was something out there, something she had no control over, something that gave perfect strangers access to her most private self. It made moments like this impossible. Whenever she started to relax with someone, or started to open up, she imaged them seeing those images—seeing her in her most playful, private, unguarded moments that were never meant for anyone but a person she'd cared about. Every time she thought about it, she felt this sick helplessness. It never went away, only receded into the background.

She cleared her throat. "Will you do something for me?"

He just looked at her.

"Will you promise you won't watch it?"

His eyebrows arched.

"It's out there, no matter what I do. And if we spend time together, someone might send it to you. You'd be surprised how people are like, 'Hey, FYI, you really need to see this, bro.'"

His brow furrowed, as though he didn't believe people could be so spiteful, but they absolutely could. She'd grown numb to it, mostly. But the thought of Brandon seeing it filled her with dread.

"Will you promise?"

"Leigh." He laced his fingers with hers. "Why would I watch something that hurts you?"

Her heart did a weird thumpy thing as she stared down at their hands, absorbing his words. He pressed a kiss to her forehead.

"I promise I won't watch it."

The knot in her stomach loosened.

"Thank you."

He gazed down at her and smiled slightly. "As long as we're putting it all out there, I should admit something." His tone was teasing, and she felt relieved that he wanted to lighten the mood.

"What?"

"When you left the other night, it did bother me a little."

She sighed. "I had a migraine."

"No, I was fine with that. It was your note."

Her mind swam as she tried to get what he meant.

"The sticky note on your bar? I put that in my purse." She frowned. "How did you read that?"

"Indented writing. It's a detective trick."

"I don't even remember what I wrote."

"You don't?"

"No."

He leaned his head back against the sofa cushion. "'Thanks for Leonard's. XOXO.'" He made a pained face. "My ego was crushed."

"I did *not* write that."

"Yeah, you did." He turned his head and smiled at her.

Well, maybe she did. She'd had a vicious headache and she hadn't been thinking straight.

"It was just a sticky note," she said defensively. "What did you want me to say?"

"How about, 'Dear Brandon, thanks for the mind-blowing sex. You totally rocked my world.'"

Leigh moved onto his lap and straddled him. "I'm sorry

I crushed your delicate ego." She rested her arms on his shoulders.

"I'll survive." He grinned and kissed her.

The kiss started out teasing, but then turned serious. The moment *was* serious, she realized. Something was happening here. She'd told him the thing she dreaded most, the thing that had been hanging over her life for years. And he'd opened up to her, too. For so long, she'd avoided intimacy, and she didn't know if she was ready for it.

But it was happening anyway.

He lifted her off his lap and shifted her beneath him on the sofa. He settled between her legs, and she stared up at him.

"What is it?" he asked.

She traced her finger over his jaw. "I should warn you. I'm kind of a mess when it comes to relationships."

He propped his weight on his elbow.

"I don't have a great track record," she added.

"Me either." He kissed her forehead.

"I have some hang-ups. The phone thing is just the beginning."

He kissed her mouth.

"And my work-life balance sucks," she said.

"Ditto." The corner of his mouth curved into a smile. "You're trying to scare me away."

"Is it working?"

"No." He kissed her neck. "Not a chance."

CHAPTER THIRTY-ONE

═══╪═══

Five Weeks Later

ANTONIO CLIMBED INTO THE minivan with a lidded cup of coffee.

"I miss anything?" he asked Brandon.

"No."

Brandon lifted his binoculars, trying to get a clear view of the bench. Antonio settled into a chair in the back of the van and sipped his coffee. They were set up behind a taco truck three blocks north of the park, which was good for concealment but shitty for watching things go down.

The hunt for Michael Lloyd had been a federal operation since Brandon discovered he was being investigated by the DEA for potential crimes in both Tampa and Dallas, where—coincidentally—two of his brother's clinics had been burglarized. Federal agents had had their eye on Michael Lloyd for nearly five years, and everything was coming to a head now, just in time to snag the case away from Brandon's department.

As much as Brandon would have liked to be the one to bring Lloyd down, he was glad for the help, especially because the feds had a confidential informant who had been working on Lloyd for months. Yesterday the CI had contacted Lloyd on one of his burner phones and told him he needed some product.

Lloyd must have badly needed money because he'd agreed to meet.

"I hate this location," Antonio muttered, lifting his own pair of binoculars and turning them toward the park.

Brandon hated it, too.

The rectangular park wasn't large. It had a pair of tennis courts in one corner, a playscape in the middle, and a line of chin-up bars in the corner closest to their minivan. A woman in a bright pink sports top stood there now, stretching her quads, about fifty yards from where a utility crew made up of federal agents pretended to be working on a telephone line.

Brandon's attention shifted back to the playscape, which was the real problem. He didn't like it at all, but Lloyd had picked this location. The CI had chosen the meeting time—seven a.m.—which was good, because there weren't any children around yet. But that could easily change.

Brandon checked his watch. It was 7:10. He wanted this op over. He was well past ready to stop thinking about Mason Lloyd and his dirtbag brother. Leigh's cut had healed, and her stitches had been removed. She still had a scar, though, and each time Brandon looked at it he felt a fierce determination to finish the job. Leigh wouldn't sleep well, and neither would he, until Michael Lloyd was off the streets.

"What's the car again?" Antonio asked.

"A gray Volkswagen Jetta or a black Honda Pilot."

Those were the vehicles belonging to Lloyd's two local girlfriends, who'd been under surveillance for five weeks. There hadn't been any sightings of Lloyd, but the feds remained confident their fugitive was being harbored by one of them.

Brandon skimmed the park, and his attention got caught on a small gray car. His pulse picked up.

"Check it out," he told Antonio. "Southwest corner, by the tennis courts."

The car pulled into a space beside the courts as Brandon's police radio crackled to life.

"Possible sighting," an agent said.

A large man climbed out of the little VW, making it look like a clown car.

"White male, approximately six-four," someone said over the radio. "Blue shirt, white baseball hat, sunglasses. Can anyone confirm?"

"That's him," Brandon muttered just as a voice came over the radio.

"It's him."

Brandon gritted his teeth as he watched Lloyd look around the park. His attention settled on the green bench near the chin-up bars, where his contact waited. The CI had three foil-wrapped bundles beside him—two of which he'd purchased at the nearby taco truck and one that contained the cash he would give Lloyd in exchange for ten oxycodone pills.

Like most of Lloyd's suspected clients, this guy worked out at the gym where Lloyd was a personal trainer. The CI had bought product from him before. Federal agents believed it was the Lloyd brothers' lucrative drug business that had motivated them to want to silence Vanessa. They didn't want her lawsuit drawing police attention to Mason or his medical clinics, which had been the target of burglars in two different states. When Vanessa became a problem they couldn't control, they tried to get rid of her. And Leigh would have been collateral damage.

Brandon scanned the park. Still no kids on the playscape. He scanned the utility crew, the pink-shirted jogger, the blond dog walker strolling past the bench.

The dog walker stopped.

"Shit," Brandon said.

"What?"

"The woman with the poodle. White shirt, near the bench."

Antonio lifted his binoculars. "That's a Yorkie."

"Whatever. She's right in the way."

The woman stood between Lloyd and the bench, stubbornly reading her phone as her dog strained against the leash.

Lloyd knelt down and tied his shoe, looking around warily as he stalled for time. Seconds ticked by, and Brandon's tension ratcheted up.

"Get off the damn phone," Antonio muttered.

Lloyd pretended to tie his other shoe. Brandon held his breath.

The dog lady started walking again.

"Finally," Antonio said.

Brandon released his breath as Lloyd stood and began moving again, his gaze scanning the park as he neared the bench.

He stopped, zeroing in on the utility crew.

Brandon's gut clenched. "They're blown."

Lloyd glanced over his shoulder at the gray VW, possibly noticing the agent posing as a jogger now standing between him and his car.

"He sees us," someone mumbled over the radio.

Lloyd took off.

He sprinted past the playscape, hurdling over a row of orange cones put out by the utility crew. A pair of agents dropped their equipment and gave chase, but Lloyd was surprisingly fast. He skirted around a pair of benches and sprinted straight toward the food truck. He grabbed the arm of a guy standing in line and hurled him to the ground. The ensuing confusion created a swarm of helpful bystanders, and the federal agents had to run around them. Lloyd widened his lead.

"He's getting away again!" Antonio said.

"Like hell."

Brandon yanked open the door of the van and jumped out. He darted behind a parked car and crouched down, watching in the side mirror as Lloyd sprinted down the sidewalk toward him, casting a frantic glance over his shoulder.

Brandon leaped out and tackled him. Fire burned up Brandon's side as they skidded across the sidewalk and crashed into a wall.

"DEA! Freeze!"

Brandon slammed his knee into Lloyd's ribs as he kept a viselike grip on the man's arms. Lloyd grunted and bucked like a bull, trying to get Brandon off him.

"I got him, I got him!" an agent yelled, grabbing hold of Lloyd's wrists.

The jogger in pink jumped into the fray with a pair of handcuffs.

"DEA!" she yelled. "You're under arrest!"

More undercover agents converged, and Brandon pushed himself to his feet and looked around for any weapons. The female agent slapped the cuffs on as another agent pulled a pistol from the back of Lloyd's jeans.

Antonio walked over, and one of the male agents glared at him and Brandon, clearly unhappy about having an assist with the takedown. The woman in pink smiled as the two utility crew workers hauled Lloyd to his feet.

"Mr. Michael Lloyd," she said. "It's about goddamn time."

LEIGH STROLLED OUT of Judge Thielman's courtroom feeling like she could take on the world. She'd persuaded the ballbuster. He'd granted every one of her motions. It had never happened before, and she couldn't wait to call Javi.

"Wait, please!" She rushed to catch the elevator and jumped inside just before it closed. "Thank you."

As she turned to face the door, she noticed the curious

looks from the other lawyers and felt them trading glances behind her back.

The attorneys and cops she dealt with didn't seem to know what to make of her lately. Vanessa's story had spread through the legal community, and several different versions were circulating. According to the most interesting one, Leigh had gotten into a shootout while trying to protect one of her clients from a stalker—which was absolutely *not* what had happened, but rumors had a way of taking on a life of their own. All the talk was distracting and made Leigh self-conscious at the courthouse. She hated being the subject of gossip. But at least this latest round wasn't as tawdry and embarrassing as the last one, and she knew the talk would die down as soon as some new scandal came along.

In the meantime, Javi was elated.

"We couldn't *buy* this kind of advertising," he'd said. "I've always known what a badass you are, and now everyone else does, too!"

The elevator doors parted, and Leigh stepped into the crowded lobby filled with prospective jurors and courthouse employees. She immediately noticed the pair of tall cops standing by the X-ray machine.

Brandon traded words with Deputy Gronk, and Leigh's heart did a little happy dance as he walked over.

"Hey," he said. "Bella told me I'd find you here. You done?"

"Yep."

They walked out together, stepping into the gusty November air. Leigh pulled a scarf from her bag and looped it around her neck.

"Want me to get that?" Brandon asked, nodding at her satchel loaded with case files.

"I've got it."

She smiled up at him, feeling giddy that he'd come to meet her in the middle of the workday.

Over the past five weeks, they'd spent lots of time

together—way more than she would have thought possible, given their busy schedules. She saw him frequently for dinner, and when neither of them had a work conflict, they'd spend the night at his place or hers. Last night, they had started the evening at her place with carryout from Mei's, but then Brandon had gotten an urgent call from Antonio and had to leave. She hadn't heard from him all night.

"You look happy today," he said as they walked around the line of people waiting to get through security.

"The judge granted my TRO. *And* he's issuing a take-down order. *And* I just filed papers this morning on behalf of Vanessa." She smiled. "*And* it's not even one o'clock, so you could say I'm having a productive day."

"Vanessa?" he asked.

"She's suing Mason Lloyd over the nonconsensual sex video. Just to add some hefty monetary damages to his list of worries. The cherry on top of his legal-problem sundae."

"Good for Vanessa."

"I know." She smiled at Brandon, noting his crisp white dress shirt. Usually by noon, he'd rolled up his sleeves. Looking him over closely, she noticed his hair was slightly damp.

She narrowed her gaze. "Did you just shower?"

"Yeah, actually. I had to run home to change."

"You guys catch a bad case last night?"

"No." He looked at her. "It was your case, actually."

She halted.

He turned to look at her, his eyes dark and serious, and her stomach filled with dread.

"The DEA set up a drug buy this morning with Michael Lloyd and one of their CIs," he said. "They took him down."

"You mean—"

"He's in custody."

Leigh's heart stuttered. She stared up at him.

"Hey." He guided her out of the traffic flow toward the side of the building. "You okay?"

"Yeah. You mean he's . . ."

"He's behind bars. Which is where he'll be staying because he's a definite flight risk."

Leigh didn't know what to say. Brandon slid his arms around her and pulled her against his warm chest.

"I can't believe it. What happened?" She eased back to look at him.

"They set up a sting op in a park." He smiled. "I wish you could have watched. The arresting agent was a woman. You would have loved it."

She wrapped her arms around him and felt him wince.

"What's wrong? Are you hurt?"

He made a face. "Just a little road burn. Lloyd tried to flee the scene and I tackled him."

"Why did *you* tackle him? I thought the feds were doing it."

"Yeah, well, it was a joint effort."

"Are you—"

"I'm fine. Just a ruined shirt, that's all."

Cautiously, Leigh slid her hand over his shoulder and cupped her fingers against his neck. Her heart thrummed wildly, and she searched his face to see what he was leaving out. But he just smiled down at her.

Michael Lloyd was behind bars. As was his brother. For five weeks, she'd been in a state of anxiety, tossing and turning at night and constantly looking over her shoulder whenever she was in public.

Brandon kissed her forehead. "Don't look like that."

"Is he really in custody?"

"He's really in custody."

He kissed her mouth.

Leigh slid her hands behind his neck and pulled him down for a better kiss. He wrapped his arms around her and pulled her tightly against him as it went on and on, with the cold air gusting around them.

He eased away. "Let's go home."

She gazed up at those simmering brown eyes. It was a look she'd come to know and love.

"Come on," he said. "I can't kiss you here."

She glanced around, aware of the attention they were attracting from bystanders.

"You *are* kissing me here," she pointed out.

"I can't kiss you here the way I want to."

She tipped her head to the side. "Are you saying you want me to ditch my important work in the middle of the day and play hooky with you?"

"Yes." He took the ends of her scarf and tugged her closer. "That's exactly what I'm saying."

Leigh's heart felt full. She went up on tiptoes and kissed him.

"Is that a yes?"

She smiled. "I could be persuaded."

MACEY BURNS DROVE THROUGH the drumming rain, gripping the wheel until her knuckles were white.

"Are you here yet?" Josh asked.

"I'm running late," she told him over the phone. "I hit traffic leaving town, and then it's been pouring the last two hours. I just crossed the bridge."

"It's—"

Noise drowned out his words.

"What?" she asked.

"It's a *causeway*. No one calls it a bridge here."

"I can barely hear you. Where are you?"

"At that bar I told you about, the one with the pool tables," he said. "You're going to love it."

Macey tore her gaze away from the highway to check the clock. It was almost eleven, and what should have been a four-hour drive had taken more than five.

"Sounds good, but not tonight. I haven't even found the house yet, and I still have to unpack the car."

"That's okay. I'm about to leave anyway. Where are you, exactly?"

"I think I may have missed the turn," she told him. "I just passed a sign that said White Dunes Park, five miles."

"No, it should be coming up on your right. You'll see it."

Josh had been on the island all week scouting locations and already knew his way around.

"You need help unloading?" he asked.

"I'm good."

"So, hey, heads up. I just found out that Channel Six is down here."

"Channel Six from San Antonio?" she asked.

"Yeah, Rayna and her crew. They're reporting on that woman who went missing two weeks ago. She disappeared without a trace."

Macey had read an article about it online. It was the type of story that normally would have captivated her attention, but she'd managed to push it out of her mind.

"We're not here to do news," she reminded Josh.

"No kidding. I just thought you'd want to know. In case you see them in town."

Rayna had once been Macey's fiercest rival, but that was months ago, before Macey walked out on her job and her life and the endless slog of the twenty-four-hour news cycle.

Her tires hit a slick patch, and she clenched the wheel. She didn't want to think about her old job right now. She just wanted to get to her destination. Her shoulders were in knots from the drive, and she wanted a glass of wine and a steamy shower.

"So, are we still on for tomorrow?" she asked Josh. "Nine o'clock?"

"Assuming weather clears. No use scouting locations in the rain."

"It's supposed to be beautiful," she said. "Let's start on the north end. We can meet at my beach house."

Beach house. She pictured the sun-drenched deck overlooking the surf. She'd been daydreaming about it since she first found the listing.

"Sure you don't need help with the equipment?" Josh asked.

"Thanks, but I can handle it."

"Okay, well, see you tomorrow, then."

She ended the call and squinted through the swishing wipers at the sign up ahead: WHITE DUNES PARK, 2 MILES.

A strobe of lightning lit the sky, revealing empty fields on either side of the two-lane highway. She was well past the tourist center of Lost Beach, past the hotels and restaurants and T-shirt shops.

She hit a bump, and the car jerked right. Her heart skipped a beat as the Honda fishtailed and skidded. She clenched the wheel and tried to get control, but it careened onto the shoulder with a jaw-rattling *thunk*. She jabbed the brakes and slammed to a halt.

Macey blinked at the windshield, shocked. Her heart raced as she tried to catch her breath. The car was tilted, and the headlights illuminated a patch of weeds and a gravelly strip of shoulder.

Macey put the gearshift in park and shoved open the door. She started to get out, but the seat belt yanked her back. She unbuckled herself and slid out. Rain pelted her as she looked around in a daze.

What the hell had happened? One second she'd been driving along and the next second it was like aliens had seized the control of the car. And she'd definitely felt a bump. Had she hit something?

Glancing up and down the highway, she saw no other traffic. She retrieved her cell phone and slammed the door shut. Her wet flip-flops thwacked against the gravel as she walked around the front of the Honda and checked for damage. No dents. No sign of an animal.

She stopped beside the front bumper. The right tire was flat.

"Crap."

She switched on her cell phone's flashlight and aimed it at the tire. Yep, flat.

Rain streamed down her face and neck. What now? She turned off the flashlight and called Josh, but he didn't pick up. She sent him a text:

SOS! Flat tire. Call me.

A car raced past and sprayed her with water. She yelped and whirled around, but the driver didn't even slow. Cursing, she glanced up and down the highway. This end of the island was fairly desolate—mostly campgrounds and nature parks. She'd passed a marina, but that was a ways back.

When she'd planned her trip down here, she had wanted seclusion. After weeks of scouring listings, she'd been ecstatic when a long-term rental popped up on the island's north end, just footsteps from the beach. The idea of being away from town, surrounded by sand and waves and the soundtrack of nature, had been immensely appealing. But now she wasn't sure. Maybe she should have followed Josh's advice and rented an apartment in town for the summer.

Macey shivered and rubbed her bare arms, chilled from the rain despite the warm temperature. Her tank top and jeans were already soaked through, and she was out here alone and stranded.

I can handle it.

Ha. Famous last words.

She went back around and reached inside once again, this time to pop the trunk. It was a new-to-her car, and she didn't know the spare tire situation, but surely there was something in the back. Macey had helped a boyfriend change a tire in college once. Well, maybe not *helped*, but she'd watched, and it had seemed pretty straightforward.

She tromped back to the trunk and slid aside the tripod

and the suitcase filled with camera equipment. After finding the corner tab, she peeled back the layer of carpet.

Score! A spare tire, along with a heavy metal tool—a lug wrench?—and what had to be a jack.

But the spare seemed . . . off. She frowned down at the anemic-looking tire. Pressing her fingers against it, she confirmed her suspicion.

The spare was flat, too.

"Crap," she said again.

Macey checked her phone. Still nothing from Josh. She hated asking a man to rescue her, but it was freaking pouring, and she was out of options.

Another lightning strike, followed by a clap of thunder. Then a jagged white bolt zapped down from above.

She looked up at the sky, awestruck. The ferocious beauty of it reminded her of why she'd been attracted to Lost Beach in the first place. She'd been lured by the film project, of course, which would pay her bills while she got her life sorted. But beyond that, she'd been attracted by the dramatic juxtaposition of nature and people. She'd been lured by the rugged Texas coast and one of the last long stretches of untamed beach and twenty-foot dunes.

Rainwater trickled down the front of her shirt, reminding her of her plight. She stared down at the useless tire.

Her trip was off to a rocky start. She wasn't superstitious—at least not usually—and she refused to take tonight as a bad omen. She was here for the entire summer, and no matter what happened, she planned to make the best of it.

A flash of light had her turning around. A pair of headlights approached, high and wide apart, like a pickup truck. The truck slowed, and she felt a ripple of unease.

But maybe this was just what she needed—some Good Samaritan here to help her.

The truck rolled to a stop and the driver's-side door opened.

Macey squinted into the glare. Nerves fluttered in her stomach as a man got out. Tall, wide shoulders, baseball cap. She couldn't see his face, only his towering silhouette against the light as he walked toward her.

As he got closer, she saw that he was *very* tall—six feet three, at least—and he easily outweighed her by a hundred pounds. Oftentimes, Macey liked being short because people underestimated her. This was not one of those times.

"Need a hand?"

The deep voice sent a dart of alarm through her.

"I'm good, thanks."

He continued moving toward her, and she took a step back.

"Is it your tire?"

She spied something in his hand, something black and bulky, like a club or—

A flashlight. He switched it on and approached the tire.

"It's fine," she said.

"It's shredded."

"I've got it handled, actually."

He took a step toward her, and she stepped back, clutching her phone and wishing it was a tube of pepper spray. She kept one in her glove box for emergencies. She'd never needed it before, but of course, now that she did, it was well out of reach.

He walked around her and shined the flashlight into her trunk.

"Spare's flat, too."

She eased away from him, and he seemed to get the hint, because he lowered the flashlight and stepped back.

"You need a ride?" he asked.

She stared at him. Did he seriously think she was going to climb into a truck with a complete stranger?

"My boyfriend's coming. He's on his way now. He's a mechanic," she added inanely.

The man stared at her from beneath the brim of the hat.

The shadows made it hard for her to make out his features, but he seemed to have a strong jaw. Beads of rain dripped from it as he stood there, looking her up and down. He was checking her out, she realized, and the back of her neck tingled.

She disappeared without a trace.

Macey's heartbeat thrummed as they stood there in the rain. He wasn't going anywhere. She'd told him she didn't need his help, and he was just standing there, looking at her.

A distant glow caught her eye as another car approached. She held her breath, watching as the low headlights drew near. Josh's ancient hatchback came into view, and she felt a rush of relief. He slowed and rolled past her, his taillights glowing as he pulled onto the shoulder.

"That's him!" Macey slammed the trunk with maybe a bit too much force in her hurry to put some distance between them. "Thanks for stopping!"

She strode toward the Toyota as the driver's-side door opened. Josh didn't get out right away, and she quickened her pace. Why hadn't he parked closer?

She glanced over her shoulder as the stranger trudged back to his truck without a backward glance.

"What the hell happened?" Josh asked as he got out.

"I had a blowout."

"How?"

"No idea. Maybe I hit something in the road."

Relief filled her as she took in Josh's familiar appearance— the ponytail, the scruffy goatee, the green army jacket. She reached up and hugged him.

"You okay?" he asked, clearly caught off guard. She wasn't a hugger.

"Fine. Thanks for coming."

He looked over her shoulder. "Who was that?"

"Some guy." She glanced back at the pickup as it pulled onto the highway. Shuddering, she watched it speed away.

"Shit, Mace." Josh walked toward her little blue Honda. "It's completely flat."

"That's what I told you."

"We're going to drown out here trying to change this."

"We can't." She strode past him. "The spare's flat, too. Here, grab a bag. You can give me a ride."

She opened the back door and reached for one of the two black duffels.

"You're just going to leave it overnight?" he asked.

"I don't know yet, but I'm definitely not leaving ten thousand dollars' worth of equipment on the side of the road."

Together, they hauled all the luggage to his car. He popped the back hatch, and they managed to squeeze everything inside. Then she went around to the passenger seat, where she shoveled fast-food bags and empty cups onto the floor.

"This is a pigsty," she said as she got in.

"Thank you, Joshua, for coming to get me in the middle of a thunderstorm," he said.

She yanked the door shut. "Thank you." She sighed. "I owe you."

"I'll add it to your tab," he said, starting the car. The engine made a little coughing sound before coming to life.

Macey grabbed a Dairy Queen napkin from the cup holder and squeezed rain from the ends of her hair. Josh looked over his shoulder, but the duffels blocked his view. He used the mirrors to check for traffic as he pulled onto the highway.

"You think there's a towing place open this late?" Macey asked.

"Who knows? You could look."

She used her phone to do a search.

"You're on Blue Heron, right?" he asked.

She glanced up. His car's wiper blades were in worse shape than hers, but she was able to make out a street sign up ahead.

"Yes, Blue Heron Trail. That's it there."

He hung a right onto a narrow caliche road that wasn't

nearly as picturesque as the name implied. They passed a water tank and a clump of squatty palm trees, then a leaning wooden mailbox. Macey peered out the window, searching for the house that the mailbox belonged to, but it was hard to see past the overgrown vegetation.

The Toyota bumped along as they passed another mailbox. This house was closer to the road, a weathered wooden cabin on stilts. It was dark and empty-looking—maybe someone's weekend place. Macey leaned forward, searching for anything that resembled the little white bungalow that she'd fallen in love with on the website.

"I still don't get why you wanted to be all the way out here," Josh said.

"We came here for the beach. I want to be near it."

"Um, no. We came here to film commercials for the tourism board."

"Well, when we're not working, I plan to hit the beach."

"You'll burn to a crisp."

He wasn't wrong. Macey's skin was even fairer than his was.

"Not to sunbathe," she told him. "I'll take pictures. Or do yoga. Or maybe take up running."

He lifted an eyebrow but didn't comment on the likelihood of her suddenly becoming athletic.

They hit a rut, and she braced her hand on the dashboard as they passed another dilapidated house on stilts, this one with a rusted boat trailer in the driveway.

An animal darted in front of the car.

"Cat!" she yelped.

Josh slammed on the brakes. "It's a possum."

"That was a cat."

He shook his head as the cat-possum disappeared into a clump of scrub brush.

"Seriously, Macey, this is the boondocks. Wouldn't you rather be in town, near all the hotels and shops and nightlife? Not to mention *people*?"

Ignoring him, she squinted through the rain-slicked windshield. Josh needed people, not her. In particular, he needed women and bars and things to do after work. Macey wasn't into all that anymore. She wanted peace and quiet, and a chance to get her life together after a hellacious spring.

A mailbox came into view, and she read the number.

"This is it," she said.

"This?"

"Yes."

He pulled into the driveway and parked.

Macey stared up at the little house on stilts. Peeling paint. Sagging gutters. A rectangular gray mark under the window where a flower box had once been. The place resembled the pictures just enough for her to know that this was, in fact, the house she'd rented for three months, for an unbelievably low rate that now seemed totally believable.

"It's a dump," he said.

She shot him a look. "It lacks curb appeal. So what?"

"You really rented this place? Like, you signed a contract and everything?"

"The inside is nice."

"Right."

"It is. I saw the photos." Macey pushed open the door and gazed up at the house through the veil of rain. "How bad could it be?"

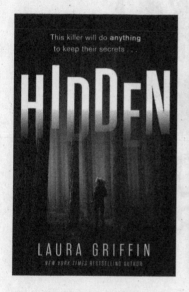
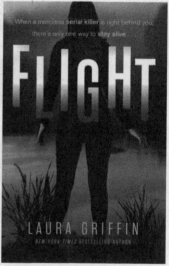

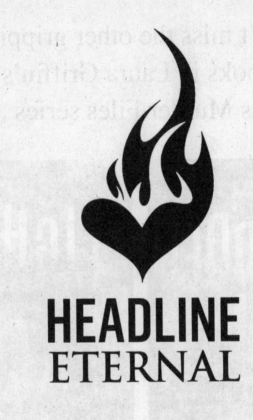

HEADLINE
ETERNAL

FIND YOUR HEART'S DESIRE...

VISIT OUR WEBSITE: www.headlineeternal.com

FIND US ON FACEBOOK: facebook.com/eternalromance

CONNECT WITH US ON TWITTER: @eternal_books

FOLLOW US ON INSTAGRAM: @headlineeternal

EMAIL US: eternalromance@headline.co.uk